SPECIAL MESSAGE TO READERS

This book is published under the auspices of

THE ULVERSCROFT FOUNDATION

(registered charity No. 264873 UK)

Established in 1972 to provide funds for research, diagnosis and treatment of eye diseases. Examples of contributions made are: —

A Children's Assessment Unit at Moorfield's Hospital, London.

•

Twin operating theatres at the Western Ophthalmic Hospital, London.

•

A Chair of Ophthalmology at the Royal Australian College of Ophthalmologists.

•

The Ulverscroft Children's Eye Unit at the Great Ormond Street Hospital For Sick Children, London.

You can help further the work of the Foundation by making a donation or leaving a legacy. Every contribution, no matter how small, is received with gratitude. Please write for details to:

THE ULVERSCROFT FOUNDATION, The Green, Bradgate Road, Anstey, Leicester LE7 7FU, England. Telephone: (0116) 236 4325

In Australia write to: THE ULVERSCROFT FOUNDATION, c/o The Royal Australian College of Ophthalmologists, 27, Commonwealth Street, Sydney, N.S.W. 2010.

SOMETHING BORROWED, SOMETHING BLUE

Twenty-seven years old, still single and, worse, still living at home with her parents in Dublin, Jenny Joyce wants something new in her life. But at her cousin Cathy's wedding, she discovers that something old can be even more fun. Hugo Hunter, her first boyfriend, has grown up, unbelievably, to be the sexiest man in Ireland. When Hugo and Jenny were fourteen, they thought nothing could come between them: they reckoned without Jenny's terrifying Aunt Lilian. Now, to their mutual amazement, they're both ready to start over. But the course of true love is running anything but smoothly . . .

JOAN O'NEILL

SOMETHING BORROWED, SOMETHING BLUE

Complete and Unabridged

ULVERSCROFT
Leicester

First published in Great Britain in 2000 by
Hodder and Stoughton
London

First Large Print Edition
published 2002
by arrangement with
Hodder and Stoughton
a division of Hodder Headline
London

All characters in this publication are fictitious and
any resemblance to real persons, living or dead,
is purely coincidental.

The moral right of the author has been asserted

Copyright © 2000 by Joan O'Neill
All rights reserved

British Library CIP Data

O'Neill, Joan
  Something borrowed, something blue.
  —Large print ed.—
  Ulverscroft large print series: romance
  1. First loves—Ireland—Fiction
  2. Ireland—Fiction
  3. Love stories
  4. Large type books
  I. Title
  823.9′14 [F]

  ISBN 0–7089–4642–9

011844

MORAY COUNCIL

DEPARTMENT OF TECHNICAL
& LEISURE SERVICES

F

Published by
F. A. Thorpe (Publishing) Ltd.
Anstey, Leicestershire

Set by Words & Graphics Ltd.
Anstey, Leicestershire
Printed and bound in Great Britain by
T. J. International Ltd., Padstow, Cornwall

This book is printed on acid-free paper

For my family, and my cousin Joan.

1

'Jenny, read this letter from Aunt Lilian,' Mum said, passing it to me.

'I haven't time,' I said, buttoning my jacket. 'Tell me what it says.'

'Cathy's coming home to get married.'

Cathy! I hadn't thought about my cousin Cathy for years. Her name had been buried under mysterious silences and unanswered questions for so long that time had swallowed her up.

'Someone she met when she was in Sydney,' Mum continued. 'The wedding's in Connemara, the weekend after next. She wants you to be her bridesmaid,' she rushed on, 'so you may have to go down a few days beforehand.'

Typical of my mother, organising everything and everyone before the rest of us has time to think.

'It's all a bit rushed, isn't it?'

'Poor Lilian's lumbered with all the preparations.'

'I'll phone Cathy myself. See what the story is.'

'Good idea. We might all drive down

together, make a bit of a family event out of it.'

Oh, no! I'd go down by train. Get a compartment to myself, read my book. Have a bit of peace.

'You should take a page out of her book. Get yourself a nice man.'

'I'm happy with my life,' I lied.

I was twenty-seven years old, still single and, worse, still living at home with my parents, Bert and Bridget, and having to skulk around when I had a hangover, hoping they wouldn't smell the beer on my breath. I glanced out of the window to avoid Mum's eyes, secretly longing for a place of my own in a nice part of town, and a nice boyfriend.

'I'm off,' I said, finishing the dregs of my tea.

Mum looked at me, knowing I was putting on a brave face for the sake of my pride. Whenever she thought of me ending up on my own she panicked. Until Paul Parker's defection there had never been anything in my life to give her cause for concern. Her fear was that I would become so desperate I would ask him to come back to me and the whole disastrous business would start up all over again. Well, there was no fear of that. Who needed him and all those females he'd lied to me about? After a blazing row I had finished with him, then saw in the New Year alone in front of the telly with a pile of invitations to parties on the mantelpiece.

I didn't care any more since I was doing fine without him. Out of sheer desperation, and boredom, I'd got myself a job in Sharp's advertising agency, a small-profile firm on the top floor of a newly built office block, overlooking Grand Canal. I found myself sharpening pencils, filing and making coffee for creative dickheads who didn't give a toss about anything except their own high-gloss images. For a graduate in marketing this was soul-destroying. Then one day, out of the blue, I was promoted from general factotum in the front office to secretary to Louis Leech, the up and coming ad exec with the biggest portfolio in the company.

'Let me know what you decide,' Mum said.

'I will. Now I have to hurry or I'll miss the bus.' I was meeting my best friend, Sophie Smith, in O'Reilly's for a drink, and I was late.

When I arrived she was slumped in a corner booth. 'Sorry I'm late,' I said.

'Let me guess. Aliens abducted you. Your car was stolen. You got a ladder in your tights.'

I threw myself down beside her. 'What a day I've had. First off I get this phone call from the bank manager telling me I'm overdrawn, and asking me to pay in some money before I use my Visa card again, as if I could pull money out of a hat.'

'Asshole.' She tossed back her long shiny black hair.

'Then I wasted an entire morning phoning around looking for a mechanic to fix my damn car.'

'That car has you broke.'

'Tell me about it. I got the name of this guy, Ian, off one of the lads at work, took it round — and guess what! He offered to fix it for free if I'd go out with him.'

'And?' Sophie's prompted.

'He's not bad-looking, if a bit greasy.' I wrinkled my nose.

'He might scrub up well.' Sophie squeaked with laughter, lit a cigarette, and sat back dragging on it, her eyes roaming round, checking out the talent.

I sighed. 'What is it with me? I can never get the guy I want.'

'Because you go for the fast, glamorous types. Your dream man probably hasn't been born yet.'

'Remember Len in Lanzarote? I quite enjoyed him.'

'So did lots of other women, and that was hot Lanzarote. This is cold Ireland, and hunks like him are thin on the ground.'

'Don't I know it!'

Sophie was a copywriter on Louis's team. She was an attractive girl with big blue eyes, peaches-and-cream complexion, and her efficient, no-nonsense attitude to work made her popular with everyone. But with men she was hopeless. She set her sights on the best-looking professional guys with prospects — lawyers, doctors — and turned down anyone else who pursued her.

Twirling a lock of hair thoughtfully, she said, 'Everyone I know is either married or has a steady boyfriend.'

'Me too. I'm sick of flirting around at boring parties full of men you can only pin down to one night a week.'

'I wonder what they do the rest of the time?' She sighed.

'Train, jog, pick their noses. Who cares?'

'Bastards.'

'Losers.'

'You've said it. What about Louis Leech?' She eyed me levelly. 'After the office party you said he was the most delectable thing you'd ever seen.'

'That was just a bit of flirting. I was drunk and he was dangerous.'

'That's what you like, isn't it?' She smirked.

'No. I'm biding my time until I find someone I really fancy.'

'Don't expect him to fall into your lap. You have to put a bit of effort in. Accept all the invitations you get,' she advised.

'Speaking of invitations, my cousin Cathy's getting married in Galway the week after next, and I'm going to be her bridesmaid.'

'That's a bit sudden. Is she . . . ?' She folded her arms, and made a rocking motion with them.

I shook my head. 'I haven't seen her for years. She's been travelling the world.'

'Lucky bitch.'

Cathy had lived in about five different countries in as many years. Unable to cope with her mother's disapproval, she had kept away from Ireland. Selfish and beautiful, she'd broken all Aunt Lilian's rules, and had remained untamed, until now.

'If we don't get hitched soon, we'll be left behind,' moaned Sophie.

We sat there in the smoky haze, guzzling high-calorie beer from bottles, eyeing the fat stomachs that came through the door, not a handsome face among them.

★ ★ ★

6

That night I phoned Cathy. 'I heard the news. It's terrific! I hope you'll be very happy.'

'Oh, Jenny! Isn't it amazing? Me, a confirmed spinster, getting hitched.'

'He must be something really special.'

'I never thought I'd meet anyone like him. He's smashing. I mean one hundred per cent smashing.' She started to laugh. 'Listen to me, wittering on. Come over soon. We'll spend the last few days of my freedom together.' She bubbled with excitement as she said, 'We'll go on the rampage.'

I picked up a photograph of Cathy and me, in the parish concert when I was eight and she was eleven, and studied it. There we stood in our long white dresses, our hair pulled up into clusters of silk flowers that sat on top of our heads like birds' nests.

My cousin Cathy was three years older than I was. I'd known her since I was eight. In that long summer of isolation, after Mum's hysterectomy and her father's death, she had befriended me when I'd come to stay at Coolbawn, Aunt Lilian's farm in County Galway. I was an only child, dominated by my parents, and to me she was the ideal companion. She looked for magic and found it everywhere: in the turn of the tide, and the changes of the moon. Throughout my summer holidays we were inseparable, sharing everything. She was like an older sister: strong, loving, full of energy, generous, wild, and resentful of anyone who came between us. I came to adore her.

A powerful swimmer, fearless in the sea, she taught me how to swim with long, powerful strokes. Together we would fish the rock pools for brown crabs, and dig in the sand for worms. Sometimes we would wade into the water in our clothes, shrieking and splattering. Occasionally she stole Uncle Tom's boat and took me fishing.

On wet days we went to the cinema and art exhibitions in the local hall. Cathy could name birds and trees, and tell stories that made sense, in a soft lilting voice that never faltered. She knew a lot about other countries too, and she could play a mean game of poker.

There was wildness in her: it was in her flame-red hair, and her deep blue eyes, in the rise of her shoulders, and her high, excited laugh. It was in the tug of her hand on my sleeve when she saw something exciting, and it was in the way she crept through the woods.

In the summer holidays we banded together and formed our own private club. We existed in our own little make-believe world. She was the leader and the instructor. I was her pupil, longing to be like her. As each summer holiday went by we grew closer. We held secret meetings in the barn, which amounted to nothing more than jeering each other and making up stories about the local boys we knew and fancied. Together we played music, danced, smoked behind the wood-shed, drank beer from bottles, sunbathed naked on the rocks in the curve of the cove, gulls hovering hopelessly around us.

Once Aunt Lilian caught us sneaking back in the evening's chill, our hair wet, our teeth chattering. She was so angry that she forced us to stay indoors in the evenings. We laughed it off and, in her old dresses, pranced around the bedroom to a *Saturday Night Fever* tape, happy.

Aunt Lilian tried to discipline us, taking charge of our day, checking us by the hour. But we didn't care: in those long summers there was the security in our happiness, and the prospect of our friendship continuing into the future. Cathy basked in my admiration, and now I couldn't wait to see her again.

Meantime, I was rushed off my feet in the office, the wedding put firmly to the back of my mind. With the promotion at work came a lot of changes for me. I loved my new assignments. One of my special projects was the organisation of a range of clothes, from

Fabia's, one of our most lucrative accounts, for the biggest fashion show of the year. The venue was the Berkeley Court Hotel, Dublin. All the details of the show had been sent to Louis. He pored over them, then gave his approval, listing the order in which he wanted each item to be mentioned. Illustrations and details were to appear in every poster advertising the fashion show and every catalogue. I had worked tirelessly, making sure that nothing had been forgotten. Faxes and e-mails had been sent all over the country. Phone calls had been made to customers and acquaintances, informing them of this new line.

I was settling the last-minute details for the launch, sifting through the artwork, making sure the illustrations would create the exact impression Louis wanted, when he came up behind me.

'Busy?' he enquired.

I tensed as I stared up at him. 'Up to my eyes.'

'Leave it,' he said, and slapped a file on my desk. 'I've something much more important for you to do.' He was just back from holiday. His blond hair, bleached by the Sicilian sun, was longer, his tan darker, his blue eyes piercing. 'I want you to make a list of all the garments and tie them in with some

10

appropriate theme, if you can think of one. I need it by this evening so I can take it to the Berkeley Court in the morning. You can do it,' he countered, when I tried to say it was impossible.

He stood there, a ravishing bully in a taupe suit, matching shirt and tie, Italian shoes. There was no arguing with him. What Louis wanted, Louis got. He had a way with women. He worked hard at it.

'You don't have to rush home, do you?' he demanded.

'No,' I croaked.

'Good girl. I'm going out for a while. I'll be back.' There was a villainous glint in his eyes.

Sandy Smith and Charlie Craven, both copywriters on Louis's team, were preparing to leave. I wanted to leave, too, because I didn't trust myself. Louis fancied me, and made no secret of it. He would be back for the report and we'd be alone. The others in the office accused me of leading him on, but his attention gave me a sense of satisfaction. That was all.

At six forty-five I phoned Mum.

'Hello,' she said.

'Hi, it's me. I won't be home until around nine.'

'This job of yours is supposed to finish at

five.' There was no sympathy in her voice for my plight.

'I know, but I've been given this report to do, at the last minute, and if I don't get it done I might just find myself back in all-purpose.'

'Have you forgotten you promised Adam you'd be home early to take him to McDonald's? He'll be very disappointed.'

Adam was the little boy Mum picked up from school and minded while his mother worked part-time in Supersavers.

'I'll take him on Saturday to make up for it.'

'I'll tell him.' Peeved, she put down the phone. Mum didn't understand the necessity for me to work overtime. Everything was black and white to her. You did the job you were paid to do and that was that. It was all right for Dad to work long hours, though. That was different. He owned a painting and decorating business.

When I finished the assignment, I photocopied it and took it in to Louis's office. Framed photographs of him, with leggy fashion models at prestigious functions, lined the wall. This office was a depiction of his success in the world, as he saw it. From here he could command his troops. From here he could plot his little schemes, and set them in motion.

Who did he think he was that he could command me to work late? By what right had he unleashed this power over me? He was only a jumped-up office boy made good. No, that wasn't quite true. He was the nephew of Sam Sharp, the owner and managing director of the company, and Sam had given the orders that had catapulted me into Louis's office, which had unleashed this unbridled passion in Louis. It was all Sam's fault: if he hadn't moved Louis to head office, none of this would have happened. Sam had the power to change the course of our lives with the snap of his fingers.

It was no use blaming him, though. I'd let Louis kiss me at the office party when I'd had a few too many drinks. It had been *only* a kiss — albeit a lingering one. Nothing to feel guilty about.

I was plunged into my own thoughts and didn't hear the whine of the lift, didn't realise that Louis had returned until he was beside me. I handed him the sheaves of paper dying to get the whole business over and done with.

'Let's see. 'Fabia's fashion line is your lifeline,' ' he read. ' 'To celebrate eight years of style we introduce our new ravishing range.' ' He leafed through it, leaning into me, his eyes glowing.

'There'll be handouts featuring all the products. I thought of using banners throughout the ballroom and came up with that slogan for the theme.'

'That's great. You're a star.'

'It was all there. I just had to pull it together.'

'Don't underestimate yourself. You're a clever girl.'

'Thank you.'

He signed his name with an expensive Parker pen he took from his inside jacket pocket. Smiling approvingly he said, 'This calls for a drink.' He pressed himself close to me, breathed heavily into my neck.

'It's getting late.' I looked at my watch and moved away.

'Just a quick one. I'll be downstairs waiting for you.' He was gone before I had a chance to say no.

I almost ran from the office, slamming the door behind me. Grabbing my coat from the cloakroom I dashed down the back stairs, and out into the car park.

When I got home, Mum was doing the ironing.

'It's ten o'clock,' she said crossly. 'You said you'd be home at nine.'

As far as she was concerned I was still her beloved miracle daughter, with flying hair and grazed knees. I was the only one of three pregnancies who'd survived to define Mum's role in life. Through me she existed, and although we didn't always see eye to eye I was still her little girl. She resented my transformation into a woman.

'It took longer than I thought,' I explained.

She frowned in exasperation and unplugged the iron.

If Dad had spent less time in the Maiden's Arms, and was less stingy with the housekeeping, Mum's life would have been perfect: her skill in housekeeping and cooking came to the fore when he was around. She was brighter, too, and more energetic.

Mum and Dad put up with each other in an exhausted sort of way. They went along placidly, their minds flung forward to a better future, their hope for their daughter, who would do them proud. Dad, a big, strong man with thick blond hair, came home every evening at half past six — when he wasn't away at the races — and fell on his supper like a vulture as he recounted his difficult day in his office.

When he saw the hat Mum had bought for the wedding he scoffed, 'A lot of fuss and nonsense, and a total waste of money.'

'It'll be a elaborate affair,' Mum said. 'Lilian's determined to push the boat out for her only daughter. All the local bigwigs will be there.'

'Why they're bothering I don't know. Marriages don't last pissin' time these days. You mark my words,' Dad pronounced, turning his newspaper inside out.

Mum nodded, as was her way, and held her tongue about her other ventures. He watched Sky Sports, then swaggered off to the pub to cram in as many pints as he could before closing time, eye up the barmaid and argue with his pals about horses and politics.

Mum had 'missed the boat', she'd often said, by marrying him. She missed her family and friends in the West too. Even though they referred to her as 'the poor relation', who had 'married beneath her' they were loyal to her and she to them. She had two sisters: Aunt Lilian and Aunt Flo but Aunt Lilian, the eldest, was the one on whose every word she still hung. She would have liked to see more of them, but her own family's welfare was all-important.

She was loyal to Dad, and would not turn against him, no matter what. He had provided her with everything she needed. But I caught a glimpse of her real feelings on the rare occasion when he went too far with his ranting and raving. Then she silenced him with a look.

When I woke up the next morning my car was outside, the keys pushed through the letterbox. Good old Ian. I'd give him a ring later.

Mum called, 'Don't work too hard,' as she waved me off, closing the gate on a roaming dog and turning back towards her sparkling windows and the colourful boxes of lobelias and nasturtiums that adorned them. I was thinking of what Louis would have to say — I had not met him in the foyer to go for a drink as he had expected, and he could be nasty.

The traffic was in full flow as I pulled out of our cul-de-sac of pre-war red-brick houses, all neat as a pin. Mum had thought Dad crazy to buy a house there thirty years ago because it was too close to the city centre, but it had been handy for his work, and she'd grown to like it.

A number of the families I'd grown up with were still living there. Mum went to their houses and they came to ours. They exchanged gossip and drank tea together, not just in the morning but at all hours of the day. Now, thirty years later, it was a desirable location, with the new neo-Georgian houses that now overlooked it. Dad hadn't approved when planning permission was granted for these 'unsightly monsters' to be built but they had raised the value and prestige of the area.

'Good morning,' the cleaner said, as she swung the floor polisher vigorously round the foyer.

'Morning, Lena.' I went up in the lift and almost ran to my office, dumped my bag on the floor and took immediate refuge behind my desk which was piled high with the morning post, newspapers and magazines. Sophie was already at her computer. I glanced towards Louis's empty office, and kept my head down, sorting the post, checking the list of important clients due in.

At midday precisely he swept in. 'I'd like a word with you, Jenny,' he said. 'In private.'

The moment I entered his office and shut the door he exploded. 'What the hell happened to you last night? How come you didn't wait to have a drink with me?' Before I had a chance to reply he thundered, 'You didn't think it worth your while to let me know that you were leaving?' He was leaning forward; his eyebrows knitted, his face like granite.

'You didn't give me a chance, and when I suddenly realised how late it was . . . ' I tried to explain.

He was furious. 'Well, thanks a bunch for standing me up,' he rasped. 'I hung around waiting for you for so long in that bloody foyer that the shaggin' security bastard locked me in.'

'What?'

'He assumed I was leaving when I said goodnight to him. The bloody cops had to come and let me out.' He was livid.

'I'm sorry,' I said meekly.

'I should bloody well hope so. Those bluebottles had a right laugh. It was only a drink we were going to have, not an orgy.'

I was mortified. 'I'm really sorry.'

He relaxed into his chair. 'You can make it up to me,' he said, with a twinkle in his eye.

For one split second I thought he was going to leap over the table, grab me and start kissing me frantically. He didn't.

'How?'

He stood up, straightened his broad shoulders and brushed back his floppy hair. 'I'll think of something. Now get back to work.'

I didn't see him again until five thirty when, sports bag in hand, he was heading off to the Riverside Leisure Club in his Mercedes for a game of squash or a jog on the running machine, while he thought up clever slogans for his commercials.

2

Next morning I went to work early in an effort to placate Louis, driving through city streets full of morning traders, fruit-sellers setting up their stalls, deliverymen hauling huge boxes out of the backs of their vans. In the office I found a note on my desk in Louis's handwriting. It read: 'Lunch with me. One p.m. sharp.'

Hastily I stuffed it into a drawer, glancing towards Louis's office. The door was open. He wasn't in. At ten o'clock he appeared, and walked over to my desk. 'OK?' His eyes were on my boobs.

Just as I was about to try to convince him that lunch together wasn't a good idea, he said, 'Ten to one in the foyer,' and made for his office.

I nodded.

The morning dragged on with the normal office routine, phones ringing, people coming in and out. At lunchtime Louis called me. 'Get your coat. We'll be out of here in a jiffy. Come on, let's go.'

Once we got downstairs, he said, 'I know somewhere where we can have a quiet drink.'

His car was parked nearby. 'Jump in.' He gave a quick glance in the side-mirror and shot off down the road.

'Where are we going?'

'My place,' he said. 'I make a terrific omelette.' He glanced at me. 'Only, of course, if you want to. Wouldn't want to force myself on you.'

'Nice,' I said, as he parked outside an apartment block in Leeson Street.

'It's handy,' he said.

'For what?'

He grinned at me.

We took the lift to the second floor. The apartment was bright and cheerful. Louis pulled down the blinds against the sun, went into the kitchen and returned with two gin and tonics. I sipped my drink while he removed his jacket, rolled up his shirtsleeves and got to work. I could hear him moving around the tiny kitchen, whisking eggs, humming to himself. We ate on a coffee table in the sitting room.

'I didn't know you were such a good cook,' I said, savouring the *omelette aux fines herbes*.

He laughed. 'That's about the extent of my range,' he said, pouring the wine.

'Delicious,' I said, taking a sip of chilled Chardonnay.

'There are many things you don't know about me.' His eyes were on me.

I glanced at my watch. 'I should be getting back to work.'

'Don't be a spoilsport. Sam's out of town, and you know what they say the mice can do when the cat's away.' He smiled that crooked smile of his, and my heart began to race. When he saw me hesitate, he said, 'Relax, everything's all right. I'm in charge. All the more reason why you don't have to rush.' He took the glass from my hand.

It was like a scene from a film. One minute we were sitting there talking, the next we were on the floor, rolling around kissing like kids. He was on top of me, his hands on my shoulders pushing me back, the room spinning. Down I went, and his muscular body covered mine. His hands on my shoulders pinned me to the floor.

'You look great down there.' He laughed. Then, leaning over me, he said in a low voice, 'I've wanted to do this for a long time.'

The doorbell rang.

'Oh, no.' I giggled.

'Shh.' His hand covered my mouth. 'Don't make a sound. They'll go away in a minute.'

It rang again, louder and longer this time.

'Damn. Whoever it is has seen my car.' He got to his feet cursing.

I jumped up, straightened my clothes and ran to the bathroom to comb my tangled hair. I heard the front door open, then shut with a slam. Footsteps went down the corridor to the kitchen and stopped. Hurriedly, I ran a comb through my hair, fixed my lipstick and escaped to the bedroom to wait for Louis to get rid of the surprise guest. I lay down, the wine making me feel drowsy.

Suddenly the door burst open and a woman came in. 'Who are you?' she asked, adjusting her glasses. 'What are you doing here?' She spoke through clenched teeth.

'I was waiting for Louis. I must have fallen asleep,' I stammered, gawking at her. 'I know you. You're the girl in the Special Spectacles commercial. I'm Louis's secretary,' I said brilliantly.

'Louis working you to death, is he?' She laughed hysterically, showing sharp white teeth.

'Yes. As a matter of fact we're very busy at the moment.'

She gazed at me myopically from the narrow space between the wall and the bed.

I jumped up just as Louis appeared in the doorway.

'Louis,' she said. 'You've got a girl in here.'

'Well, I'll be damned,' he said, scratching his head, as if suddenly seeing me for the first time. 'It's Jenny, my new secretary. Come on, let's all have a drink.'

'Not so fast.' Specs grabbed his hair.

'What are you doing?' he squealed. 'For Chrissakes, let go, Judith. Will you stop?' he yelled.

'Caught you red-handed, didn't I? I knew you were up to something.'

'What do you expect, coming up here unannounced?' he shouted, pulling free.

I made for the door. She dodged past me, barring my way.

'You can have him and good riddance,' she yelled.

'I don't want him,' I shouted after her.

'Wait, Jenny.' Louis grabbed my arm.

I shook off his hand. 'I'm going too.'

'I can explain.'

'Don't bother.' I got my coat.

'I'll take you back to the office.'

'I'll get a taxi.'

Cursing him, I stormed out, pulling the door after me, and ran to the lift. I got in, pressed the button for the ground floor, and within moments was running across the lobby and out into the afternoon traffic. Louis stayed away for the rest of the afternoon. Fortunately it was the last day before my departure for the West, so I wouldn't have to see him again for a while.

3

On the morning of my departure for Galway Mum fussed as usual. 'Have you got everything you need?'

'You'd think I was leaving for good.' I was exasperated.

'No such bloody luck,' said Dad, draining his coffee cup and making for the door. 'You'll miss the ruddy train if you don't get going.'

'Packed a woolly jumper? It can be very chilly in the West,' Mum said.

'Mum! I'm not a child.'

'That's debatable,' chimed in Dad.

'Drive carefully,' she warned Dad from the hall door, her hands at her sides, her eyes anxious.

'Don't I always?' Dad retorted.

'No,' Mum shot back.

'Bloody women.' Dad grimaced as he tore out of the gate, and stepped on the accelerator, heading fast down the hill, heedless to Mum's warning.

It was August, and we raced through the twisting streets, overtaking delivery vans and cars with caravans. Dad sped round the last corner and pulled up narrowly avoiding a holidaymaker, clad in shorts and a baseball cap, carrying a haversack.

'Bloody fool!' he exclaimed, tapping his fingers impatiently on the steering-wheel, forced to wait while the man crossed the road.

Dad set great store by punctuality. He believed that only stupid people had accidents and he wasn't one of them.

We stopped outside the station, taking up the middle of the road. Dad got out and lifted out my bag. His business suit was limp and loose, giving the impression of a relaxed man about town.

He didn't enjoy being 'dressed up like a tailor's dummy', as he put it. He was much more comfortable in the overalls he had been forced to discard when his business expanded.

'Thanks,' I called, as he hopped back into the car and slammed the door. Then he was gone, driving off at high speed.

★ ★ ★

In the train I sat in the corner of an empty compartment, legs crossed, head back, the palms of my hands sticky with heat and excitement at the prospect of seeing Cathy again. As the train trundled out of the station I leaned back and gazed out the window.

We stopped at the next station. Doors opened, and a group of high-spirited teenagers got on, opening windows, threatening one another good-humouredly. Thankfully they settled in the next carriage. The train took off again, leaving behind grey buildings, factories and office blocks. We were out in the open countryside, flying past neat fields, where sheep and cattle grazed in the sun.

The train stopped at Athlone. People got on and off. The compartment door opened. A man came in. I turned back to the window, hoping he'd get the message and disappear, but he sat down opposite me. Oh, well, it was a free country. I returned to my contemplation of the landscape. As the train started up again I kept my eyes on the view outside, sensing the man's eyes on me. I felt self-conscious, and retreated to my thoughts.

I was looking forward to the wedding: meeting old friends, the parties and discos, collapsing into bed in the early hours, and special moments with Cathy, whom I hadn't seen for so long.

We stopped at Ballinasloe. Our compartment door opened. Another man hovered just outside and moved on. I stole a glance at my companion with no more interest than anyone would give to a good-looking stranger, noticing his sexy mouth and the firm set of his jawline. He was reading the newspaper, his brow furrowed in concentration. Suddenly he looked up. His eyes held mine.

The countryside sped by, the rain-laden sky closing over the immense fields. I glanced at him again. He was staring at me. I turned back to the window, but the pressure to stare back was unbearable. I shifted sideways so that I wasn't facing him directly.

The sky darkened and the rain started, scratching the window at first, then streaking across it, blown by the wind. I took my book out of my bag, held it loosely and tried to concentrate on it. Eventually I sneaked another look at him. He caught my eye and smiled. It wouldn't hurt to smile back, would it? This was merely a pleasant interlude on a dull journey. However, no demands were being made on me, and nothing was expected, so there was no need to respond.

The train raced along, swaying from side to side. I shut my eyes briefly, intensely aware of the man, the carriage hot and stuffy, my heart thudding in my chest. When I opened them again I saw endless rows of new, expressionless houses, their façades brilliant in the sunshine. Galway City was near. In a few minutes we would arrive and it would all be over, the tension, the intimacy, and the way he looked straight into my face. Narrow gardens gave way to small back-to-back cottages, a playing-field, then grey-stone city buildings, and Galway.

I stood up.

'Let me,' he said, lifting my bag down from the luggage rack.

'Thank you,' I said.

Our eyes locked.

He wasn't smiling any more, but staring hard at me. The train jolted to a halt, pitching us together. I staggered backwards and he grabbed me. I could feel myself lean towards him as his hands steadied me. For an instant we stood still. Then the doors clanked open. Immediately he released me and I took my bag. On trembling legs I moved to the compartment door, opened it and got out.

As soon as I was on the platform I realised that Cathy wasn't in the crowd. People were rushing past, leaving me clutching my bag and looking longingly after the man. He was striding off confidently in the direction of the ticket collector, without a backward glance.

The ticket collector let me through the barrier and I stood in the entrance to the station in shadowy evening sunlight.

'You'll be lucky to get a taxi at this hour.' A

porter glanced up at the station clock. 'They'll all be at the match.'

'It's all right, I'm waiting for someone.'

At that moment a car pulled up. The doors opened and Cathy jumped out, two young men following her. 'Jenny!' she cried, hugging me with delight.

'Cathy!' I was choking back tears of joy.

Here was my cousin Cathy, recently returned from Australia, sophisticated and full of new experiences. Tall and slender, her glorious red hair tapering to her shoulders, her big, bold, defiant eyes shadowed by the brim of her straw hat, she held me away from her. In the intervening years since I'd seen her I'd adapted to life without her, but now I realised how much I had missed her.

'All grown up. You look terrific,' she said, gazing at me.

'She's right about that.' I barely recognised Drew — Uncle Tom and Aunt Flo's son — who was coming forward now, his hair dishevelled.

A tall, friendly-looking man with astonishing blond hair and solid shoulders moved towards me.

'This is Ned, my fiancé,' Cathy said.

'Good to meet you,' he said, and shook my hand heartily.

Already I could feel the excitement of the

wedding, of people arriving in new dresses and hats.

'What's in this bag? A body?' exclaimed Drew, taking charge of my rucksack and lifting it into the boot of the car.

'Mum insisted I bring my woollies.'

'She may have been right.' Drew smiled and slammed the boot lid. His car was a down-at-heel Honda and reeked of petrol fumes.

4

Beyond the station Galway beckoned, its cathedral spire glinting in the golden afternoon light. Soon we were among the city traffic. Drew slowed down. I sat in the back peering out at Eyre Square, which teemed with life and colour. Young girls in bright clothes and heavy makeup walked purposefully past gaily painted shops, and beautiful grey-stone buildings. Further on, we passed rows of houses where clothes-lines fluttered until we were in the countryside.

Once out of the city Drew took the Clifden road. Twenty miles further on he turned off the main thoroughfare and drove along a botharin that wound downhill to Kilbeg. Once again I was on a familiar road, visiting the village of my childhood. It was spread out below us, barely visible beneath the treetops, its church spire looming against the sky. Over the years it had shrunk with emigration, I'd heard, and there had been few newcomers.

Coolbawn House, Aunt Lilian's two-storey farmhouse, isolated among scattered fields, was in sight. It looked small against the backdrop of the Atlantic Ocean, which stretched endlessly beyond it, yet it was the largest farmhouse in the locality, affording my aunt Lilian the distinction of being the biggest farmer. My grandfather had built it. Over the years the farm had shrunk: some of the land had been divided between my two uncles, Edward and John. They were dead now and their share had been sold to pay my grandfather's drinking debts.

The rusty gates hung open, creaking with age and unoiled hinges, and the twisting avenue stretched ahead, overgrown and dark under the canopy of trees. But the tiny gate lodge was encased in scaffolding. Neglected for years, ivy and nettles choking its windows, grass growing out of its chimney, it was now in the process of being repaired and painted.

We passed the gap in the hedge that led to the bridge over the river. Through the open car window I could hear the gurgle of water over the stones. This was my first visit back in twelve years. I clasped my hands together to stop them trembling as scenes of my last visit came back to me. To me, as a child, Coolbawn had spelt freedom to play hide and seek through the big draughty rooms, to explore the woods, climb trees, swim on hot days, race with Cathy and the others on the beach and bury ourselves in the sand. It represented summers of warm, sunny days, of cycling with the wind in our hair, past gorse bushes and bracken, their clear scent now in the evening air.

Drew parked in the courtyard. The house stood in the sun, its slate roof glistening, and its old chimneys stark against the sky. Red geraniums blazed against its white walls, and spread their extravagant blooms, relieving its austerity. The whole place took on a magic quality as I walked up the path bordered with hedges painted with fuchsia and wild roses. Poppies danced in the adjoining field. A cat lay sleeping under a gnarled tree. Everywhere smelt of the sea.

Cries of 'Mum' from Cathy cut the air, but brought no reply. We went to the back door where chickens pecked around us and ducks waddled over to greet us. A lame collie ambled towards us.

'Spot,' said Cathy, by way of introduction, and patted his head.

The back door that had always been left on the latch was locked. I looked in through the scullery window. The churn and its wooden laths were propped against it as usual.

'Mum!' Cathy cried again.

This time Aunt Lilian swept out of the house. 'Haven't you got a key, Cathy?' Then, seeing me, she cried, 'Well, well. If it isn't Jenny! How nice to see you.'

At sixty-five she was still an attractive woman, slim with milky skin and red hair. 'How are you?' she asked, putting me away from her to stare at me approvingly. 'Come on in.'

Inside, the house was as it had always been: coats hanging on the hallstand, keys flung on top of its glove drawer, the brass hood gleaming over the open fireplace. We went past the dining room, where sunlight poured in upon dark furniture. The stained-glass vestibule door threw rose- and green-patterned light on the wooden staircase that led downstairs to the kitchen, and Cathy's Aunt Mary. I made my way along the dark passage, smelling the mingled scent of damp and cooking that had always hung in the air.

'Jenny!' Aunt Mary was out of her chair like a bullet. 'How lovely to see you. I didn't hear the car. Must be going deaf.'

'Hello, Aunt Mary.' I went into her arms.

'Let me look at you,' she said. 'You're lovely. Just like your mother.'

Aunt Mary was a small woman, neat as a pin in her flowery overall. Though her hair was streaked with grey there was softness in her rosy cheeks and youthfulness in her abundant flesh. After her brother Ambrose had brought his young wife to live at Coolbawn, she had stayed on, unwilling to

35

tear herself away from the only home she had ever known. She might have escaped eventually, had it not been for Uncle Ambrose's untimely death, but by then it had been too late.

While Aunt Lilian was the slave driver, Aunt Mary was the ministering angel. She was the one who had tended the cuts and bruises, who had listened to and kept our secrets. She knew all our tricks, doled out sympathy liberally, and spread kindness like butter. Even now her eyes still had the dreamy, romantic look of a young girl. In the early days there had been talk of a secret admirer, an ageing farmer with land, but Aunt Mary had laughed it off. Marriage to her was 'more trouble than it's worth', she'd said. Both sister-in-law and servant to Aunt Lilian, Aunt Mary took everything in her stride, gladly giving up her life to Aunt Lilian's bidding.

'Come and sit down and tell me every-thing,' she said, taking a cake out of the oven and turning it upside down on to a cooling rack. 'There,' she said, standing back, the fragrant smell wafting around her. 'A little treat to celebrate your return. I prayed to God for the day that you'd come back,' she said, ceremoniously removing the baking tin to reveal a delicious dark fruit cake.

'I came back because Cathy wanted me to come.'

'Oh, you're wanted right enough, my dear,' she said ominously.

'What's wrong?'

'Nothing as such.' She leaned towards me, and said quietly, 'But with the goings-on of this wedding there's bound to be an explosion between Lilian and Cathy. If you take my advice you'll keep your mouth shut and not take sides if either of them asks your advice.'

I went to the sink to wash my hands, mulling over her warning as Aunt Mary made tea then sat down in her chair by the kitchen window, which overlooked the walled vegetable garden. This was where she'd always sat in her leisure time, to read or sew, or recall 'the old days'.

Cathy clattered into the kitchen. 'Isn't it great to see Jenny again?' she said, pouring herself a cup of tea.

'It's wonderful, and I've cooked a special dinner,' Aunt Mary replied.

★　★　★

Aunt Lilian presided over dinner in the cavernous dining room, which was only used on special occasions.

37

'Isn't this wedding the most wonderful thing?' she said. 'I've made so many plans, and there's so much to do.' As she spoke her eyes were filled with excitement and delight.

By all accounts she had spared nothing of herself in arranging it, and had driven Aunt Mary to the edge of distraction, making her scrub and polish any surface that hadn't been freshly painted, in a superhuman effort to get the place shipshape for the big occasion. Everything had been planned with the precision of a craftsman, everything thought of. Lights had even been strung around the trees in the garden. 'I've arranged for a top Dublin band to play for the dancing afterwards.' She sat back and waited for gratitude and praise, but Cathy looked startled.

'A band? But I've booked a DJ from Galway for the night,' she said.

'Never mind, dear.' Aunt Lilian tried to suppress her anger at Cathy's foolishness. 'Cancel him. Now finish up. Aunt Flo's dying to see you both. Cathy, you'll drive Jenny over after supper.'

Aunt Mary hesitated, then said shyly, 'Perhaps Cathy and Jenny would rather be alone together for a while. They haven't seen each other for so long, and Jenny must be tired after her journey.'

'Well, of course.' Aunt Lilian drew back from the table, her smile tight-lipped, her eyes cold as the sea after rain.

'But don't stay talking all night,' she added. 'We've got lots of things to do tomorrow.' Warmth returned to her voice at the thought of her generous plans. 'We're going to have the most terrific time, aren't we?' She looked around at us all.

'Of course we are,' said Aunt Mary encouragingly.

'I'll help in any way I can,' I offered.

'That's very kind of you, Jenny.'

'If you'll excuse me,' Cathy said, standing up and going to the door.

'I know she's going to be thrilled with it all,' said Aunt Mary, to avert a crisis. 'She's just a bit nervous.'

'She'll buck up with all her own family around her on her special day,' Aunt Lilian said. 'Now, I must go too. Things to do.'

Her departure seemed to loosen a spring in Aunt Mary. She gathered herself together and said, 'See what I mean? Between you and me, there'll be trouble before this wedding's over, with Lilian on her high horse about everything. She's getting more eccentric by the day. She can be so odd at times.'

Aunt Mary had a keen nose for scenting trouble, but no aptitude for defusing it.

'I'd better go up to Cathy,' I said, excusing myself from the table.

'Certainly,' said Aunt Mary. 'It's lovely to have you back. Yes, indeed,' she added, with a smile.

I shut the door of the dining room behind me, and went up to my bedroom first, a large room at the back of the house. Its pale blue walls reflected the sea that gleamed here and there through the trees. Cathy came in to help me unpack.

'What a lovely dress!' she said, lifting my new one out of my bag. 'Spitfire red. That should turn a few heads.'

'Thanks.'

In her bedroom we examined her trousseau. 'Ned will love this,' I said, picking up a pale lilac lace basque.

Cathy's eyes were too bright, her voice too cheerful, as she said, 'I'm wearing that under my wedding dress. Which reminds me, I haven't got anything blue, and I need a couple of pairs of tights. We'll go shopping tomorrow before Fawn, my friend from Sydney, arrives. She'll be staying at Aunt Flo's. We'll have fun.' She spoke in a rush.

'I'll phone Mum and ask her to bring her blue garter from her wedding day. Aunt Lilian gave it to her and she still has it.'

'It's amazing how well those two get on,

considering Mum is such a boss.'

'That's probably the reason,' I said. 'My mum lives her real life through Coolbawn and the aunts. They're what matters most to her. In her life with Dad she only exists. How she stuck him all these years I'll never know.'

She would never consider leaving him, I knew that. It would be the easy way out, as far as she was concerned, and that was not her style.

'I'm sure she must still be an attractive woman, with a good figure and nice clothes. She could go where she liked, do what she liked,' Cathy said.

'Indeed she could, but she never does,' I said sadly.

5

Next day, after our shopping spree, we collected Fawn Fowler, Cathy's Australian friend, from Aunt Flo's, and set off for Salthill for our night out on the town. Fawn was a likeable girl, with a ready smile. Cathy, already a bit squiffy from the wine at lunchtime, took us into the bar of the Galway Bay Hotel, and said, 'I really appreciate you both coming all this way for my wedding.' She ordered our drinks, and popped one of Fawn's cigarettes into her mouth, although she didn't smoke, then sat back and puffed. 'I don't know what I'd do without you girls,' she said.

'This time the day after tomorrow you'll be Mrs Ned Wibbly,' said Fawn.

'Willoby,' corrected Cathy.

'Same difference,' Fawn said. 'And how *is* Ned? Is he getting cold feet?'

'Probably, and wet too. He's gone fishing with Drew. I haven't spoken to him today.'

'Hasn't he phoned you?' Fawn asked.

'No.'

'Get him on his mobile. Make sure he's all right.'

'For what?'

'For the wedding. He might have changed his mind.' Fawn laughed.

'He hates me ringing him when he goes out.'

'What a load of rubbish,' said Fawn. She turned to me. 'Pete, the best man, is gorgeous,' she said.

'Yes, he's cute,' said Cathy. 'A really nice fella. And, no, Fawn you're not getting your hands on him.'

'Why not if he's a nice bloke?' Fawn raised a perfectly plucked eyebrow indignantly. 'And we're all on holiday.'

Cathy drained her drink. 'He's in love with someone.'

'Who?'

'Himself.' Cathy rolled her eyes and we roared.

'Be serious,' Fawn begged.

'I *am* serious. I'm not good at sussing out men, but I can pick out the just-wants-a-quick-shag-and-no-commitment type a mile off.'

Fawn's face fell. 'Why is there always a catch?' she asked.

Cathy laughed. 'Come on, let's have a dance,' she said, looking around at the groups of people moving towards the disco like a tidal wave.

'What a jittery breed,' said Fawn, gloating at the men jumping around the floor.

A fellow with flabby jowls was pacing up and down in front of us. Eventually he plucked up the courage to come over. 'Dance?' he said to Fawn.

Cathy held her breath, fearful that Fawn would refuse, but she eyed him up and down then wiggled off with him, her hair swinging.

'Congratulations, Cathy,' gushed a passing acquaintance. 'Saw your engagement in the paper and thought, whoever has finally snared our Cathy? Australian lad, is he?'

'Irish grandparents,' Cathy informed him.

'Haven't they all?'

Suddenly a giant of a man appeared beside us, and gave a low whistle of appreciation as he looked in my direction.

'Who's *she*?' he asked Cathy.

'I'm Cathy's cousin,' I said.

'Dance?' Catching me round the waist he ploughed me through the throng, head-butting anyone who got in his way. There was no room in the middle of the floor so we danced at the edge. Suddenly, he twirled me. I slipped under his sweaty armpit, and went sprawling. With a cry of 'Gotcha,' he lifted me up and half carried me to the bar. 'You wanna watch yourself. They're a rough lot in here,' he said, tightening his arm around me, pushing some poor drunk off his bar-stool, and sitting me on it. 'What's your poison?' he asked.

'Champagne,' I said.

'No shit! You're startin' the celebrations early.'

He ordered a glass of champagne for me and a Diet Coke for himself. As he handed me my drink, he said, 'I'm Ron Ray, all the way from Sydney.'

'You don't say. Whatever made me think you were an alien from Mars?'

He laughed. 'I'm on Ned's rugby team.'

'Not drinking yourself?'

'I have to go easy on the sauce. I'm in training for the Australian team,' he said, and waited for my gasp of amazement.

'I hate rugby,' I said, and watched his face fall to the floor from behind the rim of my glass.

Regaining his composure, he said, 'And what would a snooty madam like you know about it? Huh?'

'I played five-a-sides soccer in the school team. Bruised my ribs badly,' I said, shrinking away from him.

'You don't say.' He exploded with laughter. 'Well, I wish I'd been on the opposite team. I'd have enjoyed crushing a few more of your ribs if I got you on the field.'

'Thanks,' I snarled.

Where was Cathy? Just as I had decided I couldn't take another minute of him, she swooped down on me. Breathless, her hand on my arm, she was pulling me off my stool.

'Fawn's in the loo,' she said. 'Locked.'

'No problem!' I said. 'Ron'll break down the door.'

'Not that 'locked' silly. Out-of-her-brains locked.'

'Oh, God!'

'You're not going already,' said Ron, 'just as we were getting down to a bit of foreplay?'

'You won't be alone,' I said, eyeing the big bleached blonde tottering towards us, her teeth bared.

'There you are Ronny! I was searching for you everywhere,' she squawked. Levelling a look at me, she hissed, 'Who's she?'

'Eh, I don't know. I was minding her for a friend,' said Ron sheepishly.

'Hope you win your match,' I called over my shoulder, as I followed Cathy.

'We will.' He winked, and drummed his chest. 'See you at the wedding.'

Not if I see you first, I thought, weaving through the wave of dancers.

Cathy held open the door of the ladies' toilet with one foot and I ran inside. Fawn had sat down in a corner beside a heavily

46

made-up girl who was laying out a line of cocaine on a compact mirror.

'Oh, Christ,' groaned Cathy. 'It's worse than I thought.'

'Want some?' the girl asked, squinting up at us through watery eyes.

'No!' said Cathy, grabbing Fawn. 'Let's get you out of here while you can still walk.'

'I don't wanna go,' said Fawn, crouching further into her corner.

Cathy yanked her up while I got out my mobile and phoned for a taxi.

Fawn rolled her eyes as we frogmarched her out of the loo, through the gyrating crowd, outside and down the steps to the taxi.

'Look at the cut of you,' Cathy chastised her, as she pushed her into the back. 'I just hope Aunt Flo's in bed.'

'I feel fantastic,' Fawn slurred, slipping down into the seat.

'Who'd have thought she'd get herself into this state?' Cathy moaned, dreading the prospect of finding Aunt Flo or Uncle Tom still up.

But the house was in darkness. Cathy phoned Drew on his mobile while I kept a tight grip on the collapsing Fawn. 'I'm so sorry,' she said, when he appeared in boxer shorts, half asleep. 'Fawn's passed out. I wonder if we should call an ambulance.'

'Not at all,' said Drew, lifting Fawn up in his arms as if she were a featherweight.

'Are you sure?' asked Cathy.

'Trust me. I know what I'm talking about. I've seen Mum like this plenty of times. She'll be all right once she's had a good night's kip.'

6

In the morning I caught the excitement of the wedding, picturing top hats and tails, flowers everywhere as Aunt Lilian dashed about, unpacking the good silver and cutlery. Mum and Dad had called in on their way to stay at Aunt Flo's.

'So, this time tomorrow you'll be married,' I said to Cathy, when they'd gone and we were alone in her bedroom. 'I bet you're all excited.'

'Not exactly,' Cathy said, in a small voice.

'Why do you say that?'

She shut her bedroom door and stood just inside the room, frowning. She sighed. 'Oh, don't mind me. I expect it'll be all right.'

'Why wouldn't it be?'

'Oh, you know, all the fuss. Mum's plans for a big wedding, another victory for her. As long as she has her moment of triumph.' Her eyes were misty. Then her head drooped and her hair fell forward, like water.

'You can't blame Aunt Lilian for wanting all the trimmings. She's waited a long time for this,' I said.

But Cathy would not be soothed. She said

angrily, 'Made me come home specially, and she's promised us the cottage in the lower field if Ned will consider coming to live here for a while to get acquainted with the farm. Because he's from farming stock in Queensland she thinks he might eventually take over the running of Coolbawn.'

'She wants the best for you, Cathy. Is there anything she can give you more important than this wedding? She and Aunt Mary love you, Cathy. This is their gift to you. What would you do without them?'

Cathy sat down on the bed. 'I could do without Mum and all her dashing about, lashing everyone with her tongue. I hate it all.'

'Cathy!' Aunt Lilian called up the stairs. 'Have you time to check through the seating arrangements with me.'

It was really Aunt Lilian's wedding. Everything had been carried out at her direction. She had pretended that everything was being done according to Cathy's wishes, but she plotted and planned and did everything her way. Caught up in the excitement of it all she thought only of the impression she was going to make, and forgot the importance of what was actually happening.

Cathy, with less sophisticated ideas and a

dislike of fuss, thought the whole thing absurd. And Aunt Lilian had thwarted her ideas at every stage. She would have rather died than admit defeat at the hands of her own wilful daughter.

In fact, this wedding was only a temporary distraction from the awful thing that was happening to Aunt Lilian: she would never admit, even to herself, that she was losing her power over her only daughter, over everything that happened at Coolbawn, and that her greatest enemy, old age, was catching up with her.

'Come on, Cathy. Cheer up,' I chivvied her. 'You're alive, you're in love, and that's really all that matters,' I said, thinking of Aunt Mary's advice, and that this was really none of my business.

'It's just that — ' She stopped. 'I know it seems a funny thing to say but I'd have liked a small do. I didn't want that bloody billowing tent sticking out of the side of the house like a boil ready to burst, and it's all so rushed.'

'What does Ned say about it?'

'It doesn't bother him. Why should it? She's not his mother.' She didn't look at me, just sat, her hair rippling over her face, her shoulder blades protruding as she pressed the basque back into its folds of tissue paper.

'It'll all be marvellous and he'll love it,' I said, protective of Aunt Lilian and genuinely believing what I said.

From her smile I knew Cathy disagreed. 'She thinks she's thought of everything, but what if the gods don't smile on us and it rains? And to be honest, Jenny, I'm dreading the old relatives getting together, the gossip, the drink, the mess afterwards.' She sat staring into space, rubbing the back of her neck where headaches start.

'It's only natural that you're having doubts, but you'll be fine on the day. Look, you'll be so caught up in it all you won't have time to think, and you'll be gone before the clearing up. But that's not what's really worrying you, is it?'

'No.' She glanced at me. 'Jenny, I'm only just realising that I don't know Ned all that well. There are things about him . . . ' She hesitated. 'I'm sure there are things about me that he doesn't know.'

'You have the rest of your lives to find out. Meantime, you love each other, and as I've already said, that's all that matters.'

Her voice was sharp as she replied, 'I'm not sure what love is. My whole life has been such a pretence that I'm wondering if I'm being myself now. Is what I feel real?' Suddenly she looked too young to be wearing the big emerald engagement ring she was twisting on her finger.

'Come on, Cathy,' I cajoled. 'You're bowled over by him. Anyone can see that. Now, what's really on your mind? What are you scared of?'

She looked up at me, forlorn. 'He's very wrapped up in himself and he's passionate about his rugby. It comes first.'

'Well, at least it's a ball he lusts after, not other women.'

'He's not even that good in bed. Too much tackling and not enough foreplay. I'm much better than he is.'

'Problem solved. You can teach him.'

'Teach him? He'd want to know where I learned it. And he drinks far too much when he's out with his pals on Saturday nights. Perhaps I agreed too quickly to marry him.'

'What makes you say that?'

'Oh, I dunno. We got swept into it. He was mad about me and I was flattered. Suddenly we were engaged. I expected we'd have time to get to know one another, but Mum insisted we come home straight away for this wedding from hell. She's a terrible woman when it comes to possessiveness.' She spoke of Aunt Lilian almost in tones of reverence. Turning to me she said, 'What happens if he gets bored with me, if . . . ' she trailed off.

'Oh, God, Jenny, I hate myself for saying all this but it's so awful never to be able to say what you think, always having to care about what other people feel.'

Tears flowed from her eyes and her whole body convulsed as she wept.

This was not the carefree Cathy of my childhood. Conscious suddenly of the seriousness of the situation she looked terribly young, and scared. Now she huddled into the crook of my arm as waves of terror washed over her, Cathy, loved by everyone, successful in her career as an interior designer.

'Don't worry.' I tried to reassure her. 'Ned's a solid, responsible, steady kind of bloke. It's obvious he adores you, and it's even money on your chances of a really happy marriage.'

She said, 'I hope so.'

'Well, there you are, then.'

'I'm sorry to sound so negative.'

'It's only nerves. Everybody gets them.'

'I'm glad you're here, Jenny. I need you.'

'I'll help you any way I can.' Just to be there for her was enough, I knew.

'By the way,' she said, brightening. 'Did I tell you that Hugo Hunter's coming to the wedding?'

I stared at her. 'Hugo Hunter?'

She laughed. 'Don't tell me you don't

remember him.' Suddenly, her eyes were alight with mischief. She was the old Cathy again as she said, 'Yes, that amazing creature we've known practically since we were children. The one you plied with sexual favours all those years ago.'

I put my hands to my ears. 'Stop,' I pleaded.

She laughed. 'Mum met him recently at a hunt ball and felt she couldn't leave him out of the wedding — he's the leader of the social scene in these parts.'

'Have you seen him recently?' I asked, my voice quivering.

'No. He's been abroad quite a lot too.' She looked at me. 'Don't pretend you haven't been thinking about him since you came down.'

I shrugged.

'It'll be nice for you two to meet up again. You fancied him rotten all those years ago.'

'Oh, for heaven's sake, Cathy,' I said crossly. 'It was only a teenage crush. I got him out of my system years ago.'

'You used to wait behind the barn door for him. You couldn't wait to rip off his clothes, and savage him. You used to come tearing back to tell me about it,' she reminded me.

The blood rushed to my head, and my heart was beating so fast I had to stand up.

Clutching the dressing-table to steady myself I said, 'You're cruel bringing all that up again.'

'You're blushing,' she crowed.

'Please, Cathy, stop. It wasn't that serious.'

'Oh, no?'

'Summer madness. That's all it was.'

'And that's why you were going to run away with him?' She was her old self, throwing a pillow at me. I covered my face with it.

'Cathy!' Aunt Lilian's impatient voice floated up the stairs.

She jumped up. 'Better dash.'

I grabbed my swimsuit, took off down the stairs and out of the back door. Aunt Lilian's rockery was overgrown — the garden was too much for her, I suspected. Behind the house a line of firs divided it from the farmyard. It protected the house from the harsh winter winds that blew in from the sea.

I squeezed through the well-remembered hole in the fuchsia hedge, and ran down the narrow path in the lower field to the golden meadow. There I stood, remembering long, hot lazy summer days, sheep grazing in the heather, buttercups and daisies to be picked on the grassy banks. Afterwards, thick chunks of soda bread and mugs of milk.

The summer when I was fourteen and I

met Hugo, everything had changed. Cathy had been right. It was instant attraction. We spent time on the beach, in the barn, anywhere we could be alone, our intimacy a big adventure. As I looked around at the familiar sights, I was back in the glorious time I'd savoured with Hugo. I went on down to the beach, remembering the last time I'd been here defeated, with Shep, Cathy's old collie, beside me, his ears back, his tongue lolling.

Plunging into the water I crashed through the waves and swam out until I reached the rocks. Panting, I pulled myself up. My heart pounded as I gazed up at the sky. Seagulls wheeled around me, swallows swooped as memories of that summer intruded: Hugo in his boat, and me stretched out under the sun, absorbing him, his talk, his laughter and the sea. The pair of us rolling in the hay together, hot and sweaty, Hugo returning to his college in England, my letters to him. He had written back telling me he couldn't wait for the following summer.

The next year, on my first evening back at Coolbawn, I had crept downstairs and run down to the beach. Alone, I stood looking around, scared in case he didn't show up.

Then he was coming towards me, taking me in his arms, holding me, neither of us able to speak. He kissed me slowly, deliciously. Time stopped as we clung together. At dawn I sneaked back to the house and upstairs.

Later that day I said to Cathy, 'We *did* it.'

She was standing on a rock, sleek as a seal; her hair plastered to her head. 'What?' She could hardly believe her ears.

Happiness swelled up in me and with it a longing to be questioned. Cathy, shocked and thrilled all at once, wanted to know every detail, so I told her, happy to share my secret. There was magic in the air and, overwhelmed, she took my hand and laced her fingers through mine.

We made our way home slowly that evening, past the fishing-boats — Mac, our friendly fisherman, gave us two mackerel for tea. We passed the lobster pots stacked against the stone wall, the church, the cottages, the whole village aflame in the setting sun. We met Hugo and loitered, talking to him.

'What kept you?' Aunt Lilian had enquired, her hands on her hips.

'We were waiting for the fishing-boats.' The lie tripped easily off Cathy's tongue.

Fumbling with the ironing, smoothing over the collars, Aunt Mary said, 'I love fresh mackerel.'

Cathy shot her a look of gratitude. But it wasn't enough to appease Aunt Lilian. Angrily she said, 'That's no excuse to be so late. Go to your room.'

'We weren't doing any harm,' Cathy shouted, and stormed out, slamming the kitchen door behind her.

'She's like her father,' Aunt Lilian said. 'The same way of not bothering about anyone else, keeping secrets with that same cool distance.'

The tension between Aunt Lilian and us increased. 'The idle grow weary,' she said. She didn't understand what could be gained from 'lazing around', as she put it. Furious, she tamed us with extra jobs, and messages to the village. But my hours with Hugo mattered most: there was no parting me from him. I was radiant with happiness, loving the danger of it all as we continued to meet in secret. His influence endowed me with confidence, and I was drunk with love, living in a world of new joys, wonders, oblivious to its dangers, too young and inexperienced to think that it might not last. He was everything to me, and it hadn't occurred to me that he might feel differently.

'What are you going to do about Mum?' Cathy asked. 'If she finds out you're seeing Hugo she'll go bananas.'

I shrugged. 'She won't find out if you don't tell her.'

'You know I never would.'

'Well, then, there's no problem.'

Our meetings became more frequent, and with each one there was the difficulty of keeping it secret.

One afternoon Cathy came searching for me to warn me that Aunt Lilian was looking for me. She found me in the hayrick with Hugo. 'Mum's on the warpath,' she said. 'Come quickly before she sends out a search party.'

I sat up, raking back my hair with my hand, pulling down my top. Hugo's eyes were on me, as if he couldn't bear to let me go.

'Be off before she catches you,' Cathy hissed at him.

At that moment Aunt Lilian appeared and stood horror-stricken at the sight of us. I swung myself to the floor, trembling.

White with rage she faced Hugo. 'Go home and stay at home,' she shouted. Hugo left without a glance in my direction. I ran out of the barn and down the garden path, petrified at the thought of the punishment she had in store for me.

She came after me. 'Jenny!' she shrilled. 'Come here at once.'

I slunk out from behind the hedge.

'What did you think you were doing?' she asked.

Everything was silent except for bees droning among the flowers.

'Well?' She waited for me to speak.

I was helpless in the face of her rage. I wanted to run out through the gate and off down the road. The hedge spun as she waited for my explanation.

'Have you lost the power of speech?' she asked eventually.

When I didn't reply she said, 'You're a big girl now, and you know what it's like around here when people start talking, even if it's only innocent fun.' She took a breath. 'Your association with Hugo Hunter can only lead to gossip. They're quick to jump to conclusions, too, if a girl gets too familiar.'

She waited again for me to speak. When I stayed mute she said, 'What have you got to say to that?'

Chin raised, I cried, 'It wasn't innocent and I'm in love with Hugo.'

'What?' Aunt Lilian looked frightened. 'Oh, my God, what would your mother think of this? Her own daughter to do such a thing! What can *you* be thinking of? What will people say? It's shocking, that's what it is, letting yourself get used in that way. You're too young for a start. You'll have to

61

give him up right away.'

'I won't.'

'You will so. It's not decent. You'll disgrace yourself and all of us.' She waited. 'Well?' she said finally. 'You'd better tell him. Or, better still, I'll tell him.' She began to walk away, then turned back to say, 'And don't think he'll stay around now that he's had what he wanted.'

Without a word, I walked behind her, in despair.

Next day Hugo was sent for.

Aunt Lilian looked at him sternly. 'I don't want you to see Jenny alone again. I wouldn't dare let anybody think that you two have any interest in one another, apart from a friendship.'

'Tell her, Hugo. Tell her we're in love,' I pleaded.

'And I'll tell you that you're finished in this village,' she said to him. 'I spoke to your father. He has plans for you that don't include Jenny. Now, I think you'd better be going. There's nothing more to be said.' And Hugo left, without any fight or argument. I was racked with sobs, my dreams in ashes.

'Now go to your room. I'll deal with you later,' Aunt Lilian told me.

While I waited for Aunt Lilian to decide how best she could punish me I was afraid. I rejected any kind word from Cathy, and became distant and preoccupied. Eventually she was angry with me too. 'Get a grip on yourself!' she blazed.

I set about my tasks, my head held high, but inside I felt sick with nerves.

When Aunt Lilian announced that she was sending me home I lay sobbing on the rug on the lawn. 'I can't stand this any longer,' I told Cathy. 'He's all I want. I don't care about his Manor, his education and his father's plans for him.'

Aunt Lilian didn't delay in executing her plans. In a panic she hurried me through my packing, enlisting the help of Aunt Mary, who bustled about and muttered that Aunt Lilian was making an enormous fuss about nothing. The whole affair was dealt with speedily.

On the last day Hugo appeared at the barn door. Even if I had wanted to escape from him I couldn't fight the fierce desire for him that consumed me. 'I'm being sent home,' I told him.

'When?'

'Immediately. Aunt Lilian says it's best, for everyone's sake.' I swallowed back my tears as I promised to write, feeling I'd let Hugo down by making such little protest.

His cheeks were red, his hair falling over his eyes as he explained to me that as soon as we were old enough we would run away together. A cold wind blew through me as he talked. I knew his plan was hopeless.

Back at home I tried to take up where I'd left off with Nigel Knight, a boy I'd been keen on, but I was obsessed with Hugo, thinking of him all the time. Unaware of this, Nigel couldn't understand my lack of interest. Eventually he got fed up and went off with Emily Smith, whom finally he married.

I was filled with longing for Hugo, living each long dull day minute by minute, waiting to hear from him. I wrote to him at his college, asking him to get a job in Dublin the following summer. He wrote back telling me that his father was sending him to Australia for the holidays to study beef farming with his uncle.

The letters became fewer and fewer. The dreadful day dawned when the awful realisation that Hugo was lost to me sank in. The torture of waiting months to hear from him, then the futile hope of his return was over. I thought of the past: the walks in the woods, him hurrying to meet me, the touch of his hand in mine, the laughter, the sudden delight in each other's company, the shyness in our new-found intimacy, our growing love. I remembered his smile, his assurance that everything would be all right, and cried. There was no consoling me. There was no one like him and I would never see him again.

Now, I walked back from the beach, leaving the woods behind me. The barn loomed up ahead, and I sneaked in to stand in the empty space, remembering that tempestuous time. I shut my eyes as if to block out the terrible thing that had happened. Recalling it all put a new strain on me. Years had passed since it happened. His father was dead. I probably wouldn't even recognise him when I saw him, but I was scared at the prospect of our meeting all the same.

7

The house was full of relatives from all over the countryside. Cathy's bedroom was crowded with Fawn and me, in our lilac satin dresses, Harry, the hairdresser, putting the final touches to Cathy's hair, and Aunt Lilian standing to one side in her *eau-de-Nil* silk suit.

Cathy, head tilted, eyes alert, was poised before the mirror, like a bird preparing for flight, her scoop-necked wedding dress fitting her like a second skin, her hair gleaming in the sunlight. She struck a pose. 'How do I look?' she asked, straightening up, pulling in her stomach.

'Perfect.' Aunt Lilian looked at her watch. 'Now get a move on,' she said, and left the room.

'Do you think I look OK?' Cathy asked me.

'You look fabulous,' I said, wholeheartedly. 'You'll have all the men wanting to marry you.'

'He's the only one I want.' Doubts forgotten, her eyes burned with excitement. She turned back to the mirror and pulled a face at her reflection. 'I'm not sure if that lipstick is the right colour.'

Burrowing in my makeup bag I produced mine for her to try. It reminded me of the games we played as children, painting our faces with crayons, then hobbling around in Aunt Lilian's high-heeled shoes. As Cathy wound the gold chain Ned had given her as a wedding present round her neck a clock chimed.

'Better not keep him waiting,' Fawn said.

Giggling like schoolgirls we whirled down the passage. At the foot of the stairs Uncle Tom was waiting, handsome in top hat and tails.

As the cool air hit our bare shoulders we shivered, and went slowly down the narrow path. Aunt Mary, all decked out in peach, stood awestruck, a smile creasing her face. 'Oh, Cathy,' she sighed, 'you do look lovely.' She took a deep breath and said no more as she watched her niece get into the waiting limousine.

Joe Moran, the driver, slammed the door and jumped in. Off they drove, into the golden afternoon, with us following.

The excitement was almost palpable as Uncle Tom and Cathy led the way down the path to the crowded church, the faces of the guests solemn as they gazed at the approaching bride. She stepped into position inside the door, her bouquet held aloft, then off we went down the aisle, our high heels clicking on the stone floor to the rhythm of the bridal march.

Ned was waiting at the foot of the altar, his hair almost white in the sunlight that poured in through the stained-glass window. 'Wow!' he whispered as Cathy reached him.

She took her final step and was beside him, his beautiful, nervous bride, her flame-red curls arranged around her veil. He took her hand and, together they went forward.

The flowers in my bouquet trembled as the priest said, 'Will you take this man to be your lawful husband?'

Cathy whispered, 'I will.' Her radiant smile was reserved for Ned alone, a private moment between them that sealed their vows.

'I now pronounce you man and wife.' Applause broke out, the organ played, the bride and groom went to sign the register.

We stepped into bright sunlight, guests streaming behind us, laughing and talking. Cameras clicked. The photographer pranced around, issuing instructions. 'Move that way — no, to the left. I said left. What are yis like? Don't know your left from your right,' he said, rushing up to Cathy.

Aunt Lilian stood, her cheeks pink, and her eyes on Cathy's wedding dress, which was eliciting praise from all the guests.

'You look divine,' confirmed Aunt Flo.

Suddenly I saw the man from the train. Distinguished in his tails, white shirt and pinstriped trousers, he stood head and shoulders above the crowd, surveying the scene, surrounded by a group of laughing, back-slapping friends.

'Who's he?' I asked Drew, over the noise.

'That's Hugo Hunter. Don't you remember him?'

Paralysed into silence, I moved away, anxious not to show my shock. I studied him, as he stood talking and laughing. Then his eyes caught mine over someone's shoulder and held my gaze, for a second. Cathy noticed and called him to her.

He stood over me. 'Jenny.'

'You two know each other, of course.' Cathy grinned wickedly.

In that second I had the queerest feeling that his presence here, at this wedding, was going to have a huge impact on my life. Cathy hurried off for more photographs, leaving us alone.

'Hello, Hugo.'

Time stopped as he held my hand. This powerful man with the strong, handsome face, and the self-assured manner could never be the skinny boy on the beach from all those years ago. Passion surged through me as he leaned towards me and kissed my cheek formally. 'I'm sorry I didn't introduce myself on the train,' he said.

'I didn't recognise you,' I said.

'Enjoying your stay?' he asked.

My 'Yes, thank you' was too loud. He didn't seem to notice.

'Heavens, look at the time. We'll be late back if we don't get a move on.' Aunt Lilian was running around in circles, bundling people into their cars.

We drove back to Coolbawn in a cavalcade, behind the limousine, horns hooting. In the distance, the marquee jutted towards the craggy rocks, its undulating walls shimmering, the music swelling over the lawn as we parked.

Ned and Cathy went through to welcome the guests into the flower-festooned tent, with Aunt Lilian at arm's reach of them making introductions. Aunt Flo barged through the crowd wanting to be the first one seated.

Once inside, the guests stood around in groups, holding drinks and talking. Drew handed me some champagne, and knocked back a glass himself.

Ned and Cathy wove their way to the top table. Guests cheered.

Aunt Mary's eyes narrowed as she steered a reluctant Aunt Flo to a side table. Pete, the best man, stood nervously near his seat, counting the telemessages. Aunt Lilian was engrossed in a conversation with Ned's father, her head bobbing furiously under her hat as she said, 'I was so fearful that they wouldn't do the honourable thing. I had to hide my feelings, you know.'

Cathy caught this remark and protested, 'Mum! When did you ever hide your feelings?'

'Now, Cathy, don't contradict me,' Aunt Lilian chided, heedless of her daughter's new status. 'This is a marvellous moment for me,' she gushed.

'Mum,' Cathy whispered in alarm, and turned from her to a more general conversation with others at the table.

She was giggling at some joke Ned was making when suddenly Hugo was in my sights once more, graceful as he moved through the throng to the table opposite mine. He saw me. Instinctively I looked away, but couldn't resist the impulse to look back. He smiled. My heart somersaulted. In that instant everything changed, the flowers in Aunt Lilian's hat were more defined somehow and my breathing was shallow.

The waiter served me smoked Barbary duck on a bed of salad. I broke a roll, buttered it and ate, trying to maintain an interest in the chatter going on all around me, my eyes on him from beneath my eyelashes.

Fawn Fowler was seated next to him, a bottle of wine between them. Poised, elegant, she lifted her arm and her glass as she chatted to him. He leaned towards her and poured the wine, listening politely. I toyed with my salmon. He took a forkful too, and continued listening, his laughter at her jokes restrained.

My dessert of summer fruit confit remained untouched, as I took in his rumpled hair and his handsome face. There was a disturbing air about him: it was in the depths of his blue, expressive eyes, the jut of his jaw and the set of his strong mouth. Here was a man who lived life to the full, loved and hated with no half measures. Yet he remained aloof, which appealed to me, and he had a vulnerability that was the essence of his charm.

I had looked too long. He caught my eye. Quickly, I turned my gaze to my plate, my heart fluttering. The plates were cleared away, the chatter ceased. Cathy and Ned cut the cake. Another photograph was taken. Cathy moved back, relaxed and happy, relieved that everything had gone well so far. Ned's arm was tightly around her waist.

Pete rose and called for a toast to the bride and groom. His eyes on a piece of paper he held, he spoke of how much it meant to him to be at the wedding of his best friend. Then he read the telemessages.

Next Drew thanked us all warmly for coming, with a particular message for the groom — 'Wasn't sure you'd make it.' He laughed.

Aunt Lilian, her hand at her throat, tut-tutted.

Ned, in his turn, said how much he loved his new wife and how grateful he was that she had agreed to marry him. Uncle Tom made a long-winded speech, and toasted the brides-maids. Glasses clinked. Hugo's eye caught mine.

Cathy sat down on a rug in the garden, arranged her legs, her hands, her face, and the photographer urged Ned to get down beside her. 'Now, lean towards her.' Enchanted, Cathy nestled into him but Ned got up. 'Enough. I'm going to get a drink.' Cathy, hurt, withdrew into herself, crossed her legs and sat apart.

Tables were moved to the sides of the marquee, the lights were dimmed. The band started up with 'Perfect Day', and the floor, vast and empty, beckoned.

'Come on.' Ned whisked Cathy into the centre, and everyone clapped as they danced for the first time as a married couple.

'Dance with me,' said Drew, as the band livened up with 'Last Thing On My Mind' and swept me on to the floor.

When it was over, he said, 'Let me introduce you to some of the lads.' It took some time for all the introductions to be made as he insisted on explaining to them all who I was.

The band broke into 'You're Still The One', and Hugo was beside me. 'Would you like to dance?' he asked.

He made a space for us in the centre of the floor, and danced with style, gliding and swaying, his lean body guiding me in perfect time with the music. At the end Ned appeared and stood near me. 'I've got to dance with the bridesmaid,' he said to Hugo.

'Certainly,' Hugo said, and moved away a fraction.

Cathy came forward. 'Hugo!' she said, and took his hand to lead him back to the floor. They merged gracefully together on the tide of the music as Ned twirled me away.

When the music stopped we joined the crowd drinking beer and laughing loudly. Ned and Hugo chatted. Cathy and I moved to one side.

'Gorgeous, isn't he?' she gushed.

'He was on the train the other day and I didn't even recognise him,' I told her. 'He's changed completely.'

'Champagne?' Hugo asked, suddenly beside us.

'I'd rather dance,' Cathy said. 'Come on, Ned.'

They were off again, swirling away.

Hugo and I sat with the champagne bottle between us, he topping my glass, until the band launched into 'When I Need You' and Hugo put down his drink. He took my hand, and led me back out on to the dance floor. His arms were around me, holding me close, and I leaned against him, feeling his warmth, and floated back to when I'd danced with him at our first disco. Dancing with Hugo was as magical as it had ever been. A tremor shot up my spine, which he must have shared because he stopped dancing and looked at me. 'All right?' he whispered, gazing into my face.

I nodded, not speaking, and the music stopped. Reluctantly he let me go, then caught hold of me again.

'Let's get a breath of fresh air,' he said, and led me out into the garden. The sun, sinking, blazed a trail across the horizon, leaving behind it a vast empty blackness of woods and sea. Shadowy figures loomed out of the darkness, others walked among the trees.

'I thought we'd never be alone.' His voice was urgent.

I was breathless. My cheeks were flushed, my heart was thumping, and my hands shook as I turned to him. He had the same look in his face that he had worn all those years ago before he kissed me, only then he had been shy and gauche. Now he was a well-rehearsed, confident lover. Just as he leaned towards me, Uncle Tom and Ned's mother strolled out of the marquee, and broke the spell.

Hugo's eyes were scorching me.

'I . . .' Ned cut across the lawn towards the house.

Hugo said softly, 'What's the matter?'

The band started up again and he didn't hear me say, 'Nothing.'

'It's getting cold out here. Let's go and dance,' he said, putting his arm around my shoulders, leading me back to the marquee.

My mind was racing as we danced, our whole bodies moving, the strobe light flashing.

'*Jenny!*' Aunt Lilian's voice shrilled. 'Cathy wants you. They're about to leave.' I dropped Hugo's hand and ran after her.

All the lights were on in the house, and Cathy was standing in the centre of her bedroom. 'Where were you?' she said,

unzipping her dress, letting it fall to the floor.
'I was searching for you.'

'I was outside, talking with Hugo Hunter and then we went to dance.'

She cast a meaningful glance at me. 'Flirting with Hugo, you mean.'

'Talking,' I reiterated.

'My hair's a mess,' she moaned, picking out confetti. 'I think I'll take it down.'

'Here, let me help you. We weren't flirting,' I said, as I pulled out hairpins.

Shaking it loose she said, 'Oh, well, I suppose there's no harm in it.' As if reading my thoughts she went on, 'Mum still hates that family, the Manor, and all it stands for. What am I going to do with all of this?' she said, casting an indifferent glance around her.

Gift boxes and fancy paper littered the bed. Her crammed suitcase lay open on the floor.

'Don't worry, we'll tidy everything up when you've gone. You can sort it out later. It isn't as if you're going far.'

'Cathy!' Aunt Lilian was on her way back upstairs.

'Oh, God, I can't take her fussing,' said Cathy. 'She's driving me mad.' She kicked aside her dress carelessly.

The moment had come for them to leave. The band was playing their favourite song. In Ned's arms Cathy, in a blue denim dress, a chiffon scarf round her neck, seemed to float as she held her husband, and people swirled around her, gathering to say goodbye.

The car was being loaded, and Cathy walked out to it sedately. Then she turned, to smother us all with kisses.

'Why are they off so soon?' asked Aunt Mary, shivering in the night air.

'For a bit of how's-your-father,' said Aunt Flo, giggling. 'Couldn't do it here. Not with Lilian and her decorum.'

'Flo! You've had too much champagne,' chided Aunt Mary.

'Nonsense.' Aunt Flo hiccuped. 'You've never had it, so you wouldn't understand. Haven't you ever missed it, Mary? Not even a teeny bit?'

Mortified, Aunt Mary moved away.

'I know I do,' Aunt Flo confided, moving me aside, breathing all over me. 'Your uncle Tom's not the man he used to be. Old age has got him in the goolies.' She took a gulp of her champagne.

They were driving away, waving, Cathy leaning out, her hair blowing in the wind.

'How long has she known him?' Aunt Flo asked me, as the car rattled away.

'Not long.'

'Know anything about his background?'

'Not much.'

'She kept him hidden, didn't she?'

'Not on purpose.'

'Might be a criminal, for all we know,' she suggested.

I laughed. 'That's absurd.'

'There's something about him. He looks like he's up to no good. Mind you, I prefer men like that.' She laughed mischievously.

'He's reserved, that's all,'

'Between you and me I don't think it'll last very long — and the expense of it all, just for a few hours. Is it worth it? I don't know.'

'It was a marvellous day,' chipped in Uncle Tom, coming to retrieve his tipsy wife.

'Well, and where have you been? Have you been dancing?' she asked him crossly, concerned at the red veins that stood out on his cheeks.

'I've been having a lovely time,' he said, his eyes twinkling.

'A lot of nonsense if you ask me,' Aunt Flo puffed, looking around her. 'And all just to please Lilian.'

'Nobody asked you,' Aunt Lilian snapped, from behind her.

'It's not as if they're going far, only to the Great Southern Hotel,' I said comfortingly, to a bemused Aunt Mary, whose eyes were full of tears. 'They'll be back in a day or two.'

I didn't envy Cathy — not for me the

confines of marriage, and the tiny hands of babies.

Suddenly Hugo appeared out of the darkness. 'Come on, you're missing the fun,' he said, leading me back to the dance-floor.

Pete was jumping around, forming a crocodile, pulling me in behind him, Hugo after me, holding on tight. We zigzagged out of the marquee, on to the lawn, jumped around, stomped our feet, swinging to the beat of 'When The Lights Go Out'. All around the marquee we danced, unruly children in the moonlight, the music blaring out across the sea. Fawn Fowler's eye was on Hugo as she twirled Cathy's bouquet above her head for all to see, shouting, 'I'm next, I'm next,' the world her playground. Other girls grouped around him too, laughing.

Everyone was dancing in frenzy, as the lights flashed.

'There you are.' It was Ron Ray, the Aussie monster of the hen night. He crashed through the crowd and grabbed me as if he'd won a prize.

'You're looking gorgeous,' he yelled, jerking me on to the floor. His shirt buttons were undone and his hairy pectorals danced to a rhythm of their own. 'I'm flying back to Sydney on Tuesday. How about you come with me? You'd love it there,' he asked, looming over me, nuzzling my neck. 'You wouldn't be alone. I work from home.'

The smell of his breath sent me reeling backwards. Typical! The only invitation I get comes from a hairy baboon. 'Sorry, can't. Working.'

'There's plenty of work in Sydney, 'specially for a girl like you.' He twirled and I was gone, escaping out into the safety of the dark, leaving behind the clamorous guests singing 'Take Me Home', a dirge to the dying wedding.

All was quiet in the empty house, but the lights were still blazing. Aunt Mary was in the kitchen, sipping a cup of cocoa. 'Want some?' she asked wearily.

'No, thanks. I'm off to bed.'

'I saw you dancing with Hugo Hunter.'

'Yes.'

'What did you think of him?'

'Oh, nice,' I said.

'Yes, a nice fellow. But, like all the Hunters, he presents his own dilemma.' There was a cautionary note in her voice.

I fled upstairs to bed, desperate to be alone, determined to put all thoughts of him away with my bridesmaid's dress.

8

I woke to the sound of voices, and the smell of rashers cooking. Strewn glasses everywhere marked the end of the festivities, but the house was still lively, with Mum and Dad, Uncle Tom and Aunt Flo, and Ned's mother, Mirella, joining us for brunch. Aunt Mary was cooking, Mum was serving.

'Good morning,' I said, slipping into my seat.

'Where did you disappear to last night?' Dad spoke through a mouthful of crumbs.

'You look dead beat,' said Aunt Flo.

'Why wouldn't she, after such a long day?' said Aunt Mary, putting a glass of orange juice in front of me. 'Drink that up,' she said. 'It'll bring you back to life.'

Uncle Tom banged at the kitchen door, his arms full of logs. 'You'll be needing these later on.' His face was red from exertion, his eyes still bright from too much champagne.

'Good morning,' Aunt Lilian came into the room. She helped herself to rashers, sausages and an egg, and sat down.

'That was one great wedding, Lilian,' said Mum.

'Everything went well, didn't it?' she said, and began eating without waiting for a reply, calmer now that the wedding was over and with it all the pandemonium.

'Kilbeg's never seen the likes of it,' said Uncle Tom.

'It'll never see the likes of it again,' said Aunt Flo, anxious to keep Aunt Lilian sweet for the duration of their visit.

'It will if Jenny here gets fixed up with his lordship up in the Manor,' said Dad.

'You mean Hugo Hunter?' asked a dumbfounded Aunt Lilian.

'Yes,' Dad said. 'Didn't ye see the way he was looking at her? Never took his eyes off her all night. Oh, I'm telling you, if Jenny plays her cards right, it's a match made.'

'Don't be daft,' began Aunt Flo, but everyone was talking all at once. Aunt Lilian had the weather to worry about because of the farm, and Aunt Mary was concerned about dinners for Mum and Dad.

As soon as I could I walked down to the village to get away from it all. It was a perfect day, not a cloud in the sky. There were several new shops, selling sports wear, books and renting videos. The new supermarket took up most of the corner. Next was the square, its large, elegant houses a reminder of the Victorian splendour of the previous century.

Built for squires and merchants, they were now homes to bankers and lawyers. Uncle Tom and Aunt Flo lived in the one next to the Metropole, Kilbeg's only hotel. Further along were the church and the green, the school opposite. Where the street narrowed a row of cottages squatted against the backdrop of mountains, their plain stone fronts relieved by splashes of fuchsia or pink and red climbing geraniums.

It was Sunday, and the village was quiet; the only signs of life were washing on clothes-lines visible between gaps in the hedges, and the high voices of children playing on the green.

Out of nowhere Hugo appeared. When he saw me he stepped sideways, and stopped. 'Jenny!'

'You!' I took a deep breath to calm myself.

He looked handsome in his Aran sweater, the sleeves pushed up, a strand of hair blowing into his eyes. After a minute of just standing there he asked, 'Going to Galway?' He looked at me, eyebrows raised, blue eyes dark with intensity.

'Yes. Why not?'

'Come on, I'll give you a lift. The car's here.' He opened the door and stepped back. Self-consciously, I got in. When he sat down beside me he said, 'This route is so

84

unreliable. The buses are always late or breaking down. They trot out the same old excuses all the time.'

'Nothing's changed, then?'

'You have.' He glanced at me, and smiled. 'You look stunning.'

'Thank you. Did you enjoy the wedding?' I asked, changing the subject.

'It was terrific. I searched for you to say goodbye but you were gone.'

'I was tired.'

'It's not surprising with all that hoofing around. Glorious weather, isn't it?'

'Let's hope it keeps up.'

'Yes. The countryside is wonderful this time of year.'

After that he drove in silence, a slight frown on his face. I could think of nothing to say, so studied the road ahead, the banks of daisies on either side, terrified of the silence.

He stopped the car in Eyre Square, and sat with his hands on the wheel, the engine still running. He's going to leave me here, I thought, my mind in a whirl, my hand reaching for the door handle.

'This okay?' He turned to me.

'Great.' Suddenly I couldn't bear the thought of him driving away, his car trailing into the traffic, me staring after it because I couldn't think how to stop him. I was on the pavement, thanking him, smiling, about to shut the door. 'Well, goodbye,' I said.

He leaned towards me. 'Like to join me for a drink?'

I looked away, a grip of myself. 'I've got some things to do,' I said.

'Okay, another time.'

'Maybe a quick one.' I felt myself blush.

He was grinning as he parked the car and got out. Walking beside me, he took my arm as we crossed the street. My heart surged. I was floating on air.

'This is my local when I'm in town.' He spoke close to my face, the traffic around us noisy. We entered a crowded bar full of wild-looking men in peaked caps and big boots, having a drink before heading off to Connaught Final. One or two stopped to ask about the wedding.

The barman greeted us with a slick smile and poured the drinks, talking to the men grouped round the counter. My eyes travelled from them back to Hugo, and I saw his boy's face in the way his hair fell across his forehead and in the golden light in his eyes as he looked across at me.

I sat at a table and waited. I would tell him everything about myself so that he would have to tell me about himself too. That would take about an hour, enough time to finish our drinks. I wanted to be with him all the time, talk to him. I wanted to run, jump, stand on a mountain and shout his name to the whole world. I wanted to laugh, roar, cry, race into the sea and drown myself in the impossible beauty of it.

'So!' Leaning towards me, his eyebrows raised, a smile on his lips, he said, 'What have you been doing all these years?'

'Oh, you know, this and that.'

'Tell me about yourself,' he said, without preamble.

I told him about my job, vague about the people I worked for, making an effort to keep everything light and entertaining. He listened attentively, and coaxed me to tell him more. But I was reticent, preferring to listen to him, reluctant to share everything with him, a defence against intimacy.

His face was shadowy, his eyes sharp as he talked about the Manor, its farm, and the business of making it profitable. He spoke with such energy and enthusiasm that I knew he was hooked on it. He talked about his trips abroad to view other working farms, and trips he was planning to take. This man did not require romance in his life. It was obvious that he was married to his work.

'If you believed in something would you be

prepared to sacrifice everything for it?' I asked.

'Like what?'

'Work, relationship. Anything.'

He nodded. 'Absolutely. I'm ruthless.'

I finished my drink. 'I'd better be going,' I said.

He drove me home, and outside Coolbawn he said, 'I've invited Cathy and Ned to go sailing tomorrow. Seeing as they're not going on their honeymoon yet. You'll come, won't you?' He looked anxiously at me.

'I'd love to.'

'Great. See you then.' With a wave he was gone, driving off down the road.

★ ★ ★

Cathy and Ned arrived early next morning, Cathy's sunglasses on her head, a large beach bag full of towels and swimsuits on her arm.

'Ready, Jenny? Got your swimsuit?' she asked, and gave Aunt Lilian a peck on the cheek.

Ned appeared in the doorway, said, 'Hello,' cast me a sheepish glance, and urged us to get a move on; it was a bit of a drive to Cleggan where the others were waiting at the quay, he said.

Hugo welcomed us on to his boat. In

shorts, his broad chest bare, he walked back and forth with that rolling, confident stride I remembered so well, balancing himself in the careless way sailors do as he prepared to set sail. Strong, with a natural aptitude for sailing, he leaned forward against the mast, his eyes intent on his task. My eyes were on his hands unfurling the sails as the wind picked up. I watched the long line of his neck, the deft movement of his fingers, and the heavy gold signet ring on his little finger as he worked the rigging. Intent and purposeful, the wind tugging at his hair, he steered his boat out of the harbour.

While the others talked he sat silent absorbing the sights and sounds around us, his eyes glittering. I locked my arms around myself, pressing in the excitement.

'Remember Inishbofin?' he asked, crouching towards me, his arm around me, as he pointed out the island ahead.

'I've never forgotten it,' I said, recalling past picnics there and our hot, passionate embraces. I stared at the sea, starstruck all over again. He was the best-looking man I'd ever seen. I wanted to throw back my head and shout out to everyone, 'This is it! This is it!'

Without a word he moved away and lowered the sails as we glided between fishing boats dotted around the island's tiny harbour. The sea was dark blue and tranquil. A large boat was docked at the tiny pier and people were disembarking. From where I stood the island looked enchanting.

Drew went blundering down the beach carrying the picnic basket, Cathy, Fawn and I following, Hugo bringing up the rear, the rug in his arms. 'It's going to rain,' he said.

'We might as well get wet, then. Who's for a swim?' Fawn called. Pulling off her sweater and shorts, she ran recklessly down the beach, disappearing into the water, shouting when she surfaced, 'It's lovely. Come on in.' Ned ran after her and plunged in, Hugo after him calling to me, 'Come on.' He crashed into the breakers and slowly swam out, his strong arms pulling back the water in long, even strokes. I caught up with him, swam alongside him. Fawn, winded, gasping for breath, fell back to where Ned was splashing about. Hugo disappeared. Just as I was about to panic he reappeared beside me, his hair plastered to his face.

'You gave me such a fright.' I laughed as he grabbed me around my waist and lifted me into the air.

'I'm too old for these boyish antics,' he said, lowering me into the water again, shaking his head like a puppy.

We swam back to the shore where Drew was gathering driftwood for the fire.

'Lunchtime,' said Cathy, unpacking the picnic Aunt Flo had prepared at Drew's request. She moved aside a jar of pickles to take out a bottle of wine.

Grabbing a grape Fawn said, 'I'm famished,' and piled her wet hair around her head like a wreath. Her right breast almost fell out of her swimsuit.

We sat in a circle. Cathy spread out a checked tablecloth and placed coloured plastic mugs on it then began arranging sandwiches — egg, salad, ham — mustard, salt, sponge cake and strawberries.

Ned shouted at her to get a move on and start passing round the food before it rained. She worked speedily, her face averted so that he couldn't see her embarrassment while he waited as though it wasn't up to him to do anything.

'Damn,' Hugo swore, pulling the wick in and out of the Primus stove.

'What's up?' Fawn asked.

'The petrol's flooded it.'

I was reminded of haymaking picnics. Each day we had cycled all the way up to Tully's field, passing Murtagh's farmhouse, creels of turf to one side of its gable wall, purple heather beyond. Our baskets stuffed with food, the wind in our ears, the rise of the hill slowing us down, we would arrive. The men would be waiting, stripped to the waist, their skin turning red in the sun, the smell of sweat in the air. Their eyes were on the line of our legs beneath our jeans.

Under the long shadow of the mountain we would eat. Hugo, his blue shirt tied around his waist, would peer at us, then walk ahead, taking long strides, putting a distance between us. Cathy would follow Mick Byrne, the son of the local fisherman, and stand talking to him. One day he burst out laughing at something she said and she flounced off.

No one stopped working until Uncle John called a halt. He would light the Primus, and Drew would measure water into the battered kettle. Every day was the same, the men talking about the work, what was done, what had to be done, while food was passed round. Never heeding a word that was said I would glance over my shoulder from time to time at Hugo eating quietly, his mind far away.

Afterwards, Cathy and I would walk together over the nearby fields, lie down in the tall grass, side by side, and watch the cattle moving quietly in the meadow as we waited for the work to finish. In the evening we would cycle home, our heads down against the wind. Sometimes we would stop for a quick swim to revive ourselves before carrying on to the farm. There was fun in these daily excursions, and a dangerous excitement in us. It was in our laughter, and in the gold flecks in Cathy's eyes. We formed a tight circle, Hugo and Mick at its centre. They were our chief interest, and we chased after them shamelessly.

At dinnertime we would set out the knives, forks and spoons, salt cellar, butter, milk glasses, and wait for the men's return. After dinner I would sneak off alone, leaving Cathy to make excuses for me to Aunt Lilian. Once I delayed so long that Aunt Lilian became suspicious. When I finally appeared, full of explanations, she was cross and said she'd have a word with me in private.

For the next few days we did exactly as we were told, and Aunt Lilian fell for it. We cleaned out the hen-house, picked fruit, weeded the flower-beds, quiet, obedient and undemanding. I was wholly unlike myself, and Aunt Lilian was deceived by my behaviour. I knew that Cathy was caught up in some sort of plot. What she was going to do I didn't know.

Then Cathy began to send me on all sorts of errands, inventing tasks for me as she lazed under the oak tree, or sneaked off to the lower field. I saw her less and less. Now it was my turn to explain her absence and make excuses for her. When I asked her where she was going she would snap, 'Mind your own business, don't mind mine. Kiss your own sweetheart, don't kiss mine.'

A day was long and dull without her to share it with. I would see her speed off on her bike, and wait eagerly for her return from some extraordinary adventure. She would make a sudden and dramatic appearance, her eyes glistening.

One morning early I heard the sound of a car. From my bedroom window I saw Cathy holding the gate open, while Mick drove through it. The countryside blazed in the sunshine as they left together.

Today Fawn Fowler did everything to please Ned: flung herself into his path, hurried to assist him in whatever small request he made. He laughed at something she said, and when her eyes met mine they were evasive. By the slight incline of her head towards me I knew she wanted to talk to me. I kept aloof, wondering if we'd be alone again before she left and hoping we wouldn't.

'Eureka,' shouted Hugo. 'We have lift-off. Anyone for tea?'

Cathy sat at the edge of the picnic, absorbed, silent, the brim of her sun hat pulled down over her face, no trace of the elegant bride about her.

Ned, clearly irritated with his new wife's demeanour, said to her, 'This is meant to be a happy occasion.'

'You could have fooled me,' she retorted, moving away, sitting with her back to him.

'Hugo arranged all this for us, Drew went to a lot of trouble organising the food. The least you could do is take part graciously.' He spoke in a low, aggrieved tone.

'All right, all right,' she said, raising her hands. 'Keep your shirt on.'

I went over to her. We sat side by side, our heads close. Fawn joined us, and lit a cigarette.

'Are you going to invite Hugo to Aunt Flo's party?' she asked.

'Of course,' said Cathy.

'Oh, good.'

'Why?' asked Cathy.

'It's just that we're all getting on so well together,' Fawn said, casting me a glance.

'Yes, but I'm going to be honest with you, Fawn,' Cathy said. 'You're throwing yourself at my husband, and it's making him and me decidedly uncomfortable. It's not the way to behave.'

Taken aback, Fawn said, 'What an absurd idea,' and moved over to Drew. She whispered something to him. He seemed surprised at what she had said and looked at the bad-tempered Ned, who was clearly keeping his distance.

Hugo put his hand on my shoulder. 'Jenny, over there. Look!'

He drew me towards a group of seals prone on the rocks, basking in the sunshine. The biggest one rolled over and flipped into the sea, the others followed.

'Wow!' I breathed, as the seals rolled over and over.

Hugo watched, motionless, his arm around me, blocking out everyone else. 'Are you on for a game of tennis tomorrow evening?' he asked, under his breath, a slight tremor in his voice. When I hesitated he said, 'I want you all to myself,' with a hint of urgency in his voice. 'Meet me at the pier at seven.'

The seals, their energy expended, disappeared into the water. The rain started. Ned looked at Fawn, his irritation showing as he said, 'It's raining.' Cathy began packing the picnic things.

We sailed for home, Hugo at the stern, me beside him, Fawn and Drew at the back of the boat, Cathy and Ned distant, embarrassment the only emotion they shared.

9

The next evening I walked down to the village, and into the corner shop. 'Hello,' said the ever-vigilant Pat Moran, who owned it. He pushed himself forward, leaning on the counter amid jars of rosy apple jelly and amber marmalade.

'Hello.' I glanced at him and continued looking for suntan lotion.

'And how did the wedding go?'

'Very well, thank you,' I said.

He served a woman who seemed to be in a hurry.

'It'll be yourself next up to the altar.' He smirked, as I placed the bottle of lotion on the counter and handed over the money.

I walked quickly to the curve of coloured houses at the quay, and waited near the pier. Gulls circled above me, casting their shadows on the sand below. Hugo appeared from the dark recess of the boathouse. He came towards me, smiling, and took my arm. 'How are you?'

'Fine, thanks, apart from looking like a lobster,' I said.

'You look gorgeous.'

A chasm dropped open between us as we gazed at one another. In that moment everything slowed down. A car drove by. A man cutting a hedge worked on indifferently, his ladder perched precariously on the grass verge. With his arm around my shoulders Hugo took me to his car. We drove through the deserted street, away from the sea.

Eventually we arrived at the manor's tall, impressive gates. Hugo hopped out, pressed a button and they swung back. At the top of the long avenue he crunched the car to a halt. There stood the house, its back to the sea, groups of trees on either side of it, dark green demesne fields surrounding it. I gazed up at the severe Georgian edifice, its tall windows shut against the world, its balustrade pale in the sunlight, its majestic façade cold and hostile as ever.

From nowhere a beautiful golden retriever bitch rushed to meet us, greeting Hugo with leaps of delight. Hugo threw a stick into the trees for her saying, 'Go! Fetch!'

'Come on,' he urged, leading me up the flight of stone steps. 'There's no one in.'

I could hear my own breathing as I waited for him to open the great oak door. He was taking me into his home, alone. Fraught with terror and the excitement of his nearness, I entered, enthralled.

The hall was filled with portraits of ancestors and racehorses. Hugo swept me down a silent corridor into an enormous, beautifully proportioned drawing room, its ceiling decorated with garlands of flowers in the Italian style, and its walls lined with paintings of hunting scenes. There were soft blue button-backed sofas, and matching silk curtains tied back in thin bows, and a thick cream carpet. A fire burned in a basket grate.

'So, this is my house,' said Hugo, in a husky voice, as he stood beside me.

'And what a beautiful house it is,' I said. I went towards the fire, and touched a photograph of a boy on a horse. 'This must be you.'

'Wait!' He left the room and returned with a bottle of champagne and glasses.

'Will you have some champagne?'

'Yes, please,' I said. The cork popped and I took my glass from him.

Hugo opened the french windows, took my hand and said, 'How's that for a view?'

It was breathtaking. The magnificent gardens sloped down gentle terraces, and roses, dahlias and carnations sank into one another in a carpet of colour, filling the air with their scent. Trees towered above them, their branches hanging over a high wall, the woods sloping down to our left, while the sprawling valley beneath stretched out to the sea.

'It's a beautiful place,' I said, overawed.

'Yes, it is. But it's a monster that soaks up every penny I can find. Come on. Let's have our game of tennis.' I could feel the warmth of his breath on my face as he spoke.

'Where shall I change?' I asked. I didn't have my own tennis kit with me, and was having to make do with Cathy's cast-offs.

Hugo led me to the downstairs cloakroom. 'I'll be waiting on the court,' he said.

I removed my tracksuit and put on Cathy's white shorts and shirt. Outside, I walked past the walled kitchen garden, down a dark rhododendron-sheltered path that branched off in different directions; short wooden signposts pointed to the woods, the conservatory, the pond, the animals' graves and the tennis courts. I took a honeysuckle-lined path down to where Hugo waited.

The clean, white lines of his tennis shorts made his muscular legs look longer and more tanned as he knocked balls about the court, warming up.

'There you are,' he said, coming to meet me.

My nervousness dissipated as we volleyed back and forth for a few minutes, the smell of the new yellow tennis balls, straight from

100

their green tube, bringing back the excitement of earlier summers.

The game began. Hugo flew about the court with the capability and serenity that comes from confidence. I matched him, surprising myself with my own speed and dexterity as I leaped for the ball, my racquet poised in the air for a backhand shot, my best stroke. He kept his head low over his racquet waiting as I stood poised, preparing for my next crucial serve, which would decide the game. I won. He won the next, and I rallied, swept across the court, every effort concentrated on my game. If Hugo was getting tired, he wasn't showing it. I would put the laughter on the other side of that handsome face, keep him in the losing place, where he belonged. I hit the ball back and forth as if my life depended on it.

Ten minutes later I had won. Exhausted, I was content.

'Congratulations,' he said, raising his eyebrows in surprise. 'Good win.'

My cheeks burned as we shook hands. I thought how silly it was of me to feel such emotion about winning a game of tennis. Was it a girlish crush that had made me play so hard? I mustn't let him guess too much. Subdued, we walked back to the house. The back of the Manor was a shock, its crumbling stone walls in disharmony with the front, its dark, heavy windows in need of replacement.

We went through the hall and into the drawing room to sip champagne, Hugo's favourite tipple. Then he said, 'If you'd like a shower the guest bathroom is first on the right at the top of the stairs. I'll meet you back here in, say, half an hour.'

It was quiet upstairs except for a curtain flapping at an open window. Shadows criss-crossed the wide stairs as I swept up them. In the bathroom I showered, and put on a fuchsia pink top and a short skirt, then some makeup, shook my hair loose, and went out pulling the door behind me.

The door next to the bathroom was ajar. Curious, I opened it. Light from the large window cast a pale glow on the oak furniture. The bed was unmade. This was Hugo's room, I felt sure. I stepped further in. A small glass-fronted cabinet held a collection of red rosettes and trophies, some decorated with ribbons. Photographs of Hugo on various horses lined the walls.

There, in the glow of the sun, in pride of place on his dressing-table was a photograph of a girl with huge eyes and hair twisted into a knot on top of her head. I picked it up to look at the smiling face, and in that moment the room seemed filled with sadness, so unbearable that it brought tears to my eyes. I put it down and left, my feet clicking down the stairs in my high-heeled shoes as I hurried back to him.

'In here,' he called.

He was in the kitchen, getting out knives and forks, pushing seed catalogues to one side. He took a damask tablecloth out of a drawer and spread it over the table. Then he arranged chicken, ham and salad on delicate china plates. He placed a bottle of wine in a silver cooler, found some glasses and finally added a tiered stand filled with tiny iced cakes.

'Did you prepare all this food?' I asked, unbelieving.

'Good Lord, no. I can barely boil an egg,' he said, laughing at his domestic incompetence. 'Alice, my housekeeper left this ready for us.' He poured the wine, and handed me a glass.

I sat enjoying the coolness of the kitchen, glad to play my part as guest, while Hugo tried to locate napkins.

Determined not to show the turmoil I was feeling, I said, 'It looks delicious,' picturing the overworked Alice fluttering round, fixing everything correctly.

'Alice is very formal and dinner is always in the dining room. I decided to have it in the kitchen this evening because it's her day off. More intimate, don't you think?'

My heart leaped at the word 'intimate'.

'Has Alice always been with you?'

'Ten years. My parents used to entertain on a grand scale. When my father died six years ago, Alice stayed on to look after my mother. She only lived for another year.'

'I'm sorry to hear that.'

Hugo shrugged. 'She was always delicate. Didn't want to hang on once my father was gone. She died of a broken heart, I think.'

'They must have been very happy.'

'They were never apart from the day they married.'

'Did your parents meet in England?'

'No. My mother came over from Hampshire to compete in the Dublin horse show. Dad won her heart with his prize ponies, and they were married within six months.'

'That was quick.'

'They were in love with each other until the day they died.'

'Have you ever been in love like that?' I could have bitten out my tongue the moment I said it.

'No. Have you?'

I was quiet for a minute, then I said, 'I thought I was once.'

He looked at me, his eyes unwavering.

Intuitively I knew that he knew I was referring to him. Anticipating a question, I waited. When none came I dropped my eyes. He sat in his chair perfectly at ease as he told me about his ancestors and how they had come to inherit the Manor through their bravery in battles for Britain.

I kept my eyes on his hands as he picked up a peach, caressing the skin before cutting it carefully, first a quick incision at the top, then several neat cuts to the sides. He offered me a section just as the phone rang. He excused himself and took it in the hall. When he returned he said, 'You haven't finished your meal,' on a note of mock reproach.

'My appetite has failed me,' I said.

'Such a lovely evening.' His words sounded strained. 'Let's go for a stroll down to the beach.'

'I'd love to.'

We walked out on to the terrace and down a path to the wooden deck overlooking the beach. The evening was warm, the air sweet. Seagulls tilted away from the sea, dark in the cool air. He touched my hand.

Slowly we took the path that cut into the side of the wood, feeling our way down the knotted woodland track we'd taken all those years ago. His hand clasped mine tightly. We stayed close together as we wove our way down the slope to the strand, the rocks before us, the water washing over them. On the beach I stood apart and watched the lights from the pier make dancing trails of light on the water. Hugo stood with his arms folded.

We stayed gazing at the scenery, memorising the woods, distant and dense, and the sky above them, pale in the evening light. Birds chirped as they settled down for the night. An owl hooted in the woods behind me.

Hugo stooped towards me as we continued our walk in the soft sand. In the shadows his skin was darker, his eyes brighter. We sat on a rock, heads bent, telling stories of the past. Drunk with the thrill of discovering him again, I became lighthearted and gay telling him more about my family and friends, making out that my life was more exciting than it was.

'Remember us together like this, on the beach, all those years ago,' he said suddenly.

'Yes, I do . . . Cathy searching for us to warn us that Aunt Lilian was on the warpath.'

'Childish games.'

Those words brought uncertainty to my heart.

I remembered the first disco Cathy had taken me to: getting ready, singing and swaying in the bedroom to the music blaring out from Cathy's stereo, my mind on the

106

night ahead, wondering if he'd be there. I dressed to make him notice me, staring into the mirror, seeing myself as Hugo would see me. Cathy said, 'You're pathetic,' as she watched me pout and posture in the mirror, and she saw my anxiety in my freshly made-up face and in the tautness of my posture.

'I was hoping you'd come to Dublin the following summer,' I said, with a catch in my voice.

'I wanted to, but my father had other ideas. There were responsibilities he insisted I put first, duties. I had to train to take over this place, working on farms abroad in the summer holidays.'

'It paid off,' I said, looking around.

He laughed derisively. 'Sometimes it feels as if I've spent my life putting everybody's wishes first. All those years ago I should have rebelled, but I was the only son, and I respected my father's wishes to make me a worthy heir.'

He pulled me to him, and said, 'I did miss you, and I'm sorry . . . '

His face, so close, was a blur. My heart beat wildly.

' . . . for being such a jerk.' He looked at me, his eyes unfathomable.

My heart shifted. Pain rose in my chest.

He'd driven me mad with passion, then left me with a broken heart. I'd tried hard to forget him but couldn't. Now he was taking up where he'd left off but even if I'd wanted to I could no more discuss that part of the past with him than jump to the moon. Yet I felt the security of him, a sort of shelter in a storm, which was a strange confusion, considering I'd been in love with him most of my life and had hardly seen anything of him.

'Am I forgiven?' He spoke as if it mattered greatly to him. His body was warm, his breathing harsh against my ear.

I stood up, walked away, unable to talk.

'Jenny?' he said, catching up with me, waiting for an answer.

'All that was a long time ago,' I said.

'You haven't forgotten what it was like?' His breath was warm on my face.

I watched him, noticing with renewed surprise his flashing eyes, tender under the arched eyebrow. We walked on in silence for what seemed ages.

Finally, he said, 'You've changed, Jenny. You're all grown up.'

'I should hope so. As you said, we were only children then.'

Taking my hand he said, 'You're very beautiful.'

He knew all the romantic moves, and could

ease his way comfortably through this situation. I ought to say something, do something, but I couldn't.

'Jenny, I fancied you so much back then. I still fancy you. Come here. I want to kiss you.' He pulled me to him and I could smell the clean, lemony scent of his aftershave.

The ecstasy that goes with forbidden love shot through me as his arms enveloped me. I felt myself move towards him, saw the look in his eyes as he lowered his head to kiss me. It was a moment of such ecstasy that I was as helpless as a boat on a stormy sea. With that exquisite kiss all my willpower disappeared as a charge of love shot through me. I looked up into his face and knew that something startling was happening to me. It struck me like a bolt out of the blue how much I wanted him, that I must have him and that I would never settle for anything less. I waited, barely breathing, my eyes never leaving his face.

He gripped me tightly. He must have known the powerful current of emotions that his presence moved in me because he said, 'I wanted to do that on the train.'

'Hugo . . . ' My voice was barely audible as I clung to him in the gathering darkness, abandoning all efforts at restraint, knowing that his need for me was even stronger than mine for him.

We clung together without moving for some time, our bodies melting in the heat we were generating.

I raised my mouth, aching to be kissed again, thinking of Aunt Lilian, and how furious she would be if she could see us. His lips found mine and he kissed me with a passionate force that took possession of me, thrilling me and almost suffocating me with desire. But it was all happening too quickly. I must stop. I would, in a minute. But I didn't. Instead I returned his kiss with an ardour that matched his own. Then he was kissing my neck, pulling my shirt gently off my shoulder. I was swooning, overpowered by the desire to be possessed by this man.

There was a thread of excitement in his whisper: 'I want to make love to you. Let's go back to the house.'

I pulled back. 'Maybe that's not such a good idea.'

He laughed. 'It's a wonderful idea. You're wonderful. Come on.'

The sky was dull, the trees around us huge dark eerie shapes, as we made our way back to the Manor, Hugo holding my hand, guiding me expertly along the twisting path.

In his bedroom he said, 'Don't be nervous,' and stood beside me, so still that I could hear him breathing. I could feel his eyes on me but

I couldn't look at him. Instead I gazed at the moon above the clouds. We stayed like that for a few moments. It seemed in that time that the whole world had stopped too.

He came to me naked and vulnerable, his body all warmth and motion, his hands gently catching my shoulders, pushing me backwards on to the bed, holding me down. He stroked me gently as he helped me remove my clothes. 'Hugo!' I gasped. 'I want you so much,' and we made love with ferocity.

Afterwards he lay sprawled against the pillows, propped on one elbow, looking down on me. 'You okay?' he asked.

'Yes.'

He was leaning towards me, pushing my hair out of my eyes, caressing my face, my neck, massaging my stomach, my thighs. It was happening all over again, only more slowly this time. I moaned and clung to him as we moved together.

In the dark we lay entwined. His breathing was deep and calm, as his head pressed against my shoulder. The night was warm and quiet. I lay looking at him, listening to his steady breathing as he slept. What a fool I was to have had doubts. Here he was beside me, his presence comforting, his love reassuring. I wanted to know everything about him, his most secret thoughts . . . so why was I fearful?

111

★ ★ ★

At around midnight Hugo drove me home, promising to phone me as he kissed me goodnight.

Aunt Mary was in the kitchen, doing her embroidery in the bright light, waiting up for me. I went down to her. The windows were still open, and the sound of the tide swelled in the silence.

'How was your game?' she asked.

'Very enjoyable,' I said, longing to tell her that I was in love with Hugo.

She would understand my need to share my new, delicious secret, because she was so wise and strong, but I still lacked confidence in Hugo's love for me. Instead I kissed her and went to bed to sleep away the exquisite exhaustion of being in love. I would meet him tomorrow at Aunt Flo's dinner party, play tennis with him again, perhaps. I might confide the whole thing to Cathy. But when? Cathy was gone now, sightseeing around Ireland on her honeymoon. I couldn't wait to see her and tell her my news.

10

Aunt Flo and Uncle Tom's house was full of people for the post-wedding party. Aunt Flo, in a pale blue cocktail dress, her eyes merry with party spirit, looked charming. Indefatigable as ever she greeted her guests with eager interest.

'I like your dress,' she said to me. 'Expensive?'

'It cost far too much.'

'Worth it. You look great. Get yourself a stiff drink, my dear. You'll need it to cope with this lot.' She winked as she steered me into the lounge past an endless stream of familiar faces.

Talk emanated from everywhere. Aunt Flo's high-pitched tone stopped it as she introduced Felix Mahon, the county engineer, who greeted me in a sonorous tone. Uncle Tom hung on his every word. Pete was engrossed in Fawn Fowler.

In the kitchen, bottles of wine lined the shelves while cans of beer and cartons of minerals were stacked on the table. Drew, dapper in a dark suit, saw me from the far side of the counter and came to greet me.

'There you are, Jenny. What'll you have to drink?'

While he went to get me a gin and tonic I looked for Hugo. There were people I'd met at the wedding, and people I'd encountered over the years visiting Coolbawn, all talking together. I said, 'Hello,' to the Byres, old friends of Aunt Flo's, and moved on.

Cathy and Ned arrived. Cathy, radiant once more, in a long green sleeveless dress, charmed everyone, and Ned seemed less reserved than before. The noise increased. I went out into the garden. Bees buzzed in the lavender and roses. I went down the gravel path to the part of the garden that was shaded by bushes of purple hydrangea and dark rhododendrons. There, I spotted Hugo.

He was standing by the pond with a beautiful woman wearing an expensive tight black trouser suit, the woman in the photograph beside his bed. It was the way she was holding his arm possessively and laughing up into his face that set my heart beating wildly. Where to turn? He caught my eye, gave an embarrassed smile, and made his way towards me, with the girl in tow. 'Hello, Jenny. This is Natalie.'

I hesitated, then stepped forward to greet her.

'Hello,' she simpered, flashing her perfect

teeth in a broad smile, looking up at Hugo.

She had satiny black hair, peachy skin and dark-fringed eyes that took up most of her face. Perhaps she was a model, or an aspiring actress. Whatever, she was no ordinary girl. This was a girl with ambition. But why was Hugo parading her at Aunt Flo's party?

A tall man in blue jeans came up to him. Hugo smiled at Natalie as he introduced them, and her hand tightened on his arm. I cracked with jealousy.

'I'd better get back,' I said. 'Aunt Flo'll need a hand.'

In the dining room the table was laid for a banquet, with roses in bowls, and Waterford glass as old as Aunt Flo herself among platters of food. Myra, Aunt Flo's unruffled maid, began serving dinner: roast duckling, wild salmon, all manners of salads. Cathy and I helped her.

After dinner we served coffee, the smoke thickening, the talk deafening. I helped myself to a bottle of beer while I waited to get Cathy on her own.

'Who's the girl with Hugo?' I asked her, under my breath.

'Don't know. Nice-looking, though. Jealous?' she asked, catching my eye.

'Good God, no,' I scoffed. 'If anything, I feel sorry for her. It's hard to keep having to

115

impress people all the time like she seems to be doing.'

'I thought you'd given up the hard stuff,' said Uncle Tom, his eyes on the bottle I had to my lips.

I shrugged. My head ached dully and I wished I wasn't there.

Natalie left the party early, and Aunt Flo said goodbye to her pressing a kiss on the girl's cheek. The rest of the room drifted away from me as I watched her go, her beautiful body undulating under her tight trousers, her hips swaying. Hugo followed her.

I couldn't stand there and let this happen. I pushed my way through the crowd and into the hall. There was no sign of them. I found them on the drive. He had his arm round her as he helped her into her car. She drove off as he waved. When he turned, his eyes were wary.

'Jenny! There you are.' He grasped my arm. 'I was just saying goodbye to Natalie. She's leaving for Vienna tonight.' Vaguely aware that he was in the wrong, he seemed convinced that his explanation would make it right.

'I'm going too.' I turned.

He followed me and almost shouted, 'Come back. We haven't even talked yet.'

'No thanks,' I said, my knees buckling.

He barred the way. I rushed past him,

grabbed my coat and left by the open door.

'Jenny!' He was running down the drive after me. Outside, he stood in the street shouting, 'Where are you going? Come back!'

I ran along the path, which was wet from recent rain. The atmosphere was warm and clammy, a thunderstorm threatening. Two girls screaming with laughter were running towards the beach with two young men chasing them. I could hear the distant burst of breakers on the shore.

'Jenny!'

I kept going. He didn't need me now, didn't want me. I might as well not have been there.

Hugo caught up with me. He held me, his face red from running, his smile anxious. 'I can explain.'

I kept walking. 'Leave me alone. Why do I care? What was I thinking of? I should never have . . . ' I gulped. 'I just thought you were . . . ' I slapped my forehead with my hand. 'This is where we say goodbye.'

'Don't go. Jenny, listen! I didn't mean things to happen like this. Didn't want it to. But now that it has I want to make things right between us.'

I laughed derisively. 'Why didn't you tell me about her?'

'I thought you knew.'

Until then the idea that there might be another woman in Hugo's life had never crossed my mind. I pulled away. 'How would I know?' I walked down behind the trees.

He stood before me, barring my way. I sidestepped him, moved on and gazed at the sharp rocks below, the sea stretching to the horizon.

'Who is she?'

'Natalie Mason. She's a singer. We met in Italy five years ago.'

The cold wind blew into my face. He came closer, took my face in his hands, kissed me gently on the lips.

This couldn't be happening. In a minute he'd tell me that there was nothing more to it than a casual friendship.

'Is she in love with you?'

'It's a bit more complicated than that. We were supposed to get engaged last year, but what with her concerts abroad and my work we didn't get round to it. Things have just drifted since then. I hardly ever see her.'

'Why was she here now?'

'It was just a flying visit between concerts to collect some clothes and stuff.'

I began to walk away.

Catching my hand, he held it. 'Jenny, wait! What about us?'

'There is no 'us'.'

'I think there is. Don't you realise we're falling in love?'

'So what do you want *us* to do? Play out our game of love in secret, meet and make love, part, keep each a distance from the other with not a glance to show how far this has gone?'

He moved back, looking stricken. 'I'll sort it out with Natalie. Give me another chance, please?'

Everything around us was still. He was like a small boy hovering, waiting to be forgiven. I looked at the sky, a velvet cloak dotted with splinters of stars. I was lost and I knew it.

'Please?' He pulled me to him and I leaned into him for comfort. His arm tightened around me. 'I'll tell her I've met someone else.'

I looked up and saw his reassuring smile. He kept his arm around me as we walked along.

'I'll see you tomorrow before you go,' he said.

I didn't let him kiss me goodnight.

★　★　★

'Well?' Next morning Aunt Mary's look was questioning. 'You're very pale, Jenny. You're not sick, are you?'

'No, I'm fine.'

'I'll make you a cup of tea.' It was her cure for every ailment.

'Hugo bring you home from the party?' she asked, when Aunt Lilian was out of earshot.

I swallowed. 'Yes.'

'Something wrong?'

I nodded.

'Want to talk about it?'

'He has a girlfriend. Natalie Mason.'

'I've heard of her.'

'She looks as if she'd walked straight out of *Hello!* magazine.' I sniffed. Aunt Mary put the box of tissues in front of me. 'You don't seem surprised?' I said.

'No, I suppose I'm not,' she said. 'We'd heard of her from Flo a long time ago, but then she went off to make her name abroad so I assumed it was over between them.'

'I wish somebody had told me about her.'

'I'm afraid we're not as up to date as we should be out here in the sticks,' she said, half apologetically.

I laid my head on the table and wept so hard I thought I'd burst. I could see by the puzzled look on Aunt Mary's face that she couldn't understand why I'd got involved with him again, but she was too kind to say so.

Thinking about him in bed that night I

120

decided that it had to end. I should have known from my previous experience with him not to get involved with him again. No, I didn't want any part of it. And I didn't want to think about him any more. My mind veered away and finally I fell asleep.

Next morning I said goodbye to Cathy and Ned, who were leaving that day for Australia, and returned to Dublin with Mum and Dad without seeing Hugo.

11

When I woke I still felt tired, and my legs ached. I got up and ran a bath then soaked in it for a while. Afterwards, I went downstairs in my bathrobe.

Mum was draining her teacup. 'There you are, just as I'm leaving,' she said. 'I'm taking Adam to the park.'

She went to the window and glanced down the street to see if her pal May Cunningham was coming up the road. As there was no sign of her she went outside and gave Adam his ball, cautioning him to stay in the garden and not to shout too loudly. He wanted to go to the swings and slides in the park.

'Soon,' she said, gazing up the road, admiring the gardens while she waited for May. 'If you're a good boy I'll buy you an ice-cream,' she promised. She liked the park and went there as often as she could with Adam. Sitting with the youthful mothers made her feel young again. They confided in her, and although her attitudes and manners were those of an older generation, they talked to her as if she were a contemporary. But although she loved Adam, he exhausted her, because she had him all day. 'It's too much,' she confided. 'Leaves me no time for myself. Kids are very demanding.' Her eyes were on Adam who was swinging on the gate.

Later, Dad came home unexpectedly. 'Where's your mother?' he asked.

'She went to the park with Adam.'

'Anything to eat?'

'There's plenty of food in the fridge. Make yourself something.'

He opened the fridge and unwrapped the cheese. I drank a cup of coffee looking at the phone, waiting for it to ring.

Hugo had no more intention of phoning than he had of telling Natalie about me. Our night of passion hadn't meant anything to him. Still, it was hard to believe that he had taken his leave just like that. He'd be busy by now, his herd of prize cattle to worry about. But what about Hugo the lover? Would he surface again when and where it suited him? Would I want a man who turned me on and off like a tap when it suited him? I didn't think so.

What was happening to me? A couple of weeks ago I had been happy. Life was peaceful. The whole sorry mess of Hugo had been firmly in the past where it belonged. I had been doing fine until I let him into my life again. But he had made me feel so special.

I was thinking of Hugo, tall, attractive, vibrant, elegant, sensitive, when Mum returned. 'You still sitting here?' she said. 'I thought you'd have bought out Oasis by now.'

'I can't be bothered going shopping. No energy.'

'I don't know what's got into you, but I expect it's that Hugo fellow.'

'I've forgotten all about him.'

'I don't believe that. You've been carrying a torch for him all these years.'

'Only in my dreams. He wasn't the Hugo Hunter I used to know. In fact, nothing about him was real.'

'What makes you say that?'

'We got off to a bad start again. We never get it right,' I said, remembering the brief joy of our reunion, then the sudden change when Natalie came into the picture as the dream had shattered. But I didn't want to elaborate on it with Mum so I went over to Sophie's and told her the whole story.

She said, 'He's the type of man who comes into your life and upsets everything. There are plenty of them around. You'll just have to get over him.'

'It won't be easy.'

'Stop putting yourself through the wringer,'

she said. 'Get a grip on yourself. Get a life. Get a haircut, highlights, lowlights, too, if it helps. Go shopping and buy a whole new wardrobe. You're vulnerable at the moment and lonely, but there's no use going round hoping he'll turn up again and make everything all right.'

'Oh, no. I don't harbour any hopes like that,' I said, but she knew I was lying.

I'd thought I'd never hear from Hugo again. I was getting used to the idea that he'd slept with me then dumped me. It would have been impossible if he'd lived close by, because I'd have seen him afterwards, or bumped into him in the pub, or crossing the road.

'I'll soon forget all about him,' I said.

'Well, that's half the battle. Someone else will come into your life any minute and sweep you down the aisle.'

'I don't want to get married.' I was horrified at the thought of settling down with anyone but Hugo.

'Until your hormones get the better of you and, suddenly, hey presto, you think, I want marriage and kids. And you'll find someone.'

'My hormones are dead.'

'Oh, yeah? I caught you drooling over babywear in Next the other week, remember?'

Sophie was one of the few people I knew who said what she felt. She never minded telling me things about myself that were true. She was strong medicine but good for me.

'Cheer up,' she said. 'Let's go for a drink. You never know whom we might meet.'

I shook my head. 'I'd be quite happy to live in misery for the rest of my life than bother with a man ever again.'

'You think that now but give it time. You'll bounce back. You always do. Come on, let's go. There are plenty of men out there waiting in the wings.'

'I hadn't noticed.'

In the pub we met Andy Prenderville a friend of Sophie, who bought us drinks and invited us to a party in Glasnevin. I declined.

'Oh! Come on, Jenny,' Sophie said. 'Andy's drop-dead gorgeous. Exactly what you need to help you get over Hugo.'

'Stop trying to fix me up. I'm not ready for any kind of relationship yet.'

'It's just that I hate to see you unhappy.'

'Just give it time, will you?' I shouted at her.

'Keep your voice down.'

'No, I bloody won't,' I hissed. 'I'm quite happy on my own. I don't need a man. Thank you for your concern, but from now on mind your own business.'

Work was a blessing, so much happening that I hadn't time to think, and no time to look back. In the full-length mirror I gazed at my appearance, shocked at what I saw. Huge eyes gazed out from a thin face, my hair was dull and lacklustre, and my clothes hung off me. In the short time since I had seen Hugo I had lost a lot of weight without noticing it. I pushed my hair back from my face, and studied my features. Though I hated to admit it, Sophie was right. I was avoiding life by hiding at home.

'I'm moving out,' I said to Mum, when I couldn't take another minute of her anxious eyes following me around all the time.

She didn't put up an argument, knowing my mind was made up.

The tiny apartment was on the top floor of a tall, skinny house in Ranelagh. I had found it in the *Evening Herald* small advertisements. Reluctantly Dad transported my belongings there in his pick-up, and got Ulick, his assistant, to lift the heavy boxes up the four flights of stairs. Mum had given me the bed I'd slept in all my life, and I'd brought my books and bookcases with me too. In the local second-hand furniture shop I bought a cream-coloured sofa and two comfortable chairs, and a table that doubled as a desk for when I brought work home. The sitting-room window overlooked a backyard that led to a lane.

I often sat up late watching telly, or lay listening to the arguments of the next-door neighbours through the walls. I hardly noticed the chill of the place, because my mind was usually in the past. I saw a man and a woman walking on a summer beach, laughing and joking with each other, the man with gentle assurance, the woman with excitement and delight. There would be no more intimate meetings, no more teasing between us.

I hated the loneliness of that first week, and coped with it by reading everything I could lay my hands on. When I couldn't sleep I thought of Hugo: his eyes, his exuberant hair, which he kept raking back with his long, expressive fingers, and all the different pictures I had of him in my mind. One by one I examined them: the handsome stranger on the train, whose eyes had spoken to me; the moment in the garden of the Manor when he had said easily, 'I want to make love to you,' casting a spell over me with eyes full of honesty and need. The joy of that first kiss.

In pubs and clubs, in restaurants, driving to work and back, I would see his image in front of me. Alone in my bedroom, I gazed up at the stars through the skylight window, thinking of him sad and sleepless as I was. In the lonely Manor with its gracious rooms, its rotting sash windows, its leaking roofs, its lawns, its sweeping avenue full of potholes, he would feel lost. It was too big a place, an impossible burden for him to carry alone. And yet I felt a kind of homesickness for it that I had no right to feel. I would gaze at a photograph taken of him by the official photographer on the day of the wedding, which Cathy had given me, and wonder if I would ever be free of the spell he cast over me.

The flat needed brightening up. I got a colour chart on the way home from work, and decided to paint the sitting room buttercup, the bedroom blue, the kitchen white.

'I'll get Ulick to finish it for you,' Dad said, when he called in and saw the mess I was making and the paint in my hair.

'No, thanks. I want to do it myself.'

'Suit yourself,' he said.

One evening when I went to see Mum, she said, 'Some man phoned here looking for you the other day.'

'Who?'

'I didn't recognise his voice.'

'Why didn't you ask?'

'I didn't like to. It's not as if I'm your housekeeper, or your secretary.' This was said in the voice she adopted when she was miffed. 'I said you'd moved out.'

'Oh.'

Late one Saturday evening, perched on the top rung of the ladder, my hair tied up in a scarf, I was painting the sitting-room ceiling, the windows and doors wide open. Celine Dion was singing 'Falling Into You', as the paintbrush dripped down my arm. Sweat beaded my forehead. Finally, finished, I descended the ladder slowly, my whole body aching. I made a cup of tea and sat drinking it in the gloom, waiting for the water to heat up for a bath, too tired to move.

'You've made a good job of the place.'

I nearly jumped out of my skin.

Hugo Hunter was standing in the open doorway. He came into the room, looking pale in the evening light, but he was smiling. I resisted a tremendous urge to fling my arms around him.

I revived enough to say, 'How did you find me?' and pulled my scarf off my head.

'I met your aunt Mary in the supermarket. She gave me your new address.'

'Would you like a drink? I've got Budweiser or vodka. No mixers, I'm afraid.'

'I'll have a Bud, please.'

He watched me while I poured the drinks. 'You rushed off before I could see you again,' he said.

'You hardly expected me to sit around

130

waiting to find out if you were serious about me or not?'

'But you could have given me the chance to say goodbye. We could have talked.'

'Hugo, I refuse to be a compartment in your life that you can close the lid on whenever you choose.'

'You're not a 'compartment in my life'. I haven't stopped thinking about you since you left Coolbawn. Now that doesn't say much for compartmentalisation, does it?'

There was silence.

He walked over to the window, turned and faced me. 'You thought it was just a quick shag, did you? That once I'd got my leg over I wouldn't want to see you again?'

I stood my ground. 'Isn't that usually the way?'

He looked hurt. 'No, it isn't.'

'I thought I'd met someone interesting. Someone I could care about. I'd have liked it to be more than sex,' I said.

'You made it that way by leaving so suddenly. I wanted to see you again, but there was no chance of that. You made sure of it.'

I stared at him accusingly. 'In case you've forgotten, you already have a girlfriend. It never occurred to me that anybody else existed in your life. That what we did might affect anyone else.'

'It hasn't affected Natalie.'

'I'm sure it would hurt Natalie very much if she knew about it.'

'What happened between us mattered to me, Jenny. You know it did.'

'Well, you acted as if it was the most important thing to happen to you until Natalie appeared.'

'So you think it *was* a casual fling. Well, believe me, I know what casual means and it wasn't that. For a long time now it's been casual between Natalie and me.'

'And have you told her it's over now?'

'She's still away. I can hardly do it on the phone.'

'Then what are you doing here?'

'I'm here on business. And I had to see you.'

'Well, I'm sorry, but until you sort things out with Natalie I'm not interested.'

'I've every intention of telling her as soon as she gets back.'

I gazed at him steadily. 'I don't want to get hurt, Hugo, and if I keep seeing you while you're still with her, that's exactly what'll happen.'

He took my hand, pulled me to him. 'I care too much about you to hurt you. She'll be back on Friday. I'll do it at the weekend.'

'Fine. Ring me after that then.'

He took me in his arms and kissed me with a desperation induced by separation and misunderstanding.

I pulled away.

12

Two weeks later he rang.

'Where were you?' His voice made me jump out of my skin. 'I've been calling your mobile all day.'

The sound of his voice made my heart pound. 'Sorry, I had it switched off.'

'I was hoping to see you.' There was a slight pause. 'I'm in Dublin. I suppose it's too late to make an arrangement for this evening.'

The hairs on the back of my neck stood up. I looked at my watch and said I'd meet him somewhere. I wondered if he'd finished with Natalie.

'What about the Conrad? I'm staying there.'

My voice was shaky as I said, 'Eight o'clock.'

'I'll be there.' The phone went dead.

Damn! I'd given in to him. For the rest of the afternoon I was distracted, reliving our brief past, thinking of Natalie, and remembering that they'd been together for five whole years. It wouldn't be easy to break off a relationship of such longevity.

At five forty-five I escaped to the

cloakroom, leaned my forehead against the cold tiled wall, and took a deep breath. My hair! What a mess it was. Why hadn't I had it done?'

'You all right?' Sophie asked. 'You look a bit funny.'

'Hugo's just phoned.'

'What did he want?'

'I'm meeting him in the Conrad.'

'Just like that?' She clicked her fingers.

'Yes.'

'D'you think it's wise to be seeing him until you're sure he's over his obsession with that singer?'

'It'll be interesting to hear what he has to say.'

'Perhaps you should find that out first before you meet him.'

'I'm only having dinner, Sophie, not moving in with him.'

'Since you met him you've been strung out like a piece of wire. You spend every waking minute waiting to hear from him. You should be going to nightclubs, parties, anything.'

'I'd look marvellous on my own, wouldn't I?'

'It's not as if you don't know what he's like. You knew him before. He jilted you then . . . ' She left the sentence suspended in mid-air.

'Thanks,' I retorted, furious.

'Oh, God, I'm sorry I said that. I shouldn't interfere. It's your life. You do what you think best. I'm sure you know what you're doing.'

'I'm older now, and wiser than I was all those years ago, and if there's one thing I've learned from past mistakes it's not to get involved with a man unless he's free.'

Back at the flat I showered, plucked my eyebrows, put on a short black dress with a scooped neckline, applied my makeup, removed it, washed my face and started all over again. I coaxed my hair back into a silver clip, leaving wisps sticking out. Unhappy with the effect I shook it loose and put on my dangly silver earrings.

Sophie called in on her way home, looking contrite. 'Sorry I was a bit sharp earlier,' she said.

'It's all right. I know you mean well. What'd you think?' I asked, doing a twirl.

'You look gorgeous.' She sighed ruefully. 'Promise me you won't do anything rash, at least not until you hear what the story is.'

'I promise.' We left together and I slammed the door behind me.

The city was full of people hurrying in all directions. The Conrad was crowded. I sat at the bar and waited, watching the skirmish to get the barman's attention, believing I'd been stood up. This was his way of repaying me for running out on him.

I had emptied my glass and was about to leave when he appeared. 'There you are.' He was snapping his fingers at a waiter, leading me to a table in a dim recess. 'Two vodkas and Diet Cokes,' he told the man. He eyed me up and down.

I sat bolt upright, uncomfortable at his scrutiny.

'You look beautiful, Jenny,' he said.

'Thank you.'

'What would you like?' he asked, his eyes on the Catch of the Day blackboard. 'Lobster, crayfish, dressed crab,' he read.

'I'll have a salad to start with, please, and the dressed crab. I'm not very hungry,' I added, by way of apology.

'Greek, Caesar, Blackbean?'

'Caesar, please.'

The drinks arrived. He gave the food order. As soon as the waiter was gone he raised his glass in a toast, leaning towards me, smiling. 'Here's to us,' he said.

'And Natalie? Have you told her about us?'

'Yes. I told her. It's finally over.'

My heart somersaulted in my chest with relief. 'How did she take it?'

'Not very well, as one might expect,' he said, closing the subject firmly.

The waiter arrived with the food, and set it

down in front of us. While we ate he kept up a light banter about life at the Manor, and his progress with the repairs. Over coffee his eyes were wary as he calculated the risk in saying, 'I want to make love to you again, if I may?' His eyes bored into mine as he waited for my answer.

'Yes.'

'What are we waiting for?' he said, and stood up. We went to the lift, he opened the door, and drew me into the narrow space with him. We sped to the fourth floor.

'My room,' he said, pushing open the door, reaching for the light switch, and walking in quickly.

Clutching my bag I was seized by a sudden panic that made my heart pound. What if he hadn't really finished with Natalie? I dismissed the thought. He wouldn't have lied to me.

'What would you like to drink?' he asked, going to the mini-bar.

'A glass of wine, please,' I said.

'Sure you wouldn't like some champagne? It's here.'

While he was absorbed in pouring the drinks I waited, stiff with tension. He handed me my drink, pushed back my hair, let his fingers fall gently to my neck. A shiver shot through me.

138

'You've got the most beautiful eyes I've ever seen.' He pulled me closer. My nose brushed his cheek, and the familiar lemony smell of him overwhelmed me. He bent down and kissed me. I savoured the texture of his lips, my mouth opening beneath his.

He put down his drink and mine, then engulfed me in his arms. He caught my hair, twisted it round his fingers, and clasped me to him. Our fate was sealed. It was over with Natalie. We'd be together for the rest of our lives.

Convulsed with longing I reached up for his shirt, and undid the buttons. He ripped it off and his trousers fell to the floor. I began removing my own clothes.

'Jenny, I want you,' he said, his hands on me again, so sure of himself that I couldn't help but respond. There were no preliminaries this time. So greedy was I for him that I forgot everything except my need of him. He arched up to meet me saying, 'It's all right, darling. Take your time. There's no rush.'

But I couldn't stop.

Afterwards, it was like a dream, lying in his arms, warm and safe, cars going by in the street below. I lay listening to his steady breathing, and dreaming of the future. I was wondering which of the thirty rooms at the Manor we would pick for ourselves, and what colours we'd choose for the walls, when his mobile rang, waking him.

He got up suddenly, and answered it. After a flurry of blurred words from the other end he said, 'It's no bother.'

He leaned towards me, awkwardly held my arm. 'I have to go, Jenny. Natalie's been in an accident. She's been rushed to the Galway Regional Hospital. That was Rick, her manager, on the phone. I'm sorry.'

Dumbstruck I watched him pad across the bedroom floor. I looked at him moving around in the shadows as he dressed quickly, sliding on his jacket over his sports shirt. I realised that I didn't really know this man, or what he was thinking. He was putting on his watch, calmly taking his wallet and keys from the top of the bedside locker, his face anxious.

Dressed once more, he wasn't the man who had just made love to me so thoroughly. He was Hugo Hunter, the businessman. He leaned over the bed and kissed my cheek lightly.

'It's only midnight. Get some sleep. I'll phone you when I get there.'

'You sure you want me to stay here?'

He smiled at the absurd idea. 'Of course. You get some sleep,' he said, tousling my hair. 'I love you.'

My uncertainty evaporated. All doubt gone, I turned over, unable to watch him leave. I heard him pull the door gently after him and his footsteps hurrying away.

As soon as it was quiet, suspicion and anxiety overcame me. What kind of accident had Natalie been involved in? Was she badly injured? I'd been insistent that he finished his relationship with her if I were to get involved with him again, but I hadn't bargained for this.

Did he still love her? No! I was the loved one, the one he wanted in his bed. I'd have to be understanding, though, for as long as it took. I must be wise and mature, and when he phoned I must show restraint and not bombard him with questions. Yes, I must be grown-up about this, show him every consideration. But the mistrust was there, distorting the moments we'd just shared.

I woke up in the middle of the night, alone in the bed. My watch said three o'clock. Why hadn't he phoned? I made myself a cup of coffee. Sitting up in bed I drank it, thinking of his gentle touch, his voice telling me he loved me. Five o'clock came and there was still no call.

The phone rang.

Hugo, sounding like a stranger, said, 'I'm at the hospital. Natalie's very ill. I'm not sure how much longer I'll be here. I'll talk to you as soon as I get back to the Manor. I don't know when that will be.'

'Fine.'

The phone went dead.

I fumbled for the light switch. How could this be happening? The cruelty of it made me so mad I wanted to kick something or weep, but there was no time for that. I grabbed my clothes. Where was my dress? How had it got caught up in the sheets? In the bathroom I ran the cold tap, rinsed my face. Lipstick, eyeliner, run a comb through my hair. Where were my shoes? I retrieved them from under the bed. I had to get out of here. What time was it? Where was my bag? My purse? Did I have enough money for a taxi if I needed one? Shoes. I'd got everything. Now get out.

The street lamps cast a glow on the dark street and the slate roofs. I walked quickly. It was frightening in the dark. I heard a rustle behind me. I mustn't look back. I walked on. I heard breathing. I glanced over my shoulder. A stray dog was trailing me.

'Go home,' I growled at him.

He wagged his tail, and stayed close.

The shapes of the big houses on either side of me loomed menacingly. I hailed a passing taxi. It stopped. My high heels caught in the pavement cracks as I ran to it.

'In a hurry, sweetheart?' The middle-aged taxi driver stared at me, taking in my crumpled suit, my hair all over the place, my shaky legs.

'Yes.'

He beckoned me into the back, and I jumped in slamming the door.

At home, the house was silent. I sneaked up the stairs to my flat. A cold perspiration spread across my back, and trickled down my spine as I got into bed. I spent a long time lying there, staring into nothing, thinking about what had happened, wondering what was going to happen next, and if Hugo was trying to get me at the hotel. I switched on my mobile and waited for his call.

He didn't ring.

I couldn't remember his number. Leafing through my address book I cradled the receiver. I found it, dialled, praying for him to answer. It rang for ages. Then his voicemail answered. 'I can't come to the phone right now. If you'd care to leave your name and number I'll get back to you.'

At around eight o'clock I phoned Sophie. 'Could you come over? Please? Now,' I sobbed.

A little later she was with me. 'What's wrong with you?' she asked, sitting down beside me, with her arm around me.

I told her what had happened.

'Oh, my God, poor Natalie,' she cried. 'Was it hit and run?'

'He didn't say. And now I just have to wait to hear from him.'

13

He didn't phone. In the office I went around like a robot, and sat hunched for hours over my desk trying to concentrate on my work, picturing Hugo at Natalie's bedside, his face lined with fatigue, his knuckles white with tension. I couldn't sleep. Mum insisted that I saw the doctor, who prescribed sleeping pills, which gave me weird dreams. In one dream Natalie was dead and Hugo was living a reclusive life at the Manor with Aunt Lilian. I woke up with tears streaming down my face.

Surprisingly enough, considering the gaping hole Hugo's departure had left, my life continued as before. I spent the same eight hours a day working in the same establishment, with Louis perched behind his huge desk having endless meetings or issuing instructions with a busy look on his face that said, 'Hurry up.'

The following week Hugo phoned.

'Meet me for lunch, Searson's, Baggot Street,' he said tersely.

At one o'clock sharp I was sitting by the window in the pub. There was no sign of Hugo. Oh, God, what if he didn't come

— and what if he did?

At half past one he came in, looking tired but smiling. 'Hello,' he said, his voice warm, if not completely calm, taking me off guard. I moved up to make room for him. He sat down beside me. 'How are you?' he asked.

I was trembling, rearranging myself on the seat, and trying to regain my composure.

He started again. 'How are you?'

What I wanted to say was 'You've upset me very much.' What I said was, 'How's Natalie?'

'Not good. She'll survive, but she's bad.' His voice was strangled.

'I'm sorry to hear that,' I said. 'I'll get the drinks.'

'To hell with the drinks.' He caught my hand and held it. 'I'm sorry I didn't get back to you sooner, Jenny. It took longer than I thought.' He looked at me as though he was trying to read my thoughts.

'Well, if Natalie needed you . . . ' My voice trailed off. I had been startled by the intensity of his gaze. His eyes, though pouched from lack of sleep, had a strange light in them, and his face seemed more vulnerable than ever.

When I didn't say anything he said, 'I know it's hard for you to understand, but I feel terrible about her.'

I waited.

'When it was over between us I felt

relieved, but this is different. Watching her lying there, tubes everywhere, I feel guilty, as if it's my fault. I feel I should've been there for her. She's a good person, Jenny. She didn't do anything to deserve this.'

'No, I'm sure she didn't,' I said sympathetically.

'As I told you I hadn't seen much of her in the last couple of years. She was totally caught up in her singing, always off touring, and certainly not focusing on me. And . . . ' he lifted his shoulders in a helpless gesture ' . . . I fell in love with you. I realise now that I'd no right to start anything with you while I was still involved with her. It wasn't fair to either of you.' In the silence that followed he said, 'You see, I need to believe that I loved her. That our lives together weren't meaningless, as much for her sake now as mine.'

'Of course you loved her. You spent five years of your life with her.'

He looked at me. 'I'll have to be with her until she gets better.'

My eyes filled with tears and I swivelled my head so that he wouldn't see them. I could hear music coming from somewhere.

He sat there, beautiful, inaccessible, waiting for me to give him permission to go back to her.

I said, 'It's no big deal.'

'You're wonderful, Jenny. A real trouper.'

'Don't patronise me,' I flung at him. 'I didn't expect this to happen.' I swallowed back more wounding words and stood up. It took me a minute to say, 'I don't know what I expected but it wasn't this.'

'You think I did?' he asked.

'No.' I tried to keep my voice reasonable as I said, 'It isn't something I'm prepared to endure until you may or may not be free again.'

He turned away his head as though I'd struck him. 'What do you mean?'

'I think you'd better go. You've got a long journey ahead of you.'

He looked at his watch. 'I can spare another hour,' he said.

'I'd rather you go,' I said.

'I'll phone you in a couple of weeks.'

'Please don't. I can't stand this blowing hot and cold business.'

He sprang to his feet, eyes blazing. 'So I'm blowing hot and cold, am I?'

'That's exactly what you're doing.'

'Do you know what it's like watching someone you're close to struggling for life?'

'I'm sorry I shouldn't have said that.'

'Give me some time. Until Natalie gets better.'

'Take all the time you want. Just don't

148

expect me to wait around.'

There was a stricken look on Hugo's face as he walked me to my car. I got in and he leaned into the open window. He touched my cheek tenderly. 'Jenny . . . ' he said, in a low voice.

'Don't say any more.'

'Okay.' He tried to smile and then he was gone, a man on a mission. I sat there abandoned and sobbing.

That evening I told Sophie the whole story, going through all the details, becoming more miserable as I did so, knowing that none of it reflected well on my judgement. Raising my eyes to hers I said, 'I made it worse because I was awful to him, really awful. I couldn't help letting him know how I felt.'

'What did you say to him?' she asked, girl to girl.

'I more or less gave him his marching orders.'

'That final?'

'Yes. But I went too far. He has to be with her, I can see that, but I told him I wouldn't wait for him any more.'

'There was nothing else you could've done. He's on another planet if he expects you to wait for him while he nurses Natalie back to health.'

'I love him,' I wailed. 'I want to believe that

he loves me too, or am I just fooling myself?'

'Obviously he *did*, and that's something you'll have to remember. Mind you, love is a terrible thing, and men are bastards, but in this case I don't see what else Hugo could've done. It's a rotten thing to have happened.'

'Do you think that by the time Natalie gets better he'll have forgotten all about me?' I sniffed.

'No. He won't forget you, but . . . things may not be quite the same. Only time will tell if he's the right man for you, Jenny.'

'Do you think he realises that?'

'I do.'

'I'd better try and forget him.'

'It might be for the best,' she agreed.

★   ★   ★

I continued living in the flat, much to Mum's disgust, and went to see her twice a week. She tried to cushion my sadness by cooking me appetising meals, and baking me bread and scones to take home. She bought me small gifts for the flat: a blue and yellow tea-set, a set of yellow-handled cutlery, a tablecloth, matching napkins, not knowing what else to do.

On Saturdays Sophie and I spent our time shopping, on Sundays she dragged me out for long walks in the countryside. We trudged along narrow, chestnut-lined roads, or followed boundary hedges that zigzagged for miles across fields where the view expanded to beautiful, untouched meadows. Past the 'Trespassers Will Be Prosecuted' signs we went, walking uphill or downhill, as the notion took us, saying little, thinking of nothing. I was getting on with my life, but I was deeply distressed, permanently on the edge of panic.

What really saved the day were the new accounts Louis procured. At work, I was electrified by incessant telephones, the ebullient Louis and important demanding clients.

14

Louis was in a good mood, marching up and down in front of us, waving his hands, his eyes on the storyboard as he talked about his newest potential client, Ireland West Tourism.

'This could be a lucrative account if I can pull it off,' he said, 'so I want to acquaint you all with the West of Ireland.' He paused. 'If you remember from your schooldays, historically this was a place of poverty, populated by people who were driven there by Cromwell's order — 'To hell or to Connaught'.'

'Yes,' we chorused.

'Things are changing rapidly. The western seaboard is busy reconstructing itself. It's an amazing, happening place, full of glamorous stars and film directors. With the new industry there, house prices are soaring and there's new wealth in Connemara towns, with pubs, shops and restaurants appearing virtually overnight.' He pointed to the red dots on the map of Connemara he had on his noticeboard.

'The once sleepy West is vibrantly alive. As more people move to the area, more facilities will become available, and our job will be to change the profile, bring the West of Ireland into the new millennium — transform its image, with the emphasis on sailing, mountain-climbing, and water sports to attract a younger client. Make them feel the buzz of the western coast. We also want to develop an interest in Spiddal too, and the Gaeltacht.'

'Like it's cool to speak the Irish language nowadays,' said Charlie.

'That's the idea,' said Louis. 'With information and communication, television being the catalyst in bringing our message to the people, we'll do it. I'll be touring different towns for the next month, seeing what's to be done.'

'Great.' Sophie sighed with relief.

Louis glared at her. 'The success of this campaign depends on you lot. Now, off you go and think. Think until it hurts.'

'I'm worn out thinking,' Sophie snapped.

'It's a process that's required for your job. It's what you're paid for, and if you don't come up with something good you're gone. Have you got that?'

'Yes.'

Louis turned his back on us, and was on the phone again, issuing instructions while going through lists on his computer.

A few days later he waltzed into the office

grinning like a Cheshire cat.

'I clinched the Ireland West Tourism account. As I told you, it has huge potential, and this is the best bit.' He paused, dazzling me with his smile. 'This weekend we're off to a beautiful hotel in Connemara for a conference with the Ireland West Tourism people.'

'Are you talking to me?' I asked.

'Who else? We'll be the guests of honour at their teambuilding exercise, together with management consultants, accountants, bankers, all helping to inspire new growth.'

'Oh.' I never felt less like having fun in my life.

'Don't look so glum. It's not going to be all heavy-duty stuff. We're also going to relax, unwind, play golf, party a little.'

This was what I should be doing — embarking on these fantastic, exciting, new ideas of Louis's that could put our little agency up there among the top ten and help me to get over Hugo.

'Now get your ass out of here, go home and pack.' Then he was on the phone barking instructions, like a field marshal preparing for battle.

The next day we set off early. Sophie was seething in the back, furious at having to give up her precious weekend to chat up clients and caddy for them, should the need arise.

When we came to the long, winding, empty roads of Connemara the scenery was breathtaking. 'This has got to be the most beautiful part of Ireland,' Louis said, pointing enthusiastically to the endless fields in varying shades of green, the stark, majestic Twelve Pin mountains looming above them, the shimmering silver sea stretched out below.

'Look, over there,' he said, his rings flashing as he pointed.

In the distance I could see the Castledermot Hotel, perched on the curve of an inlet that nestled between the mountains and the sea, outside Clifden. It swelled above the clear water of the Atlantic Ocean, its splendid Gothic towers and turrets reaching for the sky, its mullioned windows glinting in the sun.

'I'm nervous,' I said, thinking of the faceless gurus I was about to encounter, all eager to impart their knowledge and expertise.

Louis squeezed my knee and reassured me that it would be all right. 'All you have to do is listen carefully and take a few notes,' he said.

'I, on the other hand, have to come up with ideas,' said Sophie.

'Well, if you can't come up with good ones

in this setting you're useless,' warned Louis, half jokingly.

We turned in through enormous wrought-iron gates, and drove up an enchanting lane lined with laurel and rhododendron bushes. Louis parked on the north side of the castle, facing neatly trimmed gardens surrounded by the grey stone walls.

'It's beautiful,' I breathed, unbuckling my seat-belt.

'I knew you'd like it,' said Louis, taking the bags from the boot.

He led the way up the steps, through the gargoyled entrance into a huge, stone-floored main hall, lined with marble pillars that supported a circular gallery and a staircase that wound upwards to a stained-glass dome.

At Reception an inferno of a fire burned, throwing its reflection on low oak tables, which supported bowls of red and yellow flowers. Deep white sofas, covered with terracotta tapestry cushions, surrounded them.

'Welcome to the Castledermot,' said the uniformed concierge.

Louis signed us in. 'I've booked a room each for you at the back, with a sea-view. Perhaps you'd like to have a rest before dinner.'

Appealing as this plan was I felt a bit

strange about going to bed as soon as I arrived, especially with important-looking businessmen hovering around. 'Wouldn't it be better if we met one or two of these people first?' I said.

Louis flashed me a smile. 'Time enough for that later. You go and rest yourselves.' In that instance my misgivings about him evaporated. Perhaps he wasn't so bad after all.

'You can rest all you like. I'm going to check out the talent,' said Sophie, gazing at the handsome men assembled before her.

'And where'll you be?' I asked Louis.

'Oh, don't worry about me,' he said, throwing down his briefcase in a corner. 'There are some people I have to meet in the bar. I'll probably play a round of golf, if the rain holds off. Come on, I'll escort you girls to your rooms first.'

'There's really no need,' said Sophie.

'I insist on making sure that you're comfortable.' He took our bags and led the way to the lift. When he left us outside our rooms, he said, 'We'll meet here at seven to go down for drinks before dinner.'

I unpacked my black velvet dress with the low V neck, and hung it in the wardrobe, then lay down on the big, comfortable bed. I fell asleep instantly, and didn't wake until half past four. I rang Sophie's room, and when there was no reply I phoned Room Service and ordered tea. While I waited for it to arrive, I sat and looked out of the window. Guests strolled in beautiful gardens that surrounded a lake, wrapped up against the chill. In the distance I saw Sophie talking to a man who was taking photographs.

I watched television while I drank my tea, then I showered, using the delicious scented gel liberally. If this was what Louis referred to as a working weekend I'd be on for it anytime. Wrapped in the fleecy hotel bathrobe I dried my hair, and slowly began to get ready for the evening, applying my makeup carefully in front of the huge gilt mirror. Sophie bounced in, looking infuriatingly gorgeous in a black silk tank top that was stretched to its limit across her bosom, and matching trousers. 'Wow! You look sexy,' I said.

'I've just been talking to the most gorgeous-looking man I've ever seen in my life,' she said, pouting into the mirror.

'You say that about them all.' I laughed.

'Believe me, this guy is the business. I'm going down to the dining room early to try to nab the seat next to him at dinner.'

'Where's Louis?'

'I left him in the bar being chatted up by some leggy blonde. Oh, I forgot my eyebrow

158

pencil,' she said, riffling through my makeup as if it was her own.

'Fancies his chances there, does he?'

'He's in with more than a chance. You know, Louis has something,' said Sophie, reflectively arching a perfectly shaped eyebrow. 'To us he's *the boss*, a right pain in the butt, but to other women he appears charming, sensitive, even.'

I looked at her as if she'd lost her mind.

'Well, the evidence is there for all to see. They flock around him. For all we know he could be a great lover or something.'

'I can't imagine it.'

'What about that incident in his apartment? The woman who was about to tear you asunder when she found you in his bed.'

'Don't remind me of that débâcle.' I laughed.

'Well, we're going to enjoy ourselves this weekend, let our hair down,' Sophie said, sailing back to her room. 'See you downstairs.'

Yes, I would let myself go, flirt with the men and drink a lot. I might even flirt with Louis. Sophie was right. Away from the office he was different, full of kindness and consideration. For the next couple of days I'd forget about Hugo and enjoy myself. It was time to have some fun.

I finished my makeup, and slipped into my

dress. In the flattering boudoir mirror I looked prettier than I had in weeks.

I met Louis on the landing as arranged at seven. At the press of a button the lift hummed downwards. It stopped, the doors opened and there was Hugo, more handsome than ever in a dinner jacket and crisp white shirt. I felt my knees go weak. I'd forgotten how beautiful he was.

Shock crossed his face when he saw me. 'Jenny!' he said, as he stepped in.

'Hello, Hugo.'

Behind me Louis said, in a cool voice, 'You two know each other?'

'Louis, this is Hugo Hunter. Hugo, meet Louis Leech, my boss.'

They eyed each other quizzically before Hugo said stiffly, 'How do you do?'

'You with Ireland West Tourism?' Louis asked.

'I'm one of the directors,' said Hugo, glancing at me.

'Oh!' Unusually Louis was stuck for words. I looked away.

He recovered himself quickly and said, 'I'm leading the advertising team.'

Hugo said, 'I've heard a great deal about you,' just as the lift got to the ground floor. As soon as we stepped out he walked off without a backward glance.

Annoyed, Louis said, 'Is he a friend of yours?'

'Used to be.'

I walked with him into the lounge, as elegantly as I could with shaking knees, where the champagne was flowing.

'Hugo Hunter's here,' I said to Sophie, my composure slipping as I saw him at the far end of the room.

'Which one is he so I can go and ask him why he treated you so badly?' she asked, eyeing the crowd speculatively.

'Don't you dare,' I said, taking another glass of champagne from a hovering waiter.

'Only joking.'

'He's the tall one talking to the priest.'

'What? But that's the drop-dead gorgeous guy I was telling you about,' she said, disappointment in her eyes. 'Is he on his own?'

'He appears to be.'

On my third glass of champagne I began to relax. During dinner I sat perched on the edge of my chair, eating daintily and drinking lots of wine, occasionally joining in the conversation, which revolved around advertising and its merits. I watched Hugo surreptitiously as he talked to one of the bankers, and smiled at him when he looked in my direction.

The dinner finished with a speech from Louis.

'Introducing this magnificent part of the world to people is the first step, familiarising it with images and logos is the next,' he said. 'Good design is essential to convey to people what they need to know about this product. That is all-important. Advertising has no boundaries. Therefore the West of Ireland must have no boundaries in its appeal to all class structures. The effect of our campaign must not be underestimated. It will have worldwide appeal.'

He finished by saying, 'I would like to name it the West Awake Campaign, and officially launch it. Here's to a successful weekend. And here's to us,' he said, beaming like a beacon.

There was clapping and cheering.

'Enjoying yourself?' he asked me, touching my arm as he sat down.

I smiled at him. 'So far so good,' I said, the alcohol helping me to keep up the bravado, and giving me confidence to flirt shamelessly with him. As soon as I'd finished my coffee I excused myself. 'I'm just going out for a breath of fresh air. I feel a bit dizzy.'

Louis said, 'Want me to come with you?'

'No. You stay and dazzle them some more.' I left, weaving my way through the tables.

162

15

The cold sea air hit me like a slap in the face. I walked down the path to the sea wall and sat looking over at the lights of Clifden twinkling in the dark, sobering up.

'Jenny!' I turned. Hugo had followed me out.

'I was dying to have a chat with you. How are you?'

'I'm very well, thanks.' My teeth were chattering as much from nervousness as the cold. Hugo took off his jacket and draped it around my shoulders. We didn't touch or speak, but the flood of feeling that passed between us was so strong that it forced me backwards. I hugged his jacket to me.

'Let's walk,' Hugo said. 'It's too cold to keep still.' He went on, 'Louis's got off to a good start. He has them eating out of his hand.'

'He certainly knows his job,' I agreed, concentrating on walking steadily beside him to reassure myself that I was sober.

'Have you been seeing much of him?'

'Every day for the past few months.'

'Lucky man.'

'Oh, no. You've got it all wrong. Louis's my boss. There's nothing between us,' I said.

'He's totally besotted by you,' Hugo said.

We stood facing each other.

'How have you been?' I asked.

'Miserable. How have you been?'

'Lost. Lonely.' Blinded by tears I kept my head down as I struggled to stay calm.

He slipped a hand under my arm, and guided me on down the path. 'I didn't phone because you asked me not to, but I desperately wanted to see you.'

'Did you?'

'I wanted to talk to you, but I knew how you felt, and I didn't want to upset you.'

I couldn't look up into his face as I said, 'How are things at the Manor?'

'It's beautiful this time of year. The sunsets are stunning. I've been watching them lately, *alone.*'

Silence.

Hugo said, 'I wish I could turn the clock back to where it was.'

I faced him, my whole body suffused with a warm tingling sensation. I wanted to fling myself into his arms and say, 'Forget about everything, make love to me,' but I said nothing.

'Would that be very wrong of me, Jenny?' He stood with his back to the sea, his eyes dark with desire.

'I don't think so.' I could hear the tremor in my own voice.

'I've been thinking of things, getting everything into perspective.' He turned to me. 'Damn it, Jenny,' he said, slamming his hands against a tree-trunk. 'You should be there with me.' His voice snapped with anger.

'Stop,' I said, trying to quell the pain that was rising in my chest. I walked a few steps away from him to gather myself together.

'I've missed you.' His quiet words, and the wretched look on his face, wound a string of pain round my heart.

I caught my breath. 'I've missed you too,' I said.

He turned to me eagerly, lifted a strand of my hair and brushed it against his cheek. He moved closer. He was holding me, and my hands were on the sleeves of his dinner jacket, its texture as smooth as the cheek that rubbed against mine.

Burying his face in my neck he said, 'Jenny,' and leaned down to kiss my cheek just as I turned.

He caught me full on the lips, sending shock waves into every bone and muscle in my body. 'You feel so wonderful. Just like you always did.'

I wanted to turn and run but he held me

firm. His lips met mine, warm and urgent, and I turned my body completely to his. His hands moved over my velvet dress touching my breasts. I pressed against him, lost in his kiss, oblivious to the world around us, the party going on behind me. He slipped his hand inside my dress, and I was losing control. It was all the fault of my body. It knew what it wanted and was taking it.

'Oh, Jenny,' he moaned. 'I want you.' His hands on me were gentle, and I was giving in. I wasn't imagining the joy I was feeling.

'Yes,' I said.

He wrapped his arms around me tightly. I looked up at the moon and stars, their glow lingering on the sea and the rocks, enfolding us into its embrace. Yes.

'I want you so much,' he said, and I said 'Yes,' once more, the wind ruffling my hair, my face.

It was heaven in the shelter of his arms. There was strength and comfort in them. We were flying to the place where I wanted to be, where I should be. Where he would hold me for ever, where no one could hurt me, where I didn't have to think for myself. Trust. Ah! That's what it was all about. With all my heart I longed to be able to sleep in his arms and know he would be there in the morning when I woke up. For richer for poorer, in sickness . . . Sickness! I was jolted back to reality, sobered by the thought of Natalie.

'Stop!' I wrenched myself away, staring at him.

'What's the matter?' Hugo looked down at me, puzzled.

'We can't do this.' I turned away, smoothed my dress. 'It's not right.'

'It was a kiss.' He was pulling me to him, seeking my lips again.

'What about Natalie? She's still in your life.'

'I haven't slept with her since I met you again. I swear it, Jenny. I couldn't because I never stopped loving you.'

Strangely enough I believed him. 'But you're still with her.'

He nodded, letting me go. 'We're just going through the motions until she gets back into the swing of things. If she were well we'd be parted by now. As far as I'm concerned, you're the woman for me. You're gorgeous, you're perfect, and you're the only woman I want. I just wish we could go away and make love.'

'I do, too, but I keep thinking of Natalie and how much she needs you. As long as she's still in your life there's no place for me.'

He sighed. 'I thought that by being there with her I could help her get better. But it's difficult. She's changed. She was always so confident in the past. Now she's insecure about everything. She's very unhappy. I tried to talk to her, but she refuses to discuss it.'

'Wouldn't it be better if she knew the truth? About us, I mean.'

He shook his head. 'I don't think she's able for it at the moment. It might slow down her recovery and, physically, she's making good progress.'

'Well, then, you should make a fresh start together.' I looked into his eyes. 'I mean it, Hugo. You don't seem to have an alternative.'

Before he had a chance to say anything else I left him and went back inside.

Next day I saw Natalie arrive just as we broke for lunch. In the lobby she paused, her back to us, as she explained something to the concierge. I took in her sweep of black hair, the too-narrow waist, and too-thin legs.

Hugo went to meet her. 'Natalie, you remember Jenny,' he said, shifting awkwardly from one foot to the other.

Her eyes blazed dramatically as she said, 'Nice to see you again,' unafraid in her greeting, poised beside Hugo.

'Jenny's with Sharp's advertising agency.'

'What a coincidence.'

With an effort I faced her. 'I'm glad you're well again,' I said.

'Thank you,' she said, and turned away to talk to Hugo.

I went out through the french windows, down the path, past the flower border by the old wall. I stood holding on to the crumbling wall, shell-shocked and confused. I knew that Natalie was here to assert her ownership of Hugo. 'Hugo is mine,' was written in her sweet, possessive face. I watched them walk away together, his head bowed towards her, his hand on her elbow, guiding her. The awful feeling of insecurity I'd had since I met her reasserted itself. She'd got her man. She hadn't been able to hold on to him before, but she'd got him now, and I wondered to what awful lengths she'd gone to achieve that.

16

'What's with the sunglasses in the middle of October?' Charlie Craven asked, at work the following Monday morning. 'Louis been bothering you again?'

'I did warn you about going to Connemara with that Jack-the-lad,' said Sandy Smith, perching himself on my desk, the whiff of gossip in the air too much for him to ignore.

'So did I,' said Charlie. 'Tell me, did he . . .'

I shook my head miserably. 'It's nothing to do with Louis.' My face crumpled.

'Leave her alone,' said Sophie, marching between them with all the subtleties of a Rottweiler.

Louis arrived. 'Did nobody tell you that the weekend is over?' he barked. Then he looked at me. 'What's the matter with you? Are you coming down with something?'

'A cold,' I said, clutching a handkerchief to my nose.

'Look, I've got a meeting in the Shelbourne at ten so I'll take you home, and put you to bed with a hot-water bottle and a couple of Disprin on my way.'

'No, no.' I shuddered. 'I'd rather work through. I'll be all right.'

'Then I'll book us a nice lunch somewhere. I want to talk to you about the weekend.'

'Sorry, I'm meeting someone,' I said.

'Bad idea,' he said, rolling his eyes to heaven in the manner of praying for patience. 'Now, come on, everyone. Work!'

At lunchtime I escaped with Sophie to O'Reilly's. In a corner we ate bowls of spicy chicken washed down with pints of beer.

Sophie said, 'Spill the beans. Did you sleep with Hugo?'

I shot her a sharp look. 'No, I bloody didn't. We talked, that's all, mostly about Natalie. She doesn't let him out of her sight.'

'Silly cow!' said Sophie. 'He should get rid of her. Still, if he's prepared to be a martyr, that's fine, good luck to him. I've no sympathy for him.'

'Soph!' I said in frustration. 'You've got to see it from his point of view. She's still fragile after her accident.'

'There's nothing fragile about her. She's as tough as old boots.'

'Not since her accident she isn't. According to Hugo.'

'He'll probably see sense and escape from her eventually, then come looking for you.'

'I don't think I'll ever see him again,' I said sadly.

'You'll be seeing plenty of him. Have you any idea how much work's involved in the West Awake account? Now, let's change the subject. Did I tell you I'm going to have a party?'

'You are?'

'I've invited Colin, that nice banker from Belfast we met at the weekend. I told him to bring a friend.'

'Oh, God!' I heaved a sigh. 'What do you want me to do?'

'You don't have to do anything. I'll organise it all.'

'Booze is all anybody is interested in at a party,' I said knowledgeably.

'We'll buy some beer,' she said, taking out her notebook and pen, making a list.

They'll bring wine.'

'Lots of it, I hope.'

'I'll make salads,' I said, warming to her enthusiasm.

'Colin's nice.' Sophie sighed.

'He's a banker,' I reminded her.

'Have another beer. Cheer us up.'

'Hello!' said a loud voice from the other side of the bar.

'Hi, Louis.' I waved.

'Enjoying your lunch?' he enquired at the top of his voice.

'Yes, thanks.'

'Be back at two sharp.' He pointed to his watch.

'Twat!' said Sophie.

'He's sulking because I wouldn't have lunch with him, and when he's sulking he goes off on his own.'

'He can't bear to think of anyone enjoying themselves without him.'

'Let's get out of here before he comes over.'

We passed him on the way out.

'Where are you going?' he asked, his eyes on his watch. 'It's not two o'clock yet.'

'Out into the traffic to jump under a bus,' I said.

'Don't be late back.'

'You're awful to him.' Sophie laughed.

'He drives me mad.'

'It's not his fault. It's that awful job he does. Always having to encourage everyone to buy things they don't want. Maybe we should invite him to the party.'

'No,' I said. 'I see enough of him every minute and hour of the day. Doesn't give me a minute's peace. 'Jenny, do this. Jenny, do that.' He bores me rigid.'

'He thinks the sun shines out of your arse. He can't stand not to have you under his nose. He'd be much nicer to you if you were nicer to him.'

But I wasn't really thinking of the party or worrying about Louis and his loneliness at that minute. I was thinking about Hugo, and wondering if he'd moved Natalie into the Manor permanently.

Next day Louis collared me. 'You've got to have lunch with me today. I want to talk things over with you.'

Oh, God! Was he was going to fire me for refusing to have lunch with him, and for moping around the place? For the rest of the morning I buried myself in work taking out my self-pity on my keyboard. Natalie's beautiful face kept coming up before me. Well, at least I knew now where I stood. Hugo would stay with Natalie while she was recuperating. There was a sense of relief in not having to wait for the phone to ring or cancel anything at the last minute. I worked on in a daze until lunchtime.

The restaurant was packed, the noise deafening, as Louis battled his way to our table. No sooner were we seated, the drinks ordered, than he said, 'Well, tell me what the problem is.'

'It's just this cold, that's all.' I sniffed.

'Sorry to be such a misery.'

He leaned forward. 'You've been on tenterhooks ever since you bumped into that Hugo Hunter, haven't you?'

I nodded miserably.

'Want to tell me about it?'

'Not really.'

'I saw you talking to him. How you didn't freeze out there I don't know. He stayed in the bar for a long time after you left him, drinking brandy.' He gave me a sharp look. 'You can tell me to mind my own business, if you like, but in a way it does concern me. The thing is, Jenny, whatever's going on is interfering with your work.'

'Oh!' Here we go.

'Let's order.'

'I'm not very hungry.'

'I'll order for both of us. Two chicken tikkas, two side salads, and a bottle of house Chardonnay,' he said to the waiter, handing back the menus.

'When do you want me to leave?'

'Leave? I don't want you to leave. On the contrary, I need you more than ever.' He swirled his drink. 'You see, Hugo Hunter has this idea of opening his idyllic gardens to the public to keep the wolf from the proverbial door. It's a big place, apparently, and the upkeep's enormous.'

'I know. I've been there.'

'He's hosting the press launch for the West Awake promotion at the Manor soon and wants me to have a look round with a view to taking him on as a client. Obviously, this is going to affect you. I'd like to know how you feel about it.'

He was waiting, his eyes boring into mine. Where to start? How much to tell him? I plunged in giving him a sketchy version of the story while trying to keep the tears at bay. 'So you see,' I finished, 'it was over before it had started.'

He covered my hand with his. 'Don't blame yourself, Jenny. It's not your fault. He was a fool to get mixed up with you in the first place. How were you to know he was involved with another woman?'

'Exactly. But that doesn't make it any easier,' I said bluntly.

'So, what are you going to do now?'

'As long as Natalie's in his life I'm going to keep away.'

'Sounds like a good idea to me. You're right to leave him to sort himself out. The thing is, I'll need you with me when I go down there in a couple of weeks' time.' He drained his glass and sat back. 'Do you think you can handle it?'

'Doesn't look as if I have a choice, does it?

I've got to deal with it and get on with my life.'

'Sensible girl,' he said, wiping his mouth with his napkin. 'Now, let's have coffee and get back to work.'

★   ★   ★

Two nights later there was a knock on my flat door. It was barely audible because rain was hopping off the ground and thunder rolling in the distance. The knock came again. 'Hello, Jenny.'

Startled, I cried, 'Cathy!' I opened the door and ushered her in. She let me hug her briefly, then moved back and I got a good look at her. She was a bag of bones, and her beautiful hair was cut short. She looked like a demented creature who had escaped from an asylum.

'What on earth's the matter?' I asked, putting my arm around her.

'It's Ned,' she said, in a high-pitched, hysterical voice, her eyes huge and shiny with apprehension.

'What?'

'It's over. I've left him in Australia and I'm not going back.'

I was silent for a moment as I let what she'd said sink in. Then I took her arm and led her to the kitchen. 'Why don't I get you a drink? Come on, sit down,' I said.

She sat on a chair at the kitchen table while I busied myself getting the bottle of whiskey and a glass out of the cupboard. 'Here, get this down you.'

Through chattering teeth she thanked me as though I was a stranger. She sipped in silence for a few minutes. Eventually I said, 'It mightn't be as bad as all that.'

She broke into frenzied laughter. 'It couldn't be any worse. I've left him, for God's sake!'

'Do you want to tell me about it?'

'There were all these rows, mostly over his drinking. He was the boss, the one who made the decisions, stupid things like how we were going to spend our weekends. We always did what *he* wanted to do, and saw who he wanted to, and there's Fawn.'

'Fawn?'

'Oh, yes. She's got very pally with him. Ever since the wedding. They were always . . . I don't know . . . huddled together.'

'Cathy, calm down and take off your coat. It's wet.' I was fussing.

She stood up, slipped off her coat, and sank back into her chair. She sat quieter now, her head drooping. It was then that I saw bruises on her neck.

Astounded, I asked, 'Did he hit you?'

'It was his parting gift.'

'What?' I knew Cathy was used to verbal abuse — she'd taken it regularly from Aunt Lilian, but physical violence, never. I thought of Ned with his perfect manners and his quiet ways, how much Aunt Lilian had liked him.

'I've had it. I can't take any more.' She began to pace up and down. 'What am I going to do?'

'You'll have to see him at some stage, talk to him.'

She sat down again, and settled into her chair. 'Too late for talk. The damage is done.' Her voice was high and strange. She stared at me and said, 'Fawn told me she had been with him before he met me. I hate him, Jenny, and I think he hates me.'

'I doubt that.'

'It's true. He wants me to have no views, no interests and no opinions of my own. The only opinions that matter in our marriage are his. He says I'm dumb and selfish and only care about things that affect me personally. But he's the selfish one, the arrogant, conceited bully.'

'But you were in love with him. What happened to that?'

'Marriage, I suppose. It all changed as soon as we got back to Australia. Now I think it's

179

time for a divorce.'

'It's not that easy to get one, and Ned may not agree.'

'Oh, don't be ridiculous,' she scoffed. 'Of course I'll get one. I'll cite Fawn.'

'You'll have to have proof, and I think you have to be separated for five years.'

She wasn't listening. 'Can I stay here? I don't want to go to Coolbawn just yet. I couldn't face Mum.'

I sprang to my feet, hugged her. 'Of course you can.'

Next morning she displayed none of the emotion of the previous night, but slumped in a chair, showing no interest in anything. I forced her to have some breakfast. Later on I heard her moving around in the bathroom. When she emerged, in jeans and a jumper, her skin was taut, almost transparent, but her hair was fluffed up and softer around her face, accentuating her strong jawline. Her eyes were brighter, too.

'You're looking better,' I said.

'I feel it. I'm sorry to drag you into this, Jen, but I had to leave him. I was so fucked up I had no choice.'

'I'm glad you came to me.'

'If I could get some cash together I could start my own interior-design business here in Ireland. That's my dream.'

'The first thing you'll have to do is start eating properly. You're far too thin.'

'That's another thing. Once we were married Ned took charge of the finances. He didn't believe in spending money on food. Booze and cigarettes yes, but food . . . ' Her voice trailed off.

'How did he manage that?'

'He ate out all the time, on other people's expense accounts mostly, and he probably assumed that I did the same.'

When I got home from work that evening Cathy was sitting down, breathing deeply, the window behind her wide open.

'It's freezing in here.'

She sniffed. 'I'm trying to relieve the tension.'

She relaxed a bit over supper, to talk about her business ideas, and what she thought she could do if she could raise some capital. Once or twice she alluded to Ned, her eyes darkening, but she didn't seem to want to talk about him.

Around midnight, when I was in bed, the lights turned out, I heard the creak of the floorboards as she moved around in the sitting room.

Next morning, Saturday, I woke late. Cathy was in the kitchen cooking rashers and sausages.

'I had a dream about Ned,' she said, and spilled out the details of a blazing row she had had with him in the dream.

'He's made you so unhappy. You deserve to be with someone nice who'd appreciate you and not treat you like some kind of fool.'

'Haven't you noticed that there's a shortage of nice men?'

'It's just that you haven't met any.'

'I'll have to get a life of my own and spend more time enjoying myself. Meantime, I suppose I'd better get over to Coolbawn, and break the news.'

'I'll drive you down next Saturday morning. Stay for the weekend to give you moral support, if you like.'

'You're an angel,' said Cathy.

17

Early Saturday morning we packed our bags and set off. We drove through the quiet city streets, Cathy nervous as a kitten at the prospect of facing Aunt Lilian. Once we were on the motorway she sat back, pretending to be full of confidence.

'Cheer up, it won't be too bad.' I smiled to cheer her up.

'Not as bad as what I've been through with Ned, I'll grant you.'

'Well, then, what are you going to tell Aunt Lilian?'

'I wish I didn't have to tell her anything but what choice do I have, without a job or a penny to my name and just a few sketchy plans for a business?'

'Won't you miss Australia?'

'I'll miss my rich clients, and the sunshine, but I won't miss sitting in the traffic trying to get to some client's house and being late, the crowds, or Ned and the rotten Saturday-night parties he always dragged me to — all those tedious full-backs clutching their beer, talking crap about their dreary matches. No, give me the wide-open countryside every time.'

'You're still a country girl at heart.'

Cathy laughed. 'I sure am,' she said, in an American Western drawl.

'You must have made some friends of your own. Won't you miss them?'

'The people I worked with were good mates but seeing them outside the office was impossible. As I told you, Ned was only interested in his own crowd.'

'Well, you earned a good living in Sydney and there's no reason why you shouldn't do the same here. There are lots of wealthy people in Ireland now. All you have to do is flush them out.'

Cathy said, 'I can't imagine the farmers of Connemara having much use for an interior designer.'

'The community isn't just comprised of farmers. There are conference centres, hotels. There are doctors, dentists, solicitors, bankers, computer programmers. Galway attracts the best talent in the arts, and the Irish Film Board is based there. What more could you want?'

'Butchers, bakers, candlestick-makers?'

We laughed.

I told Cathy about the West Awake campaign, and how Louis had masterminded it. 'He knows exactly how to whet the appetite of the unsuspecting public, and he's no scruples when it comes to making money. He'll be a millionaire by the time he's forty.'

'He must love it.'

'Oh, he loves getting people to spend their money, all right. He has the knack of making them believe they can have a better life if they buy whatever it is he's selling. Mind you, he can be a narky bastard to work for. He loses his temper if things don't get done his way. Still, as long as he has them flocking to the Manor when they see his ads.'

'It'll take a lot of money to put the Manor right,' Cathy said. 'The roof's been caving in since I was a child. Somehow, I can't see Natalie getting swamped under all the tea she'll have to pour,' she giggled.

'Oh, Natalie won't get bogged down with all that. Hugo'll probably employ a manager once the thing's up and running.'

'The Manor means everything to him,' I said. 'He's the driving force. It wouldn't be the same without him at the helm.'

'Will they stay together, do you think?' I could feel Cathy's eyes on me.

'I haven't a clue.' I kept my eyes on the road.

'I wonder if you'll see him this weekend.'

'Hardly, and certainly not without Natalie. She hasn't let him out of her sight since her accident.' I told her about Natalie arriving at the Castledermot hotel to cart him off home.

Cathy groaned. 'Poor Hugo. I don't envy him.'

We talked about Natalie's accident. I told her about Hugo's attentiveness towards her since it happened, and his insistence on staying with her until she got stronger. Aunt Flo had told me that she thought Natalie had caused it deliberately to snare the straying Hugo. Cathy gave this some thought. 'Aunt Flo's pretty batty but I don't think she'd make up a thing like that.'

Yet the idea of Natalie, beautiful, sophisticated, elegant, doing something as drastic as that to keep her man still didn't make sense.

Near Galway Cathy said, 'Why don't we stop for a bite to eat? I'm starving.'

'Good idea. I could do with a break too.'

We parked in the picturesque village of Oughterard, and walked down the street to a pretty pub overlooking the Corrib lake. Cathy led the way to the back of the cosy lounge full of deep, comfortable chairs strategically placed in nooks and crannies. We sat by the roaring fire, sipping vodka and Diet Coke, giving our order to the waitress, a young, pretty girl with bright, friendly eyes and a big smile. She served us bowls of fresh chowder with homemade brown bread, followed by the most luscious prawn salad I had ever tasted,

186

at a table overlooking the lake.

Time slipped by as we dawdled over our coffee, gazing out at the swans, savouring our last peaceful moments together before facing the wrath of Aunt Lilian. I studied Cathy carefully, wondering how she had got herself into such a terrible mess, and what she was going to do stuck in Coolbawn, the middle of nowhere. Surely a talented, successful woman like her should be in the heart of the West End of London, designing homes and offices for the wealthy. And what if Aunt Lilian threw her out? We finished our lunch and I advised Cathy to stay calm in the face of whatever came her way, and praised her for having had the courage to walk out on Ned. Finally, we left the pub and wandered slowly past the lake back to the car.

Cathy was reluctant to get into the car. 'I'd like to stay here for ever,' she said.

'You can do what you like, live wherever you like, once you establish yourself.'

As we drove through Connemara, the roads narrowed. The Twelve Pins loomed high over lonely green fields divided by drystone walls, their pattern broken only by grazing sheep and cows, and an occasional thatched cottage. At last we swung through the old iron gates of Coolbawn, and drove slowly down the narrow, potholed lane, my stomach in a knot, Cathy pale with fear.

Aunt Lilian was in the vegetable garden, digging. She straightened when she heard the car, and hurried down the flagged path to greet us.

'Cathy! Jenny!' she said, expectancy in her posture. 'Where did you spring from?'

Cathy stepped out of the car gracefully. Taller than Aunt Lilian she bent to kiss her, her smile bright, giving the false impression of gaiety. 'Thought I'd come home for a visit.'

'All the way from Sydney? Where's Ned?'

'I've left him.' Cathy kept her eyes on the garden.

'You've left Ned!' Aunt Lilian repeated, like a parrot.

Cathy held herself together as she said, 'Yes.'

'Let's go inside and talk about this properly.' Aunt Lilian ushered us in at the back door. In the sitting room, she said, 'Now, what's this nonsense all about?'

Cathy, keeping her voice steady, said, 'It's over between us.'

'But it can't be! You're married such a short while.'

'Don't remind me,' said Cathy, her eyes swivelling away from the danger she saw in Aunt Lilian's.

'But why? What on earth went wrong?'

188

'Everything,' retorted Cathy, collapsing into a chair. 'He's a cheat and a bully.'

'I don't believe it for a moment.'

'It's true.'

'So! You're not a child, Cathy, you're a grown woman. You can't give up just like that.'

Cathy's vision of herself as the wronged wife shifted, leaving her doubtful and defenceless. She cried, 'Well, if you think I'm going back to him you can think again because I'm not.'

'Stop.' Aunt Lilian sprang up from her chair. 'You can't mean that. Rushing off at the first sign of trouble never got anyone anywhere. I went through it once and, believe me, it wasn't pleasant, but we got over it.'

Cathy sniffed. 'I'm not interested in sorting it out.'

Aunt Lilian considered this. 'And what has Ned got to say on the matter?'

'I didn't ask him.'

'You walked out of your marriage without consulting your husband?'

'Yes.'

'But have you talked to anyone? Asked anyone's advice?'

'No.'

'Well, then, you'll have to talk to Canon

Devine. I'll phone him, ask him to come over tonight.'

'Don't bother. He'll only try and talk me into going back to Ned, and I don't want to. I can't speak plainer than that.'

Aunt Lilian slammed her fist on the table, her face flaming. 'You'll talk to Canon Devine.' She wore the same horrified expression as she had all that time ago when she caught me in the barn with Hugo.

Cathy leaped up setting the cups rattling in their saucers. 'No, I won't. Now, if you don't want me here I'll go away.'

Aunt Lilian's eyes softened as she said, 'Perhaps a cooling-off period wouldn't do either of you any harm. I wasn't suggesting you go racing back to him this minute. You can stay here for the present, but there'll be no talk of separation or . . . ' She hesitated, unable to bring herself to say the word 'divorce'. 'Or anything else,' she finished.

'But you don't understand.' Cathy covered her face with her hands.

'I understand a great deal more than you realise,' interrupted Aunt Lilian, 'and, believe me, I know what's best for you.'

'Like the big, embarrassing wedding you foisted on us when I begged you not to?'

'That has nothing to do with this separate, unpleasant matter, which must be resolved.

190

Now, no more arguments. The subject is closed.'

It was obvious that Aunt Lilian's sympathies lay with Ned, and for the rest of the evening Cathy had to listen to her condemnations of people who gave up too easily on their marriages. She could find no escape until Aunt Mary came lumbering in.

'Cathy! Jenny! What a surprise,' she said, looking enquiringly from one of us to the other.

'I missed you,' Cathy said, and went over to hug her.

Aunt Lilian diverted the conversation to other matters, then left us, saying to Cathy, 'Go to bed early and have a good sleep. You'll feel better in the morning.'

Aunt Mary said to Cathy, 'Tell me everything.'

When Cathy had concluded her story, Aunt Mary said, 'Ah, my poor child, my poor baby.'

The next day Aunt Lilian marched around like a prison warder, dispensing orders, her authority unquestioned. Cathy suppressed her desire to argue. A perplexed Aunt Mary said little. She didn't want to be accused of fuelling Aunt Lilian's anger with talk of Cathy and Ned's predicament. But Aunt Lilian's lack of understanding drove her mad.

As far as Aunt Lilian was concerned,

though, there was nothing to understand. 'We must have a serious talk,' she said to Cathy, lips pursed in disapproval, 'so we can understand things better.' Not that Aunt Lilian was given to listening. Cathy couldn't explain anything to her without causing a row.

Aunt Mary was upset, too. 'All this talk of leaving Ned alarms me,' she whispered to me, when we were alone.

'It doesn't seem as if she had a choice, Aunt Mary.'

'I'm afraid I'm out of it,' she said, and pointed out that her life had been devoted to the care of the house and that her knowledge of the world was slight. 'But I won't have Lilian being unkind to the poor child. There's no telling the harm she could do,' she concluded.

That Sunday evening, after tea, I returned to Dublin, promising Cathy I'd come to visit her on my return for the West Awake launch at the Manor.

18

Louis and I drove up the avenue to the Manor for the press reception of the West Awake campaign on a golden autumn Friday. Dressed in its winter coat of red creepers, its windows glinting in the sunshine, the Manor seemed warm and welcoming. Louis parked opposite the great, open doors, through which I could see people milling around inside and sense the opulence in the air.

'Sumptuous,' said Louis, awestruck. 'You never told us how glorious it was. I could sit here all day surveying this scene.'

'I was only here once before,' I excused myself.

'You should have remembered to tell me about it. Is it this grand inside?'

'Not throughout. It needs a lot more work done to it.'

'All the same, I think I'll persuade Hugo to open it to the public too. He could charge more.'

The lunch was in full swing with a noisy, merry throng. My heart gave a lurch of excitement and pleasure when Hugo came into the room. There he was, tall, tanned from playing golf, talking to Bob Crowe, a hotel owner, an entrepreneur in his late fifties, who managed to convey, by his joviality and the tone of his voice, that he was a keen supporter of Hugo. Hugo, his hair windswept, his eyes shining, looked gorgeous as he hovered among the throng. My head swam as he chatted easily to the hotel owner. I'd gone for weeks trying not to think about him and now, suddenly, I was gripped with such an overpowering ache for him that I couldn't breathe.

For a moment I stood collecting myself then went over. 'Hello, Hugo.'

'Jenny, how lovely to see you!' he greeted me. 'How are you?' He spoke to me as if I was on my own, and hadn't come with Louis at all.

'Sorry we're late,' said Louis, coming forward. 'The traffic in Galway City held us up.'

'I know. I know,' said Hugo, taking my arm, steering me towards the drinks table in the centre of the hall, Louis following. 'It's such a long journey. You'll feel better when you've had a drink.'

'You've got a lovely place here, Hugo,' Louis said, sipping his drink. 'You should open it to the public.'

Hugo said, 'The renovations aren't completed. Maybe when we get ourselves sorted out, if we ever do.'

Louis said, 'I'll need to check everything out.'

Hugo nodded. 'I'll show you round later.'

The hum of conversation surged around us. Louis, mollified by the obvious success of this press reception, was more carefree than he'd been on the journey. Uncle Tom, lawyer to Ireland West Tourism, was listening to Louis, his mottled face intent and his eyes wary. Behind him I spotted Aunt Flo, shivering in a natty silver velvet coat, her wavy hair caught up in a little hat with a feather stuck out like an antenna. She was gazing up proudly at her husband, who had the power to improve things in the region and was intimidated by no one but his wife.

'Jenny, my dear! Fancy seeing you here,' she said.

'Hello, Aunt Flo!' I kissed her cheek.

The talk moved to markets and prices, and Aunt Flo's face took on a jaded expression. Excusing herself she withdrew to talk to the timid wife of the hotel owner about the weather, the flowers still in bloom at this time of year. Hugo and Louis disappeared to Hugo's office to go over the blurb for the brochures.

Alice, Hugo's housekeeper, was rushing around like a whirlwind, chivvying the girls from the village who had come to help with the lunch.

★ ★ ★

'Come with me,' Hugo said, as soon as he could extricate himself from his guests.

I walked out with him to the library, away from the crowd, the noise and the scent of expensive cigars. It was full of magnificent flowers and a great quantity of ancient books. As soon as we were alone he said, 'Sit down,' pointing to the wing-backed leather chair by the window. He sank into the chair opposite me, all swagger and importance gone out of him. 'Sorry I didn't get to talk to you sooner. Things are chaotic around here today. I'm not as organised as I should be. It's so difficult to get help.'

'Is Natalie not helping you?'

'She's away on tour at the moment.'

'Oh!' I caught his eye. In that unguarded moment he looked vulnerable, and troubled. I instantly wished I hadn't mentioned her.

'She's well again, then?'

'Yes, thank you, quite recovered and, as they say, life goes on. She's only happy when she's singing, so there was no point in her

196

refusing the offer. I've got this place to worry about, getting the gardens going and organising the planning permission for the cottages in the lower field.' He ran his hand over his eyes wearily.

'Louis has loads of ideas for the advertising. He'll ensure the gardens are successful.'

'I'm sure he will.' Hugo smiled, pleased by my enthusiasm. 'Meantime,' he said, gazing at me, 'I missed you.'

A silence fell. In that flash I was able to answer all the questions that had been puzzling me. I was still in love with him, and he was in love with me. My thoughts sprang to Natalie, and the possibility of her leaving him. But no, she looked on him as her saviour. I would wait for him, with nothing to go on but my own interpretation of his look. I needed no further confirmation.

Hugo stood up and walked over to the window, his hands thrust in his pockets. 'I'm sorry I've embarrassed you.'

I said, standing up too, 'No, it's just that — '

The door burst open and Louis barged in.

'There you are, Jenny. I was looking for you everywhere. I've got hold of the boys from the *Galway Gazette*. Come on, they're waiting to take photographs.'

'It's my fault,' Hugo said. 'I kept her.'

197

'This isn't the time or place. She's working,' Louis said rudely, and headed out of the door.

Hugo looked down at me with a grin. 'Sorry about that. We'll talk again later.'

I followed Louis, who was waylaid by a woman in a red coat who said, 'I've been wanting to talk to you.'

'Yes, it's rather wonderful this time of year,' I heard Aunt Flo say to a distinguished-looking man. She went on about the wonders of Connemara, hoping to impress him. When she spotted me she insisted on introducing me to Mr Dickens, a journalist from *Country Matters*, nudging me to make sure I acted impressed. 'Mr Dickens is quite passionate about fishing,' she said, looking up at him in the worshipful way of older ladies towards gentlemen.

Mr Dickens nodded casually, his eyes on the drinks and the pretty waitress who was serving them.

'Isn't he most attractive?' said Aunt Flo, as he moved off after the girl.

I agreed with her.

'So, what are you doing here?' she asked. 'Still chasing that rascal Hugo?'

'Oh, nothing like that, Aunt Flo. We're doing the advertising for the West Awake campaign.'

'I see. Does it include this old ruin, then?'

'Yes, I believe Hugo wants us to look it over with a view to including it in our advertisements,' I said, as diplomatically as I could.

'I thought so.' Lowering her voice she said, 'Take my advice, dear. Don't bother with him. It's all very well fancying yourself as the lady of the manor but, believe me, he's not suitable and time's racing by. You don't want to end up like poor old Mary. Never had a man in her life.'

'So you said before.'

'Not that that's your problem, I'd say.' She laughed, her eyes twinkling.

'And how are you?' I asked, in the hope that she'd change the subject, but she wouldn't be diverted.

'Busy. I'm on the West Awake committee, but to get back to what I was saying, I strongly advise you to get yourself a more suitable young man. What you want is a city chap with a reliable, corporate job, not a struggling farmer, with a crumbling old pile and a load of debts.' In a hushed, conspiratorial tone, she added, 'And a woman so desperate to get him that the poor wretch tried to kill herself.'

'You told me that before, Aunt Flo, and it's nonsense.'

'Believe me, it was no accident!' said Aunt Flo. 'Tom was told it by Hugo himself.'

She'd had a few drinks too many. Where was Uncle Tom? He should take her home before she said anything else. I looked around but there was no sign of him.

'Girls these days are so foolish. Throwing yourself at a man is one thing, but trying to kill yourself for him is another. Now, why would a lovely, eligible girl like you want to take on a drip like him with all that baggage? Surely not just to get yourself a manor and some status? You realise you're not in his league socially, dear. There'd be talk. Your poor mother married beneath her, and look what happened. She was ostracised by her own people, a social outcast. Now you wouldn't want that for Hugo, would you? He could so easily stick to his own class.'

Into the centre of the conversation came Hugo, smiling warily, only too aware of Aunt Flo and her small concerns.

'We were just saying that your place here is wonderful, Hugo,' said she.

'Yes, indeed,' said Hugo, knowing that she had little feeling for either him or the Manor. His eyes were riveted on me as I said, 'I'll see you later, Aunt Flo,' and moved away.

He followed me.

'Hugo!' Another member of the West

Awake committee, an elderly man, cornered him to compliment him on his work with them, and asked him to select a venue for the Flower Growers' Festival. Evidently Hugo was valuable to the committee — especially since he entertained them royally, putting his home at their disposal for occasions like these.

But why did Aunt Flo think that Natalie had tried to kill herself? It couldn't possibly be true. Silly old bat.

'Jenny!'

There was Aunt Flo again.

'Natalie's father's big in banking. He invested heavily in some of Hugo's schemes before he retired to Madeira. Some say he's backing all Hugo's enterprises.'

'I'm sure Hugo's a good investment,' I said, wondering what it had to do with me.

'He'll leave you in the lurch, you know,' she hissed.

Uncle Tom rescued me: he took her arm, saying, 'You spreading gossip again, Flo?'

'No!' she protested loudly, reaching out for another glass of champagne from a passing waitress as he steered her away.

I found Louis deep in conversation with a group of men, obviously setting out his stall for the campaign, delighted with the credit he was getting for his innovation. I drank more champagne. Hugo was talking about blood-stock with another group, but keeping me in his sights. Eventually, people were coming to say goodbye, thanking him for the most marvellous time. The thought of being left alone with Hugo and Louis filled me with dread, but I knew there was no way out. I was here to work.

'You surpassed yourself this time,' a woman in mauve silk said to Hugo, as she left.

Eventually, when everyone was gone, Hugo took us to inspect the gardens. 'Come on. Let me show you what I've planned.'

Corners of the shrubbery had been dug up. The laurels and rhododendrons had been cut back, and airless parts of the woods had been dug out too so that the lawns, richer now in the sunlight, stretched further down to the slope of the blue-tinged woods where cattle lay in the bracken. I took notes as Hugo elaborated on his schemes and plans, which would take up all his skill and imagination.

I could see the visitors arriving, spending the long summer afternoons pottering about. They would all be keen gardeners, who understood gardening, had ideas of their own. I could imagine the end result: terracotta pots full of geraniums, jasmine and japonica tumbling down the terraces, banks of blue and purple hydrangeas along the edges, and clusters of cardinal red roses in the centre beds. I could visualise exotic nights, Hugo with friends, Natalie flicking back her long silky hair as she chatted to important business acquaintances.

'It's a marvellous place,' Louis said, taking out his camera, moving away, snapping with enthusiasm.

'What do you think?' Hugo asked me, putting his arm around me, drawing me to him, forgetting about Louis.

I was excited, not by the garden but by him. I fought to get rid of this feeling, but the quiet, secret thrill of having him near me was too strong.

'It's wonderful,' I said, forcing myself to concentrate on the garden.

'The trouble is, it all costs money. We've added more cattle to the herd too.'

We walked past the yard and the milking parlour, which was pristine, the cows standing contentedly as the milking-machines hummed. Louis asked Hugo about crop yields, acreage and livestock. I took more notes.

'I've bought a couple of yearlings. Thought you might like to see them.'

'I'd love to,' I said.

Louis, not a lover of horses, went off to talk

to the farm manager.

Hugo, his jacket open, led me to the paddock. Haze and drifts of smoke from chimneys merged, and pale apples hung heavily in the orchard. Beyond the boundary hedge, in a lush green field, horses grazed. The yearlings were standing in the stableyard, heads up, tails brushed, coats glossy.

'They're beautiful,' I said, going forward.

Hugo's hand held me back. 'They're not as docile as they look,' he said. Our eyes locked. I could hear my own heart beat in the stillness as he turned fully towards me. Never taking his eyes off me he said, 'It's not wise to go too close to them.'

He didn't say any more, just stood there looking at me, his back to the beautiful scenery that was part of the glory around us. Then he reached out and kissed me. It was a long, slow kiss, full of passion that seemed to go on and on. It was like waking out of a deep sleep, like the calm before the storm. But there was Natalie to consider, wasn't there? Out of my depth I pulled back. I said, 'You shouldn't have done that.'

'I'm sorry,' Hugo said. 'I've been aching to kiss you all day. It's seeing you again, and having you here. I thought it would be all right, that I could handle it.' His voice was gruff.

'I don't want to hurt anyone,' I said, recovering.

'You won't.'

'Aunt Flo intimated that Natalie's accident wasn't an accident at all.'

Hugo's face went bright red as he looked at me. 'Trust Aunt Flo to come out with that one.'

'I didn't believe her.'

'It's a long story, Jenny.' He took a deep breath. 'We need to talk.' There was a note of urgency in his voice as he said, 'Have dinner with me tonight.' His voice was soft, his eyes pleading. I couldn't bear to hurt his feelings by refusing him outright.

'Louis's expecting me to have dinner with him at the hotel.'

'Make up some excuse.'

'I'll try.'

The West Awake account was important to the company, Hugo's approval essential. I didn't want any falling out between Louis and him over me.

As soon as Hugo and I returned to the house, Louis said, 'Right, we're off. I want to put a few ideas on paper,' and made for the door.

When he was out of earshot, Hugo said, 'I'll pick you up around eight?'

On the way back to the hotel Louis said, 'They liked my presentation,' satisfied with his day's work.

'Louis?' I looked at him. 'I won't be having dinner at the hotel tonight.'

'Why not?'

'Hugo's invited me to have dinner with him.'

Dumbstruck he looked at me, 'He didn't let the grass grow. I've booked a table for us at the hotel.'

'I know, and I'm sorry. I didn't like to refuse him. Thought it might look bad for business.'

'Hmm,' he growled. 'OK, fine. If you want to have dinner with him, then, fuck it, have dinner with him.' He sulked for the rest of the drive.

Poor Louis! Just when he was at the height of his brilliant success, I had to go and spoil it.

206

19

It's only for tonight, I told myself, looking into the mirror. What should I wear? Should I look sweet and innocent, wild and wicked, or shy and mysterious? I had only this one night to impress him.

In the end I wore my black halter-neck top with the silver band, my tight black skirt, and my silver hoop earrings.

Hugo came sauntering up the steps of the hotel to meet me, divine in a razor sharp dark suit, a blue shirt and matching tie.

'You're gorgeous,' he said, kissing me. 'I've booked a table at the Waterfall. It's one of my favourite restaurants. Is that all right with you?'

'Sounds wonderful.'

On the way to the restaurant he made small-talk, mainly about the press reception. Pushing open the door, he stood back to let me in.

'Mr Hunter.' The maître d' smiled. 'How nice to see you again. Your usual table is ready if you'd like to follow me, sir.'

'Thank you,' Hugo said.

All eyes followed us as we were led to a

table in a corner. I held my head high and followed Hugo.

As soon as we sat down Hugo ordered gin and tonic for us both.

'Everyone's staring at me, wondering who I am,' I said, looking round furtively.

'Take no notice,' he said, handing me the menu.

I gaped at the prices.

Hugo smiled. 'Have anything you like. You've been working hard. The fish is good here.'

Suddenly, realising how hungry I was, I plunged in, deciding on prawns in filo pastry, and red snapper to follow, with a side salad.

The waiter brought the drinks.

'Here's to the West Awake,' Hugo said, raising his glass, his head tilted, signs of strain around his eyes.

I raised my glass. 'To the West Awake,' I repeated, sampling my drink.

'So, Louis has an idea for a documentary programme on Connemara for the spring, he tells me.' Hugo looked at me enquiringly.

'Featuring all aspects of the Manor.'

'It's a great idea,' he said enthusiastically.

'Hugo!'

'Natalie,' Hugo spluttered, and jumped to his feet.

I turned round. Sure enough there she was!

What was she doing here — and what should I do? I could run to the loo, hide there until she'd gone. But she was just arriving, obviously back from her glittering tour abroad, and would be here for the evening. Anyway, it was too late. She'd seen me.

While Hugo was talking to her I studied her intently. If she was taken aback by the sight of us having a meal together, she didn't show it. Beautifully groomed in a black leather coat, her long legs encased in black leather boots, her hair sleek, eyes sparkling, she looked self-assured and confident. She leaned over and kissed his cheek, then sat beside him. A waiter had unobtrusively brought up a third chair and laid a place for her on the table.

'I flew in this morning,' she said. 'My concert in Cologne was cancelled, so there didn't seem to be any point in hanging around.'

Oh, God! What a mess! Panic-stricken, I pushed back my hair. At least I had nothing to hide.

'You remember Jenny, don't you? You met her at the conference in the Castledermot.'

'Hello,' she said, taking my hand briefly, one arched eyebrow raised.

I said, 'Hello, Natalie,' as casually as I could.

'Rick's parking the car. He'll be joining us in a minute.' She glanced towards the door. 'Oh, I've had an awful time.'

Hugo said, 'Jenny came down with her boss, Louis Leech, from Sharp's today, for the press reception.'

'Oh! I see,' Natalie said, then gazed at me with dislike. I shot Hugo a pleading look, but he was staring towards the door.

'Here's Rick now,' he said, and got up to greet him.

'Hello there,' said a tall, freckle-faced man with red hair, shaking Hugo's hand.

'This is Jenny,' Natalie said. 'Your surname escapes me.' She raised a quizzical eyebrow.

'Joyce,' I stammered.

'Rick Stevens, my manager.'

'Hello, Rick,' I said, extending my hand.

'Hi,' he said, shook it and sat down.

'Rick has made all the arrangements here for the tour, so I thought, Why don't I pop over early? I was feeling a little *homesick*.' She emphasised it for my benefit I was sure.

Hugo said, 'Why didn't you let me know you were coming?'

'I thought I'd surprise you. You're not mad at me, darling, are you?' A waiter was hovering and she ordered a bottle of Bollinger.

'No, of course not,' Hugo said, with slight

irritation, 'but if you'd let me know I could have arranged to meet you.'

Her eyes held Hugo's, excluding me from the conversation. If only I could slip away into the night, I thought, but there was no chance of that.

'When Alice said you were coming here for dinner I thought you'd be with the West Awake committee,' Natalie remarked. 'How was I to know you were entertaining Miss Joyce?'

'How indeed?' said Hugo.

'Of course, when Daddy told me that the garden project was under way I felt I had to come. You should have told me yourself, Hugo. I'd have been here sooner.' She spoke lightly to hide her fury.

'You'd got your concerts to worry about, and I'd got all the help and expertise I needed.'

'So I see,' she sneered, shooting me an unfriendly look. 'From now on I'm going to take more of an interest in everything.' She reached out and patted his hand.

I sat there stupidly, watching her, and she went on, 'I'm glad of the break anyway. All that travelling, the late nights, have exhausted me.'

Hugo's arm pressed against mine, giving me support.

'I was turned out of my suite on the last night of our stay in Munich,' Natalie complained. 'I'd stayed on an extra day to do some shopping, but the hotel had to have the suite for someone who'd booked it in advance. I was given a room that was unbearably noisy at the top of the building, in a turret, for God's sake. And there was nothing we could do about it. Was there, Rick?' There was a haunted look in her pretty face as she spoke. She shut her eyes quickly, then opened them again. With a tremendous effort she smiled, and her face was smooth again.

'They're immoral some of those cretins who run hotels,' Rick said indignantly.

'Where did you say you were staying?' Natalie asked me.

'At the Castledermot.'

'Good. Comfortable?'

'Very comfortable, thanks.'

'How long for?'

'Until Sunday. We're back at work on Monday.'

Another long pause. Why didn't I make up some excuse and leave now, before she found a way to really humiliate me?

'So tell me about your concerts here,' Hugo said to her.

'I'm at the leisure centre here on the tenth,

212

the Point on the twelfth and Belfast on the twenty-ninth.'

While she had his full attention I excused myself and escaped to the ladies' to wallow in anger and jealousy. Only a short time ago I'd been the centre of his world. Now I felt sordid and ill at ease, all my contentment with Hugo gone. It was obvious that Natalie didn't want me anywhere near him — and what was going on between them was anybody's guess.

Suddenly Hugo, the Manor and all the things that had mattered so much less than a half an hour ago repelled me, but I had to return to the table. I stumbled, excruciatingly, to the end of the meal, lost in the long pauses between the small-talk.

At last it was over, and Natalie was yawning as Hugo paid the bill.

'I'll drop Jenny off at the hotel,' Hugo said to her, as we left the restaurant.

'Don't be long. I'll be waiting for you,' she said, giving him a peck on the cheek.

'It's a beautiful night,' he said, as we set off.

Heartbreaking was the word I had in mind.

He stopped the car outside the hotel, switched off the engine and sat back into his seat.

'I'm sorry Natalie turned up like that,

giving you a hard time.'

'That's putting it mildly,' I said. 'It was the second time I've been put in this awkward position with her, and I'm fed up with it.'

Hugo's voice cracked as he said, 'I don't know what to say. Look, Jenny, I quite understand why you don't want anything more to do with me, but I'd like to explain about the accident, if you'll let me.'

'You don't have to.'

'I want to, so you'll understand things better. I'll never know what really happened that night,' he said. 'What I do know is that Natalie's accident didn't make sense. She was a good driver, not given to speeding.' Pain was etched on his face. 'I can't forget the way she looked at me when I told her it was over between us. She said, 'You always do what you want to do, Hugo.' Then she had stood and yelled at me about duty and honour, and how cowardly I was, backing out at the eleventh hour. I just took it thinking, I deserve this. I've done this to her. I made her act like this. Then, when I got that phone call to say she'd had the accident I drove straight to the hospital after I left you. She was just out of surgery when I got there. I was allowed to see her, but only for a few minutes. She was swathed in bandages with tubes coming out of her nose and her mouth. She'd been driving at high speed, the surgeon said, had lost control and her car had smashed into a wall. He asked me all sorts of questions about her, if she'd been depressed or if anything out of the ordinary had happened to her. Then he questioned me about our relationship. I said we hadn't been getting along recently and he looked at me suspiciously. I'd just come from being with you so you can imagine how terrible I felt as I sat there staring at her, thinking about how strong and beautiful she'd been, how talented. I thought, I did this to her. She's lying in this bed seriously injured, and all because of me. I'd given her the push that had sent her over the edge. I thought about all the times she'd left me to go off on her tours, glad to get away from me, and how I'd resented it, feeling second best. I'd felt humiliated and inferior, as if my failure to keep her by my side had been my fault.

'I read the signs all wrong. She had to spread her wings. With her enormous capacity for success, her ambition a driving force, her career was consuming all her energy. It was all about winning with Natalie, and it had been nothing to do with me, really. But it drove us apart.

'Anyway, there she was on that hospital bed, and I swore to make it up to her.

Whatever she wanted I'd do for her to help her get better. But I couldn't see a future for us, not after meeting you again. Still, I made the promise that if there was any hope of a recovery I'd be there for her. I realise now that I was riddled with guilt, and that's how I got into this mess.'

He struggled with pent-up tears. Eventually he said, 'Things were all right while she was convalescing. She allowed me to look after her, and she didn't complain. She made a good recovery and then, as soon as she was well enough, she took off, touring around Europe with Rick and her band. She sent a card occasionally from some big city or other, and that was all.'

He rubbed his eyes and sighed deeply. 'I thought I could help her to rebuild her life, after all she'd been through, but she doesn't seem to need me. She's happier with Rick and the band, and she doesn't feel the same way about me as she did before the accident, and that's fine. I just want us to sort ourselves out, like a couple of mature adults. But she won't talk about it.'

'She seems to want to hold on to you.'

He sighed. 'I feel I owe her something, Jenny. That's the difficult part.'

Maybe he did owe her, but as I tried to imagine what it was like to come home to an empty house, your partner gone God knows where, I realised how difficult it was for him too. Of course, he was asking too much of himself.

'Maybe she should cut down on the touring. She hasn't time for a relationship.'

'When Natalie wants something she lets nothing stand in her way, and she's completely single-minded about her career. It suffered a setback when she had the accident, with cancelled engagements, and her fans hearing rumours and not knowing the truth.'

'You must still love her, Hugo.'

He shook his head. 'No, I fell in love with you, and now we're being kept apart because I'm not brave enough to abandon Natalie. It's a crazy situation.'

'It's that strong sense of responsibility of yours. Remember when we were teenagers? You followed your father's wishes, all in the line of duty. Now Natalie's happiness has to come first. What about your own? Does that not count for anything?'

'Yes, it does, but I've known her a long time. I don't want to destroy her confidence just as she's regained it by dumping her.'

'Very commendable, but not really surprising.'

'What do you mean?'

'Well, all those years ago I waited for you to

come to Dublin. You never came. Not even for a holiday.'

He stared at me, his eyes burning, his face pale. 'I should have,' he said reflectively. 'In spite of my dad.'

'And it's the same now. Aren't you committed to Natalie? Aren't you in too deep to get out of it?'

'No!' Hugo said hotly. 'All I'm saying is that it'll take time.'

'What do you want of me? If it's an affair the answer is no. I just couldn't bring myself to do that.'

'Certainly not. I wouldn't dream of dragging you into something as sordid as that. I want you to give me a little more time.'

'And what'll I do in the meantime?'

'Carry on as normal, but keep yourself for me. I know it's asking a lot but it'll be worth it. I promise. We're perfect together, and you know it.'

'Yes.' I had to admit it. It was just a pity that Natalie kept getting in the way.

I gazed at the dry-stone walls in front of me, the dark fields behind them. There was a lonesome look in the stark outline of the mountains, which I hadn't noticed before.

I got out of the car. 'I'll see you tomorrow night — and don't worry, I'll be a true professional. I won't put a foot wrong.'

'I don't doubt it for a moment.'

'By the way, thanks for inviting the aunts and Cathy. Looking after them will keep me busy.'

'That's the idea,' said Hugo, as we walked slowly across the gravel to the steps of the hotel. 'I'm sorry it has to be this way, Jenny.' He put his hand on my arm.

I went inside without looking back.

I was sorry, too, sorry to be in love with him.

20

Louis was in the foyer waiting for me.

'You're back early,' he said, glancing at his watch. 'You look upset. What's wrong?'

'I'm all right.'

'Come and have a nightcap with me.'

He led me to the bar and ordered us a brandy each. Arms folded, he leaned forward. 'Tell me all about it.'

Damn! All I wanted was to escape to bed. I ran my hand through my hair. 'It's nothing, really.'

'You discovered that Hugo's only chasing you for your body?'

'Shut up.'

'Sorry. I shouldn't have said that. I know you're upset.'

I looked at his face, inches away from mine. His eyes were kind, and he was not to be deterred. 'What is it? Tell me,' he said.

'It's nothing.'

'I've got all the time in the world, if you want to talk.'

I shifted in my chair. 'Natalie turned up at the restaurant, out of the blue, with Rick, her manager,' I said.

Louis whistled. 'She orchestrated that well.'

'Alice told her where Hugo was dining, and she thought he was with the West Awake committee, and that she'd join him.'

'So she found that it was just you and him. What a surprise she must have got.'

'Not half as big as mine.'

'What did Hugo say?'

'After he got over the initial shock he was all right about it. She's home for a concert tour. Says she's going to devote more time to the Manor and the campaign.'

'Oh!' Louis looked surprised. 'Well, that won't do us any harm. She's rich, famous and she's got connections. Her father's loaded too, by all accounts.'

'But why is she bothering?'

'She's obviously after the lady-of-the-manor title. Having a pile like that to entertain her celebrity friends in, and be photographed in can do a lot for her image.'

'You don't think she's holding on to him *just* for that reason?'

'People do all sorts of things for all sorts of strange reasons. But maybe her intentions are honourable. How would I know? I only know that from what you've told me there's not much love left between them.' Leaning forward he said, 'Look, Jenny, joking apart, if Natalie's serious, and she's going to be around for the next couple of months, I'd watch out. She's quite likely to turn up and pick a fight with you, especially if she knows Hugo's been hounding you.'

'Maybe I should abandon ship now before she strikes,' I said sarcastically.

'You're angry.'

'Bloody right I am,' I stormed at him. 'I can't say I'm thrilled to bits with you sitting there passing judgement. In fact I don't even know why I'm having this conversation. I didn't hit it off with Natalie, and I don't give a damn what she does. She can invite all the famous people she likes to the Manor. It's really nothing to do with me.' I burst into tears.

'Don't cry,' Louis said, giving me his laundered white handkerchief.

I wiped my eyes and blew my nose. 'It was such a shock seeing Natalie standing there. I couldn't believe it.'

'Must have been a nastier shock for Hugo,' he said. 'Anyway, you've nothing to feel guilty about. It's not your fault that you were having dinner with him when she turned up.'

I shook my head. 'No, it wasn't.'

His eyes were bright, as he said, 'Look, don't worry about it. Stick with me tomorrow night at the Manor. I'll take care of you.'

The idea of being constantly at Louis's side

filled me with horror. 'Thanks, but I can take care of myself,' I said. 'It wouldn't do to have you throwing your weight around. You intimidate people.'

'Only trying to protect you,' he said into his drink, hurt.

'Why?'

'Because I feel responsible for you.'

'You're not responsible for me.'

There was a strange look in his eyes as he said, 'Strictly speaking, I am. You're here because you work for me, and I don't want to see you hurt. Look, Jenny, forget Hugo. He's nothing but trouble. What you need is a bit of fun.'

'With you, I suppose.'

'That's not a bad idea.'

'Look, Louis, I like you, but . . . '

'I fancy you rotten, you know I do. I've been giving you enough hints.'

'I never took you seriously. Now, I'd better get to bed. It's late.'

As he turned away I saw the disappointment in his eyes.

Next morning I woke early and went down to the dining room for a peaceful breakfast alone, thinking Louis would have a Sunday morning lie-in, but he was already there.

'Good morning, Louis,' I said politely.

'Morning,' he muttered sulkily.

'Will you drive me to my aunt's house, please?'

'What? At this hour?' he said, looking at his watch. 'It's only half past eight.'

'I promised I'd go over as soon as I could get away.' I was being brutal, I knew, but I wanted to get away from him, and I badly wanted to see Cathy.

He drove to Coolbawn at high speed.

'I'll pick you up this evening,' he said, screeching to a halt outside the house.

'Thanks, Louis, I'm very grateful.' I sounded like one of his business letters.

He said quietly, 'We could have a drink together, later on tonight, if you like.' He was revving up his engine, waiting. 'Talk things over.'

'If you like,' I said, to get rid of him.

He roared off in a cloud of dust.

When she saw me Cathy hugged me. 'Jenny! It's great to see you.'

The kitchen was warm and cosy, the windows fogged up, Cathy looking like a nymph in a thin cotton nightdress.

'How did the press reception go?' she asked.

I told her all about it, and about Natalie showing up in the restaurant.

'Bloody hell! That was awkward.'

'That's putting it mildly. It'll be worse at

the dinner tonight if she's there.'

Cathy nodded. 'She's bound to be.' She looked at me. 'So what are you going to do about Hugo?'

'Nothing. Not while he's got Natalie.'

'He might be using her to make you jealous. Let you see what you're missing.'

'Oh, I don't think so. It's far too serious for games like that.'

'You know what men are like. They love the idea of women chasing them all over the place. Can't resist letting us know how desirable they are.'

'Well, he's succeeded,' I said, seething.

'Why don't you use Louis to make him jealous? Beat him at his own game.'

That idea didn't appeal to me one little bit. 'What about you? How have you been?'

'Oh, Jenny! I don't know what to do.'

'What is it?' I asked.

With her long arms wound round her knees, her head up, she spoke of her new freedom. 'I'm just scared Mum'll tell Ned I'm here, and spoil everything.'

'He'll have to be told some time.'

'Not yet. I know this place isn't ideal. It's lonely here. There are so few people around to talk to, and I have to be so careful not to cause any gossip, but at least it's peaceful.' Her face was pale in the light from the

225

windows, and her cheeks were sunken.

That evening, while Cathy was in the bath, I sat gazing out at the sea, my heart aching for Hugo, thinking of his anguished face as he recounted the details of Natalie's accident ... Funny, I mused, how Natalie always seemed to know where to find him, and how her timing was spot on. The night she'd had the accident she knew exactly where he could be located, and at the meeting in the Castledermot Hotel. Then there was the restaurant. How weird! Until now I has overlooked these coincidences.

I wasn't going to dwell on them right now, though, because I was in danger of bursting into floods of tears, and Cathy was calling me to come and change, that we were going in half an hour.

Upstairs, I found Cathy trying on my new red top over her velvet skirt. I perched on the side of the bed, assuring her that she was absolutely gorgeous in it. 'You can borrow it just for tonight. I want it back first thing in the morning or I'll forget it. Now, I'd better get ready.' I had a quick shower, put on my black trouser suit and my makeup, carefully applying my lipstick and mascara, all the time thinking there was no comparison between Hugo and Louis. Hugo was handsome, sophisticated, desirable, while Louis — well,

Louis was attractive, there was no doubt about that, but in a wild sort of way, funny sometimes, kind on occasion, and often sulky. Through the window I saw his car arrive. I ran downstairs to open the door for him.

'Sorry if I was rude to you last night, Louis,' I said. 'I didn't mean to take it all out on you.'

His expression softened. 'Who could blame you?' he said. 'Bad timing on my part.' He changed the subject. 'Are you ready?'

'Yes. Can my cousin Cathy have a lift with us?'

'Of course,' he said, pacing up and down.

I called up to Cathy to hurry. 'How was your day?' I asked, sounding like a wife.

'I was snowed under with paperwork. Then I went to the Manor to have a chat with Hugo.'

'Was Natalie there?'

Louis looked at me sheepishly. 'Yes. She was making all sorts of changes to our schedules to fit in with hers. She talked about fencing in the garden to keep the punters from straying into the farm. It was strange having to deal with her too.'

'I wonder how pleased Hugo is at having her involved.'

'Not very I'd say,' Louis replied. 'She's a difficult woman to deal with. I can't see her living there permanently as the country squire's wife. It doesn't fit in with her image.'

'Ready,' Cathy said, appearing at the top of the stairs.

Louis whistled under his breath. 'Stunning,' he said, eyeing her up and down. 'Come on, or we'll be late.'

21

When we arrived at the Manor Hugo, charming and distinguished-looking as ever in a grey suit, welcomed us. Alice took our coats and made us comfortable in the conservatory, where we sat looking out into the garden, with only its groomed outline visible.

Hugo said to Cathy, 'Jenny tells me you're planning to start your own business.'

'In a small way to start with, working from home,' Cathy said.

'You shouldn't find it too difficult to set up,' said Hugo. 'You've got lots of experience, and there are plenty of potential clients around.'

'I'm dying to get going but for the moment I'm enjoying my freedom.'

Hugo laughed at that remark. 'You haven't really changed from the fun-loving tomboy you used to be.'

Cathy said, 'I've got a lot on my mind, not least Mum breathing down my neck.'

'You won't have that for long,' I said.

'I'm sure you'll sort yourself out. It'll be all right. Everything takes time.' Hugo's voice and his words were reassuring.

Aunt Lilian and Aunt Mary, Uncle Tom and Aunt Flo arrived. Hugo went to greet them.

'Do you mind if I tell you something?' Cathy said, when we were alone.

'No.'

'Promise you won't mind.'

'What is it? I said, exasperated.

'Hugo's mad about you.'

'How do you know?'

'The way he looks at you. It's written all over his face.'

'Oh, go on with you! You're just an incurable romantic. What about Natalie?'

'What about her?'

'Do you think I ought to take what I want and bugger the consequences?'

'Yes.'

'Seriously, Cathy, you've no idea what it costs me just to be here,' I said.

'You've no choice. It's your job. Come to think of it, where's Natalie?'

'I've no idea, and I'm certainly not going to ask.'

More guests arrived, among them Bob Crowe and his wife. A little later, Alice popped her head round the conservatory door to tell us that dinner was served. The dining room was brightly lit. Hugo stepped over to the sideboard and poured wine for everybody. 'Here's to our good health,' he said, raising his glass.

'And to new beginnings,' added Louis.

We all raised our glasses. 'To new beginnings,' we chorused.

The meal was a delicious mêlée of lobster, crab, shrimps, all served with crisp vegetables. The conversation flowed. Aunt Lilian, seated beside Mr Ruane, the bank manager, discussed with him her farm and its success after years of struggle, smiling graciously, but casting anxious glances at Cathy. Cathy regaled us with tales of adventures from her time in Australia, studiously avoiding the mention of Ned.

I began to relax, glancing at Hugo from time to time, smiling at him, comfortable with him in company. He talked about the pressure he'd felt when he first took over the Manor and his father's debts, and what a change real farming had been from the agricultural college in England where he had studied.

Louis told us about his early, difficult years in advertising, and the challenge to come up with new concepts and ideas.

'So, it looks as if your job here is more or less done,' said Uncle Tom to him.

'Not quite,' said Louis. 'We'll be back later

on to do a few shots of the Manor to tie in with our Ireland West Tourism television commercial for the spring.'

Hugo talked to Uncle Tom about his idea for a golf course at the Manor.

'That's a very good idea,' said Uncle Tom enthusiastically.

'You'll have people flocking here from the four corners of the globe to play on it,' Aunt Mary said.

'I'm dying to see the brochure,' said Aunt Lilian. 'Mind you, the Manor sells itself. It's absolutely divine here in the summer, what with the mountains and the sea all around.'

'You'll miss your trips to Connemara, won't you, Jenny?' Aunt Flo winked at me.

'Yes, I will.' I glanced at Hugo. His face was impassive.

'So what are your plans?' he asked me quietly, while the conversation buzzed around us. 'Will you stay on at Sharp's?'

'For the moment. Eventually, I hope to move into marketing — that's what my degree is in — maybe open my own business when I get more experience.' And more confidence, I added to myself.

'Good for you. I admire enterprise.'

At that moment Natalie stepped into the dining room, exquisite in a short black figure-hugging dress.

'Natalie!' Hugo said, going forward to greet her. 'You made it.'

I watched her as he poured her a drink. How confident she was as she stood at his elbow, chin up, eyes smouldering, smiling her pouty smile. She was back to her old self, sweet to everyone, telling us that it was lovely to see us all again, taking her place beside Hugo.

'I hope you're staying for a while this time,' Uncle Tom said to her.

'I'm not going anywhere for a long time,' she assured him. 'I want to help Hugo with the gardens. I plan to plant a wilderness of daffodils and tulips down by the gorse bushes.'

'It'll be divine in the spring,' said Aunt Lilian.

'Last spring was lovely, before your accident. Do you remember?' said Aunt Flo, bringing that unhappy event back into everyone's minds, and halting the conversation.

After a pause Natalie began to reminisce about the accident. 'It was quite strange, really, how it happened. You see, at that time I was losing Hugo,' she said, casting him a glance. 'Of course, we should've got married a long time ago but I'd my career to think of.

It took up practically all of my time. It was exhausting.'

'It's extraordinary how people worship you when you're at the top,' said Uncle Tom.

'Yes, indeed,' said Natalie. 'I couldn't work myself hard enough, and I went on killing myself. I thought there was plenty of time later to get married and have children. Can you understand how upsetting that was for Hugo? It was torture for him, poor darling, not knowing when we'd settle down. When I think back on it, I realise I was monstrous to him.' She sighed sadly. 'Of course things started to go wrong between us. Then I had the accident. And where was Hugo?' She raised her eyebrows at him. 'He was off somewhere on business.' She glared at me.

'People can be so cruel, just when you need them,' sympathised Aunt Flo, giving Hugo one of her looks.

Hugo sat silent, alarmed, clearly wishing with all his heart that Natalie would stop.

'That brought me to my senses,' Natalie said.

'Don't you ever feel, Natalie, that there's still a sort of contest going on between you and your career?' asked Cathy, with veiled sarcasm.

'Yes, but I'm coping better with it. I'm not frightened of it any more. The past's behind me, and I've recovered. I'm content for the time being to be here whenever I can, to recoup my strength. It's such a tonic. No matter where I am I love coming back to it, and to Hugo, of course.'

'You make it all sound so romantic,' said Aunt Mary.

'It is. I've won Hugo back, and I'm not letting him go again.' She gave Hugo a long, piercing look, which said, 'I have him where I want him.'

Did I imagine the cruelty in her eyes? Hugo said little, intent on keeping the fragile peace. He knew the satisfaction Natalie was getting out of ruling the roost.

Alice popped her head round the door. 'Phone call for you, Mr Hunter.'

Hugo excused himself, and I slipped away to the cloakroom. I brushed my hair, dabbed on more makeup, replenished my blusher, and mascara, and still felt terrible.

'There you are,' Natalie said, waylaying me in the hall.

We stood eyeball to eyeball, gazing at one another.

'You must be delighted your work here is done. Hugo tells me it's been hard work for you all.'

'Well, yes, I suppose it has.'

'There'll be big changes around here.'

235

'Now that everyone's going to know about it let's hope so.'

'And that's not all. Hugo and I agree that it's time we settled down.'

'Oh. Well, well.'

'Hugo has had enough of being on his own. He wants me here. I've insisted on taking over the proper running of the Manor as soon as we're married so that I don't get bored.'

'That's very self-sacrificing of you,' I said.

'Oh, no! It'll be fun. The reason I'm telling you this is to make sure that when you leave the Manor this time you never come back. For everybody's sake. It's too embarrassing.'

'What do you mean?'

'Oh, don't act the innocent with me. Everyone knows you made a play for Hugo when I was away on tour, and that you've been chasing after him at every given opportunity. Not that you're the only one. All the women are after him. He's such a sweetheart. I'll never forget the way he nursed me after my accident. If it weren't for him coaxing me back to health I don't know what would have happened to me. You see, we've been in love for a long time now. There's no one else for either of us, really. That's something we've discovered the hard way.' She cast me a look that made me shiver.

As she spoke, though, the joy and laughter

of my days and nights with Hugo the previous summer were uppermost in my mind. Go away, I wanted to say. Go away and don't ever come back. But there was no chance of that: she was making it clear that she was back to assert her authority, and ensure that her influence endured. She would always be around to impose her will on him, and the Manor, and it was the strongest will that had ever ruled the place. I excused myself and left her. Shaking, I walked down the corridor, and out into the garden, loathing Natalie and myself, railing against what Hugo had done in getting involved with me, yet which I could not wish undone. In that stolen time with him I had experienced more rapture than ever before in my life, and I cursed Natalie's interference. He had loved her and would, I suspected, love her again. In doing her wrong he'd hurt himself as well as me.

'A penny for your thoughts.' It was Louis, putting his arm around me. 'Don't let her get to you,' he said, trying to comfort me. 'For once, I don't think she'll get what she wants.'

'I think you're wrong. Hugo'll love her again all right — he won't be able to help it.'

'The swine,' Louis said, then swore under his breath.

I looked at him, and over his shoulder saw

Hugo coming towards me. 'Jenny!' Are you all right?'

'No,' I gasped.

'Was Natalie giving you a hard time?'

'Yes.' I looked away to hide my tears. 'I'd like to get out of here.'

Cathy was coming towards us.

'Get the coats,' Louis said to her. 'I'll make our excuses.'

'I'm sorry,' Hugo said. 'I'll speak to her.'

I couldn't look at him.

'Come on,' Louis said, taking my arm. He loaded us into his car, slammed the doors and tore off down the drive. I looked back to see a desolate Hugo standing on the steps, watching us as we sped off. Oh, what a mess.

'What did Natalie say?' Cathy asked.

'She was letting me know that she was back in action, and that Hugo was hers. Warned me not to come back.'

Louis said, 'Bossy bitch.'

'Evil cow,' said Cathy. 'Cruel, too, holding Hugo to ransom like that. She's terrified of defeat.'

'If I were Hugo I don't think I'd live at the Manor under those circumstances,' Louis said.

'I think they have the queerest life ahead of them. What she's doing is positively danger-ous,' Cathy said.

'Dangerous?'

'Natalie's too full of her own importance to be as concerned about Hugo as she pretends. And Hugo! Did you ever seen such despair in anyone as in him? I tell you, when Natalie was talking about her life and her accident, there was a savage look on his face.'

Louis dropped us off at Coolbawn. In the bedroom, I lay thinking of Hugo. It was only him that I wanted. Seeing him again, and being back at the Manor, had made me sick with need for the love he couldn't give me. I shut my eyes, trying not to think of Natalie and Hugo lying side by side, his arm flung around her, her hair spread out on the pillow.

22

I went for a walk the next morning, after Aunt Lilian and Aunt Mary had gone to town, leaving Cathy to tidy up after breakfast. Slowly I made my way along the path to the woods, but as I drew near to the house on my return I heard a man's voice I recognised, and saw the back of his head and his shoulders through the window. I hurried up to the door.

'You've got to come back. It'll be different!'

'Don't,' shouted Cathy's voice.

When I barged in she was sitting at the kitchen table.

'Ned!'

He was standing over her, and didn't seem to notice me.

'I could skin you alive the way you walked out like that.' His voice was hoarse, his handsome face twisted in rage.

I waited, frozen.

At last they both turned to me.

Cathy said, tears pouring down her bewildered face, 'Jenny, he's come back.'

I stood still adjusting to the chill in the atmosphere and the change in Ned. There was no softness in him this time. He was hard, ready to use force if necessary to have his own way.

'I want her to come home,' Ned said to me.

Cathy lifted her head and gave him a strange look. 'Why should I? Our marriage was a disaster.'

'Did you hear that, Jenny?' he asked, his eyes as cold as steel. 'I've come all the way from Australia, not knowing if she'd be here for sure, and now she's telling me she won't come back. I don't even know what I've done wrong.' I felt the tension mount as he turned back to her. 'Call me dumb, if you like, but I don't understand it. You love me, you told me so.'

'That was before I realised what you were really like.'

'And what's so bad about me? I'm no different now from what I was when we got married.'

'You drink too much.'

'You can't pick on me for that. You're pretty good at it yourself.'

Rigid with temper she said, 'And there's that thing you have about Fawn.'

'There's nothing going on between me and Fawn,' he shouted.

'I don't believe you. I want you to leave. Right now.'

241

'You'll regret this, Cathy,' he said, and to me he said, 'She's being a bit hasty. I mean, we're barely married.'

I could feel Cathy bristle. 'Oh! I won't regret it,' she said.

'I think you might, later on, when you simmer down.'

'I won't,' Cathy reiterated, standing up and folding her arms. 'I'm not interested in the kind of marriage you have to offer me. In fact, I'm not interested in any kind of life with you, and I'm getting bored with this conversation.'

He grabbed her arms and pushed her on to the sofa. 'I'm not going to let you go that easily.'

'You don't have a choice.'

'You can't mean that. You can't forget the lovely times we had together in Sydney. I want you to come back with me. I'll give you everything you need.' His eyes were bright with pain.

He sat beside her and caught her to him. Cathy was pinned to the sofa, helpless. 'I don't love you any more,' she said.

He released her. 'I knew it the minute I walked in the door. So who is he? An old flame?'

'No one yet,' she said bluntly, not caring if she hurt him.

'It's going to be hard on your own,' he warned.

'So what? I *expect* things to be hard,' she flung at him.

'I mean, really tough.'

Cathy's eyes flickered nervously over his face. 'What are you saying? That you're going to close the bank account to punish me?'

'I've already done it.'

She shrugged and said, 'Marriage is not for me, and that's the end of it.' Her words held the ring of finality, and a certain superiority, too.

'You'd rather fuck your way around the world, living like you did before you met me?'

His words were not what she had expected to hear, and their meaning took time to sink in.

'You never change, do you?' she said eventually, her voice trembling. 'I shouldn't have come home. You were bound to find me here.'

They stared at one another. Cathy's face was wet with tears. Finally she said, 'You'd better get going.'

He caught her arm in a vice-like grip. 'Come on, come back with me.'

'You're hurting me!' She yanked away her hand, then jumped up and spun away from him, running for the door. 'You *made* me leave you!' she shrieked.

Ned raced after her.

I sat staring at the phone, listening to the rain, which was now pouring down, wondering whether to call the police. At last, she reappeared, her hair wet, her clothes saturated.

'Has he gone?' I whispered.

'Yes.' She glared, her cheeks flushed. 'And I hope he never comes back.'

'Where on earth did he go?'

She flopped down on the sofa. 'I've no idea,' she said. 'And I don't care. I'm so sorry you had to walk in on it, Jen. It's not true what he said.' She sat down, put her hands to her face. 'I've had such a terrible time with him.' She began to laugh. 'I was brutal to him too. The things I said to him.'

'You *were* rather blunt.'

'I couldn't help it. He went on and on. He's such a liar,' she said.

'Don't feel bad, Cathy. You'll get over it.'

'He's jealous because I'm getting along fine without him. He can't pin me down and that's bugging him.'

'You're secretive, Cathy, that's what's getting to him.'

'Am I?'

'You know you are.'

'In what way?'

244

'Well, nobody knows much about Ned or how you two met.' I looked at her mistrustfully.

She laughed. 'Let's have a drink and I'll tell you all about it.'

'Maybe we should go to bed, discuss it in the morning.'

'I'm going to tell you now. We all lived in the same house in Sydney, in a group. There was this guy called Walt, a friend of Ned's. I was with him when I met Ned.'

'You lived with him?'

'Sort of. I'd just arrived in Australia. Walt showed me around, took me places. It wasn't serious. I had been out of touch with Mum for a long time, I was working in a fashion store while I tried to find a suitable job. My money was running out. Walt said I could move in with him — it would be cheaper than having my own place. By then I liked him a lot so I didn't see the problem. Then Ned arrived. He had never lived with a woman, except his mother, of course, and he'd left home years ago.' She laughed brightly. 'We fell for each other. When he got the job in the stock market he swept me off my feet saying that there was no excuse for us not to get married, that we could afford it.'

I watched her face while she was speaking and the sardonic curl of her lip. Her life had not been dull — at least, not until she settled down in Sydney with Ned.

'I think we should go to bed,' I said, standing up. 'Will you be all right?'

She reached out and took my hand. 'Thanks, Jen, for listening,' she said. 'I feel better for talking to you.'

'Do you think you might ever go back to Ned?'

She tilted her head sideways, 'I'd rather be dead,' she said, and went silently into her bedroom.

★ ★ ★

The next day Aunt Lilian and I went for a walk. Warm in her winter coat, and sensible shoes, her mind was on Cathy and Ned. She was disappointed with Cathy, she said, and tired of her high-handed ways.

'Give it time. It might work out all right,' I said.

Cathy was still young, she conceded, and perhaps she would settle down at Coolbawn, with Aunt Lilian's prize herd, the chickens, the pigs, and reap the rewards of her hard work. Everything she had done on the farm was for Cathy, she said. She'd put her strength into it.

Aunt Lilian liked Ned. As far as she was

concerned, he was a well-mannered young man, and his quiet acceptance of her generosity at the wedding had won her over completely. He had told her he might take leave of absence from his job in Sydney to work on the farm, and learn as much as he could for the future.

Her mind went back to the past, to when Cathy was a child and Uncle Ambrose had been alive. Sometimes, in dreams, she heard Ambrose calling her, she told me, and after such a dream she would long for him. It was worse than a nightmare, she said. She might talk to Ned, she said, to see if she could smooth out the trouble between him and Cathy. She didn't see any harm in that.

The words Ned and Cathy had spoken to each other were chasing around in my head. Cathy had let go of her marriage, loosened her hold on respectability. What was she going to do now? And there was another problem. Ned wasn't the only one who was drinking too much. So was she.

23

When we got back to the office Sophie was waiting for me. 'I'm glad you're back. We're up to our eyes here.'

'I won't be long getting through that lot,' I said, looking at the bundle of papers on my desk.

As soon as he got in Louis pounced on me. 'I don't want to rush you but we've got to get down to work immediately if we're to make the schedule for the advertising literature,' he said, throwing a list of e-mails for me to send on to my desk. He snapped his fingers at Charlie Craven, then headed for his office, with Charlie at his heels.

'Right, then, let's get down to it.' I groaned, opening up my computer.

'What's wrong with him?' Sophie grimaced, reflecting my feelings.

'I'll tell you later.'

Over lunch I told Sophie the whole story about Natalie showing up in the restaurant, and the chat Louis and I had had in the hotel afterwards.

'Do you think there's a chance that Hugo will leave Natalie?'

'I don't know. He says things haven't been the same since her accident. I think he's hoping she'll leave him.'

'Do you honestly think she'll let him off the hook that easily?'

'She doesn't love him, and he doesn't love her.'

'Maybe not, but that's not the point. There's a lot at stake here, Jenny — the Manor, her father's investment, not to mention the history between her and Hugo.'

'What are you saying? That they'll stick together through thick and thin?'

'I don't know if they will or not. I'm just being practical because I don't want you deluding yourself. Let Hugo make his own decision, one way or the other, but he shouldn't expect you to hang around in the wings while he dithers.'

'He's suffered over it. Believe me, he's suffering now,' I said.

'I'm sure he is, and he's making you suffer too. How could you bother with a man like that? Face it. The man you love belongs to somebody else.'

'Thanks,' I said, and stormed out of the pub.

I fumed all the way back to work. One look at my screen and my head throbbed. I rubbed my eyes, leaned back in my chair, and looked at the ceiling. What did Sophie mean, did I think Natalie would let him off the hook? She had a bloody cheek! Who did she think she was? And what if Natalie really loved him? Hadn't she been keeping tabs on him secretly all the time, perhaps having him watched? A spasm of jealousy overtook me as I thought of her in the Manor, with her secret smiles and sexy ways. I pictured them sitting down for dinner together, a huge cluster of diamonds on her wedding finger sparkling in the firelight.

I gripped my desk, and gazed around the office, the desks crammed together, the faces behind them tired and depressed. Here I was, stuck in this rut, while she swanned around the Manor in the heart of the most glorious countryside in Ireland. Would I be happy to give up my life here and live there with Hugo if I had the chance? Yes, I thought, I bloody well would. She can't have him back, I thought. He's mine! He said he wanted to be with me, didn't he?

'All done?' Louis asked.

'Yes,' I said, concentrating on my screen, pretending to be working.

* * *

About ten days later Aunt Mary phoned me in a terrible state.

'Is Cathy with you?' she asked, a quiver in her voice.

Fear gripped me. 'No. Why?'

'She's disappeared. We don't know where she could have gone.'

'She'd hardly leave without telling someone,' I said, remembering all the times Cathy had cleared off in the past without a word, leaving everyone to guess where she was.

'Not a sign of her since the evening before last,' Aunt Mary continued. 'She went off to Galway, and when she hadn't returned by ten o'clock Lilian thought she might have decided to stay the night with friends.'

'Did she seem all right to you when she was leaving?'

'A bit vague. I wondered if you'd heard from her.'

'Not a word.'

'What could have been so urgent to make her rush off like that? Supposing something's happened to her.' Aunt Mary's voice shook.

'I'm sure it's nothing to worry about,' I said unconvincingly.

'It's most peculiar,' said Aunt Mary. 'For all we know she may have been abducted — or worse.'

'Never!'

'Anything's possible in these dreadful times. You hear terrible stories. I try to reassure myself that these things don't go on in Kilbeg, but only last week there was a burglary up at the Manor and some of the priceless antiques were stolen. The itinerants parked up the road from it are getting the blame. But I know some of them and they're decent folk with nice, friendly children.'

Aunt Mary was cordial to itinerants, sympathetic to their plight but careful of them at the same time.

'Nothing's sacred any more,' she said.

'Did you phone the guards?'

'Lilian doesn't really want to drag them into it.' Her voice was wistful. 'And what would we say to them? They've got their hands full with drugs and violence and big crimes.'

'You could tell them she hasn't been at home for the last couple of days and you're concerned about her. Did she take much with her?'

'She didn't take any of her stuff. Everything in her bedroom is just as she left it, as if she might appear at any minute. We don't want to raise the alarm if she's only gone off for a few days.'

'Would you like me to come down tomorrow for the weekend?'

'That would be great. If it's not too much trouble,' she added.

I knew that Aunt Lilian would take out Cathy's disappearance on Aunt Mary, and that her demands and pressures would make Aunt Mary's life hell. If I was there Aunt Lilian would be more circumspect.

Where *was* Cathy? Wild, attention-seeking, misunderstood Cathy was at it again. The more Aunt Lilian tried to knock her into submission, the more Cathy did as she liked. I thought of Cathy's words: *I'd rather be dead than go back to Ned.* Had she flaunted her perfect body and her flame-red hair once too often? Was she dead in a ditch somewhere? Or had she killed herself? I thought of the sea closing over her. Or perhaps she'd gone into the woods, put a rope round her neck, climbed up a tree, knotted it to a reachable limb and dropped down into the dark, root-twisted, forest floor.

No. Cathy loved life too much, and she'd all sorts of plans for her future. Where had she gone when she went missing before? I racked my brains. Suddenly I remembered her father's old caravan, hidden in the sand dunes on Kilbeg beach. It had been Cathy's secret hiding place when we were kids. Was it still there?

On Saturday I drove straight there. Kilbeg

beach was deserted. I parked and took the path that ran alongside the undulating sand that stretched as far as the eye could see on one side and was bordered by a pine forest on the other. The day was bright, the sea like a mirror, the air fresh with the heady scent of pine and seaweed.

Fishing-boats and pleasure-craft were moored alongside one another on the tiny quayside where a few men were sorting their nets, passing the occasional remark. Shielding my eyes I walked towards the dunes, wondering where exactly the caravan used to be parked. One of the men gave a low whistle as I passed.

'Looking for someone?' another of the men asked.

'I'm looking for my . . . a woman.'

'Could you be more specific?'

'Tall, short red hair. Beautiful,' I said.

He pointed to the pine forest. 'Over there, in a caravan hidden behind those trees. I've seen a woman coming out of it.'

I found the caravan and stood outside it, postponing the moment of finding her.

She was lying on a camp-bed, a half-bottle of vodka beside her.

'Cathy! What are you doing here? What is it?'

'Jenny!' She collapsed in floods of tears.

'It's all right,' I said, taking her in my arms. 'I'm here now. Tell me, what's the matter?'

'I don't know,' she mumbled. 'I feel so rotten.'

'That's not surprising. You've been drinking,' I said, taking the bottle from her. Then I got up and made coffee.

'Here, get this down you,' I said, holding the cup to her lips.

'No, no. I'll be sick.'

'Why did you clear off without telling anyone?' I asked, gently wiping away the perspiration from her brow.

'I felt so ill. I couldn't stand Mum finding out and sending me off for tests.'

'How long have you been like this?'

'A couple of weeks.' She looked at me anxiously. 'Supposing it's something terminal?'

'Of course it isn't. It's probably stress from everything that's happened to you recently.'

'I tried to get back to normal. Honestly I did, Jen. You know I did. But I couldn't even do that much,' she said, grabbing the bottle back, her mouth closing over its neck, her throat constricting as she swallowed its contents.

'Are you sick in the mornings?'

'Yes. Usually in the mornings.'

'When was your last period?'

A tremendous blank overtook her features. 'I haven't a clue.'

'Think back, Cathy. It's important.' I sat and held her. 'You might be pregnant.'

'Pregnant? Oh, God. I couldn't be.'

'It's a possibility.'

She looked at me aghast. 'Oh, no. Sure I left Ned ages ago,' she said, horror in her eyes.

'Did you have sex with him before you left him?'

'Yes. It still happened now and again, even though we weren't getting on.'

'And if you weren't taking precautions . . . '

'I don't want to go back to Coolbawn,' she said, struggling to come to terms with it all. 'When Mum finds out she'll freak. She'll make me go back to Ned. Maybe it's a false alarm,' she said.

'There's only one way to find out. You'll have to see a doctor. Just to be on the safe side.' I hated to be adding to her problems but it seemed the only sensible thing to do. 'Come on I'll take you.'

'I don't want to see a doctor.' She sank back on the bed, her hand on her head, her eyes closing.

As soon as she was asleep I sneaked out of the caravan, ran to the car, and drove to the chemist's in Kilbeg to buy a pregnancy-testing kit. When I returned she was still asleep.

I waited for her to wake up. When she did, I made her do the test, dreading the result.

'It's gone blue,' she said, slowly making her way back from the lavatory, with the little stick in her hand. 'Positive. Oh, no,' she wailed. 'I can't be this unlucky.'

'It's not the worst thing that could happen to you.' I tried to sound convincing but failed miserably.

'It is, if it grows up to be like Ned,' she replied, despairingly.

I laughed. 'Don't forget, it'll have your genes as well.'

It was all too much for her. 'Jenny, what'll I do?' she wailed. 'I'm all alone. How can I bring up a baby?' She burst into fresh floods of tears. 'Oh, my God. This is awful.'

I put my arms around her. 'You're not alone. We'll see this through together.'

Calming herself, she said, 'Does this mean I'll have to go back to Ned?'

'No, of course it doesn't. But it might make you feel differently towards him. You might need an active father for your baby.'

She shook her head, 'I doubt that. Maybe it would be better to have an abortion.'

Shocked, I looked at her. 'Oh, no! You can't

do that. You'd never forgive yourself after-wards.'

'But I won't want it, Jenny.'

'You'll feel different when you've had time to think about it.'

'I thought living with Ned was bad, but this is the worst thing that could have happened to me,' she said, through her tears. 'No wonder I felt so sick. I'll have to go away somewhere and hide until it's all over.'

'That's out of the question,' I said, looking around. 'You need rest, nourishment and someone to look after you properly. We'll go for a walk and talk it over.'

Slowly we plodded along the beach in the mist, hunched into our coats and woollen scarves, our arms linked. Cathy, pale and subdued, stared straight ahead, her mouth set in a thin line.

'It's cold.' She shivered, burrowing into her scarf, digging her hands deeper into her pockets. She gave a short, derisive laugh and said, 'Why did it have to happen?'

'It's not the end of the world.'

'I'm going to get big and fat. I won't be able to go out.'

'Try not to think about it now. Just walk, and try to relax.'

She pointed to the boulders at the end of the beach. 'I come down here sometimes, and sit on the rocks over there. It's peaceful, with only the gulls to disturb me. I like it here. It makes me forget my problems. Or it did until now'. We gazed at one another. 'You see, I'm scared of having no structure to my life, and with the thought of what lies ahead . . . God, I feel I've lived a lifetime in the few months since I got married.'

'Will you tell Ned you're pregnant?'

'Not if I can help it.' She paused. 'I was foolish to come back here.' Suddenly she was angry. 'That was my first mistake, and assuming that Ned would accept that I'd left him and let me go graciously, was the second.'

A look of desolation took hold of her as she said that. We were at the point, looking at the granite boulders sleek as seals from the previous night's rain, when a downpour started. We hopped across the boulders to the boathouse to shelter from the rain. There we sat down on an upturned boat, and stared out at the grey sea. In the silence the pull and suck of pebbles in the receding waves sounded like the clang of chains and the bolting of doors. Cathy shut her eyes, her face tired and pale, an inexpressible sadness in the droop of her mouth. Then she said, 'Do you remember swimming here when we were little, the pebbles catching in our toes, the sea beneath us?'

I nodded. 'We used to get out of our depth and start screaming.'

'I'm out of my depth now.'

'The days were always hot, and you had a pink swimsuit.'

She smiled. 'I loved that swimsuit. Aunt Mary bought it for me in Galway.'

'You used to hide down here. They never knew where you were. I remembered.'

'I stayed down here, after Daddy died, hiding from Mum. I felt he'd abandoned me, and this was the only place I could feel close to him. I used to be with him here when he was repairing his boat or fixing his fishing-rods. We'd play ball on the beach, and swim. Sometimes, when he was too tired to do either, he would sit smoking, gazing out to sea, while I collected shells, or fished in the rock-pools for crabs. You see, he kept the caravan down here to hide from Mum. He used to sleep in it sometimes. Then he died. It happened so fast. One minute he was there, the next he was gone. That's when Mum assumed the position of control that we all found hard to take. I felt like an orphan, as if I'd lost both parents, which was silly because I still had Mum. But she changed overnight.'

It was the first time Cathy had spoken to

me in any detail about her father's death. She had been ten when he died, the year before my first visit to Coolbawn.

'You still had Aunt Mary.'

Cathy nodded. 'She was wonderful. She tried to keep everything smooth. She was like a rock. I don't remember much about that time, apart from Mum screeching. Aunt Mary said then that Dad was the only one who could reason with her when she got into one of her tantrums, and now that he was gone she didn't know what to do.' Cathy hunched into her jacket. 'Reminiscing about Dad makes me long for those days again,' she said, and blew her nose.

'Me, too,' I said, tears in my own eyes.

'I stayed down here once for a week, shut up in the caravan with no heat, dreaming of sailing away in a big ship, to some exotic location where I could forget about everything. Mum had taken me to stay with my friend Jean in Galway. After a couple of days I told her parents I had to go home. But I didn't. I sneaked down here. When I finally did go home Mum had the police out scouring the countryside for me. Apparently Jean's parents had phoned to see how I was. Aunt Mary wouldn't let her scold me. She said I was emotionally withdrawn because of Dad's death, and that I should be taken to see someone. Shit!' She let her head drop onto her chest as tears engulfed her.

'What would Dad make of this pregnancy? Why did he have to go and die?' She sniffed. 'And Mum's expectations were always so high, pushing me into a career, something she'd always craved. 'Keep your nose to the grindstone,' she'd say. But she still wanted marriage for me, above everything else. She pushed me into it when she heard about Ned and his job on the stock market. Just as everything was going well, and I was enjoying being independent.'

A passion of rage against her mother surged through her and the tears welled up again, but she fought to control them. I held her and rocked her as I gazed over the sea, feeling her heartbreak for the father she'd lost so young. A man who'd adored her, and who'd been able to control her when Aunt Lilian couldn't.

Gradually her sobs lessened. 'I often imagined what it would be like to be pregnant but never expected it to be like this. I thought it would be wonderful.'

'It'll be fine. I'll help you through it.'

She sniffed. 'Soon it'll be noticeable. Oh, God!' She sat still, taut with the agony of Aunt Lilian finding out, something fixed and dangerous in the way she stared at the sea.

'I'll go away for a while until all the fuss dies down,' she said. 'I'll write to Mum but I won't tell her. *You* won't tell her, will you?' Her voice was strained.

'Of course not,' I assured her. 'But it's not a good idea.'

'Why?'

'You'll still have the problem to face when you come back.'

'You're right. It's not a good idea,' she said. 'I wish I was dead.'

'Don't say that.'

'Why can't I have a quiet, normal life like other people?'

Eventually we got to our feet. 'Come on,' I said, 'before we freeze.'

As soon as we got back to the caravan she got out another bottle of vodka. 'I was dying for that drink,' she said, after she'd taken a hefty swig.

She was blurring her senses into a numbness that helped her overcome her fears, and forget the horror of what had happened and what was about to happen. Finally I managed to coax her into the car.

'I don't want to go,' she wailed.

'You have to come home, Cathy. Aunt Mary's worried about you. Just for now until you get yourself sorted out. Then you can get a place of your own.'

24

Back at the house, I helped her down the hall, along the passage into the kitchen where the reassuring smell of cooking greeted us. Aunt Mary was whipping cream and, on the range, blackberries bubbled in a black pot.

'Oh, Cathy!' she said, clutching her to her flowered apron. 'I'm so glad to see you. Where were you?'

'I went to Dad's caravan,' Cathy said.

'You should have let us know. We were so worried about you. Now, you must be dying for a decent cup of tea.' Aunt Mary reached for the brown teapot, confident in its restorative powers.

'I'll just have a glass of water,' Cathy said. Tea now made her feel sick.

Aunt Lilian came into the kitchen. 'You're back,' she said, and without any enquiries as to where Cathy had been she continued, 'Your conduct is disgraceful, and you look terrible. I'm phoning Dr Kelly to ask him to come over immediately.'

'I'm not sick,' Cathy protested.

'You look sick to me. I don't intend to

discuss it, at least not until Dr Kelly has examined you.'

There was nothing to be done except bow to her will. The doctor was called. He examined her thoroughly. 'How long since your last period?' he asked, his eyebrows raised into question marks.

Cathy said she thought it was about two months.

'You're pregnant.'

'I know,' Cathy said.

'What?' gasped Aunt Lilian. 'And your husband thousands of miles away.'

'You must rest, take nourishment and have someone to look after you properly. There's nothing wrong with you that a complete rest won't cure,' said the kindly doctor, ignoring Aunt Lilian's outburst. 'No long walks for a few days, and no more drinking.'

'Don't worry, I'll make sure of it, and I'll insist she stays in bed,' Aunt Lilian said.

'No way,' said Cathy. 'I'm not staying here.'

'You'll do as you're told,' said Aunt Lilian sharply.

'Bickering won't do her any good,' said the doctor. 'You must be calm. Give the baby a chance to develop.'

Cathy was put to bed by Aunt Mary and me, while Aunt Lilian went off with Dr Kelly, firing questions at him. I stayed with Cathy, feeling her vulnerability and uncertainty in that lonely room.

Exhausted she slept. Much later, when she woke up, her head wasn't pounding any more, and her stomach felt steady. 'I'm sorry I put you through this,' she said to me, sitting up, fighting her despair.

'How's the patient?' asked Aunt Mary, coming into the room quietly with a tray of scrambled eggs on toast.

Aunt Lilian was close on her heels. 'Well, how are you?' she enquired.

'I'm fine,' Cathy said.

But as soon as they had left the room Cathy turned to me and said, 'Oh, Jenny, what am I going to do?'

'I'll stay on here and look after you, keep Aunt Lilian off your back,' I volunteered.

She tossed her head hopelessly. 'How can you? You've got to go back to work. I'm finished, Jenny. I'll never be happy again.'

'Don't say that. You'll be all right,' I told her, but the more I looked at her, the more I doubted it.

Poor Cathy! This was all my doing. I had brought her back to the wrath of Aunt Lilian. What could I do for her now?

Aunt Lilian returned and, determined as a jailer, came into the room to look down on Cathy with unfriendly eyes.

'Can I not come downstairs?' asked Cathy, meek as a child.

'You'll stay where you are,' Aunt Lilian said, with a key in her hand.

'You don't have to lock her in,' said Aunt Mary, coming up behind her. 'I'll keep an eye on her.'

Aunt Lilian stalked off in a huff.

'I'm so sorry about all of this, Aunt Mary,' Cathy said, in a shamed voice.

'Don't upset yourself,' said Aunt Mary. 'I'm sure you can come downstairs as soon as Lilian has cooled off.' She added in an undertone to me, 'Lilian's too hard on her. She'll have no luck for it, you know. After all, Cathy didn't choose this pregnancy.'

★ ★ ★

After lunch on Sunday Aunt Mary suggested that Aunt Lilian let Cathy have the gate lodge. 'That'll give you both a bit of space. The beds are aired. It won't take long to make them up.'

The gate lodge had been redecorated for the wedding and was bright and clean, and Cathy was thrilled when her mother agreed reluctantly. 'I'll move in now,' she said, taking the key from the hall table.

We walked fast down the drive, past the

trees, their limbs stark and elegant in the winter sunshine, birds fluttering about them.

From the road the gate lodge looked dull and lifeless, its walls covered in ivy, its windows empty, a pile of turf stacked against the gable wall. But the back overlooked the wilder, more picturesque side of the valley, with fir trees and rocks chasing one another down the steep slope to the beach.

'We'll soon have it shipshape,' said Aunt Mary, arriving immediately after us with a basket of essentials and some things she knew Cathy wouldn't have thought of, like a lamp, a tea-set, soap, shampoo, coffee and fruit. We opened every window to air the place, made up the beds and lit the range.

Aunt Mary cooked a lovely meal of roast chicken and vegetables from the garden, serving it with understanding and sympathy to tempt Cathy's appetite. Then she glanced out of the window at the square of front garden boxed in with hedge.

'We must plant now for spring,' she said. 'I'll order some bulbs, and there's nothing like flowering shrubs to liven up a place — and keep our minds off Lilian and her grievances.'

We were chatting happily when Aunt Lilian came down the flagged path, her lips pursed. Cathy bristled when her mother insisted she had her meals up at the house, ostensibly to make sure that she was eating properly, but really to make sure she hadn't run off again.

I left for Dublin promising Cathy I'd ring her as soon as I got back.

What would be the end of it all? I wondered as I drove along. After the next months of waiting, the outcome would be more calamitous than anything that had gone before. Still, a baby for Cathy to care for! What joy might it bring? I mused.

I drove home on a delightful note of hope.

★ ★ ★

The following Monday morning, Sophie said, 'Have you seen this week's copy of *VIP* magazine?'

'No.' I looked at her dubiously.

She took a copy from her desk and handed it to me, open at the centrefold. There were photographs of Natalie posing in front of the Manor and the headline screamed:

SINGER NATALIE MASON TO MARRY WEALTHY LAND OWNER HUGO HUNTER

The lines blurred. I couldn't read on. It had never occurred to me that it would be

269

announced like this, though why I don't know. Probably because I had thought that it would never happen. Hadn't Hugo told me he was only waiting for Natalie to get stronger? That it was only a matter of time before they would go their separate ways? Hadn't he asked me to wait for him, for God's sake?

Sophie brought me some coffee, looked at me over the rim of her cup, her eyebrows raised, as if she'd made a mistake in showing the magazine to me. My face averted, I handed it back, my bottom lip trembling. She pulled up a chair beside me and put her arm round me.

'It must be awful for you.' There was genuine sympathy in her voice.

'It's a nightmare! I shouldn't have believed him when he said that they weren't getting on, but I did. I trusted him, Sophie. I thought he loved me. It felt like he did. God, this is awful! Look at me, I'm falling apart, and for what? Bloody Hugo Hunter, who's never going to leave bloody Natalie Mason. I don't know anything any more. I don't even know myself.'

'It's not your fault,' Sophie assured me. 'Maybe you'll have better luck next time, with a nice, uncomplicated chap. Someone like Charlie there.'

'I'm never going to fall in love again. I'm going to be sitting on the shelf long after everyone else has settled down.'

'You don't really believe that, do you?'

I looked at her. 'I'm beginning to.'

'Look, Jenny, you've got a good job, a boss who's crazy about you, great friends, and you've still got plenty of time to meet Mr Right. All you have to do is pick yourself up, dust yourself down, and go out there and find him.'

'They're all married out there, or as good as.'

'Drink that coffee while it's still hot. We'll go clubbing on Saturday night, somewhere new. God, is that the time? I'd better get some work done before Louis gets back and catches me swingin' the lead.'

All afternoon I kept myself half anaesthetised with endless cups of coffee, the thought of Hugo's engagement making me feel sick. I worked on, trying to dispel the feeling that I was going to break down in front of everyone. In the cloakroom I washed my face with cold water to keep the tears at bay. At half past four Sophie stopped work and came over to talk to me. I pretended to be busy.

'Feeling any better?'

I nodded.

'You're not saying much,' she observed.

I shrugged. 'It's not that I don't want to talk, I just can't.' All I wanted to do was get away from her sympathy, and out into the fresh air.

She glanced at her watch. 'Why don't you go home? Louis's hardly going to turn up at this hour. He'll never know,' she said, handing me my bag, almost pushing me out of the door.

★ ★ ★

I walked into the flat, let the door slam behind me and sank into the sofa. On my own at last I sat in front of the television screen, tears falling fast and furious. I thought of Natalie tripping down the aisle of St Clement's Church, Kilbeg, her nervous, tinkling laugh as she faced Hugo, her seven bridesmaids bunched up behind her.

I could face most things but not him loving someone else. My handsome Hugo with *her*! But I didn't want to think about Hugo and I certainly didn't want to think about Natalie. No! I blew my nose, reached for the phone to call Mum and put it down again. She'd probably have heard the news by now, so she'd probe me about how I'd taken it and it would be the same thing all over again.

Sitting in front of the television I fell asleep.

Later I woke, confused, from a tangle of dreams, the television still blaring. I must have been dreaming of Hugo because his presence was all around me. With Hugo I'd been a different person, living in a different world. He was apart from everything else. But, regardless of how much he'd protested his love for me, he had another great love, the Manor. His love of his home had drawn him into his quest to restore it in its entirety, and discover all its possibilities. He'd gone further than his predecessors in battling to overcome his debts. He'd let Natalie's father invest in it. It made sense that he should settle down with her. She was a rich, exotic creature, a real catch in every sense of the word. I was only the girl-next-door type. No, worse than that, I was the poor relation of the girl-next-door. And the boy I'd fallen in love with all those years ago didn't exist any more.

Hugo was gone. He'd done the right thing. Natalie's happiness had been at stake and he wasn't prepared to leave her.

I made an omelette, and ate it in front of the television because I couldn't be bothered to set the table. The thought of being without Hugo for the rest of my life was too much to bear. If I could keep going for the moment, fill the present so that I need not look forward or back, I might find some ease of mind. I should get out, go somewhere, anywhere, to assuage my loneliness and lay the ghost of Hugo Hunter to rest.

I phoned Louis.

'Hello?'

'Louis, it's me, Jenny. Fancy going to the pub for a drink?'

'Jenny, I'd love to.'

'See you in about an hour.'

I wore my new black and silver sparkly top with my black pedal-pushers, and made up my face with plenty of eye-liner and lip-gloss.

25

Synnots was packed with people, vibrant, beautiful women everywhere. Louis pushed his way through the crowd, and went up to the bar. The women's eyes followed him as he brought the drinks carefully back to the table. He looked attractive in his new black leather jacket, his blond hair flopping seductively over his eyes. Being out made me feel better. I was right to try to enjoy myself instead. Hiding away in my attic wasn't the answer. I would drink a lot, forget my troubles and flirt with Louis. I mean, really flirt with him like I used to before Hugo came back into my life.

'Would you like something to eat? The food here's good.' He went to the bar to get the menu.

Out of the corner of my eye I spotted Charlie Craven coming towards me. 'Was that Louis I saw with you a few seconds ago?' he asked.

'It was.'

'So you've finally succumbed.'

'Sorry to disappoint you but we're only having a drink together. Nothing to get excited about.'

Charlie laughed. 'Must be very frustrating for someone like him to get strung along. He's used to having women falling at his feet. Still, you're right to make him wait.'

'You think so?'

'He's fancied you for ages. Not that I blame him. You're the best-looking chick in Sharp's.'

'Thanks, Charlie.'

Louis, returning, heard the tail end of the conversation. His eyes shone with delight. 'She may be the best-looking, but she treats me rotten,' he said to Charlie.

Charlie said, 'If they get wind of this in the office they'll have you two paired off.'

'All right by me.' Louis laughed.

When we were alone again he said, 'I heard about Hugo and Natalie's engagement.'

'Thought you might have. Announcing it in magazines like *VIP* is bound to draw people's attention to it.'

'She's not exactly a shrinking violet, old Natalie. She obviously wants everyone to know that she's nailed Hugo to the mast.'

'To the cross, you mean.'

Louis laughed. 'Yeah, she's not the most charming woman in the world. Not someone I'd care to be trapped by.'

'Hugo has a tremendous sense of duty.'

'Too polite to tell her to get lost, you mean.'

'Oh, far too well-bred to do a thing like that. She's got a stranglehold on him.'

'I know that, but isn't it about time you were honest with yourself, Jenny?'

'About what?'

'About Hugo. He was always going to marry Natalie.'

'Do you have to be so hurtful?'

'I'm trying to get you to be honest about it. And don't think you'll die of it either because one of these days you'll wake up and realise that not only are you over him but that you positively hate the bastard for what he put you through. That's if you ever get to the stage where you're honest enough to admit it to yourself.'

'Why are you being so cruel?'

'I'm trying to get you to see things the way they are. Let's drink a toast to them.' He raised his glass. 'To Hugo and Natalie.'

'May they rot in hell,' I raised my glass vindictively.

'That's going a bit far.'

'May they crumble in their manor, then.'

'No way. Not after the effort we put into promoting it.'

Louis could continue putting effort into the Manor, but not me.

We drank, and drank, and when Synnots closed we repaired to the Kitchen where we continued drinking. Energised, we danced to a bad version of 'Let's Go Round Again', and 'Viva Forever', punching the air, laughing, carefree, advertising and Hugo Hunter temporarily forgotten. The fun and excitement drove me on, and made me forget my sadness. I smiled at Louis as I danced my feet off, swaying this way and that on the tide of the music. 'More Than A Woman', the last dance, had Louis holding me in a tight embrace, his lips against my hair. I didn't seem to belong in my own body any more as I drifted around the floor, letting myself go.

On the way out we bumped into Charlie Craven swilling beer at the bar. 'So you two lovebirds are off for a bit of nookie?' He smiled knowingly, slapping Louis heartily on the back.

I whispered to him, 'Don't tell Sophie you saw us together. She's lethal when it comes to Louis.'

'What's it worth?'

I thought quickly. 'I'll make your coffee every morning for the next week. No complaints.'

'Sounds tempting, but I'll have to think about it,' he teased.

Glad to be out of the stuffy atmosphere we

walked back to the flat.

Louis said, 'I enjoyed tonight, Jenny. You're good fun. You were beginning to forget what it was like to enjoy yourself. You need someone to remind you every so often.'

'That someone being you.'

'Yes, of course. Why not?'

'I had a great time, thanks.'

'Good. That's all that matters. For what it's worth, it's been hell these last few weeks watching bloody Hugo making you miserable. I don't know how many times I've wanted to punch his lights out.' He banged one fist against the other.

'That wouldn't have been very clever, would it?' I said.

'No,' he agreed.

I sighed. 'I'll get over him.'

Louis turned to me. His eyes were intent as he said, 'D'know something? As far as I'm concerned, you're bloody lucky to be rid of him before he messed up your life completely.'

'You're beginning to sound like a counsellor.'

'I know a bit about the subject, and you're too young and beautiful to write off romance just because of what's happened with Hugo.'

'That's not to say I intend getting involved with anyone for a long, long time.'

Louis said, 'I'm in no hurry. I can wait.'

'It might never happen.'

'I'll take a chance on that. Meantime I'll settle for a cup of coffee.'

By now we were standing on my doorstep, Louis hovering while I searched for my key.

'Coffee it is,' I said, weaving up the stairs, Louis close on my heels.

'This is cosy,' he said, gazing around the sitting room. 'You've made a nice job of it.'

'Thanks.'

Louis drank his coffee quickly.

'If you don't mind I think I'll go to bed now,' I said, when there was no sign of him leaving. 'It's almost three o'clock.'

Reluctantly he got to his feet. 'I really did enjoy myself tonight, Jenny, thanks.'

'I did too.'

'Any time you need a laugh, or a shoulder to cry on, just call me.'

'Thanks.' I gave him a peck on the cheek.

He caught me in his arms. Our eyes met and his were full of lust. Before I realised what was happening I was sliding backwards, pinned beneath him.

'Louis.' I was struggling to sit up, gasping for breath. 'We're not ... we agreed ... Louis!'

'Jesus, Jenny, you've no idea how much I fancy you, you're gorgeous.' I was thrown

280

back on the sofa like a doll, Louis leaning over me, kissing me.

'Lou-is!'

'Relax, sweetheart, go with the flow.'

It was a long, slow kiss, which must have aroused something in me that temporarily dominated my senses because when I surfaced for air I was panting.

'Stop!' I said, struggling to sit up. 'We can't do this.'

'Oh, Christ! I can't stop now. I've wanted to do this for so long,' he said, kissing me again. 'You're so gorgeous, irresistible.'

A sucker for a compliment, I shut my eyes in a moment of abandon. Down I went, Louis on top of me, moaning unintelligibly. His hand came up under my top, tugging it. 'No!' Pinned to the sofa I was struggling like mad.

'Oh God,' he groaned, writhing around.

'Get off me,' I screeched, and my fist connected with his eye.

Jumping to his feet, dancing in agony, he said, 'Sweet Mother of Jaysus! What did you do that for? What did I do wrong?' He gave me a bleary, startled look out of his good eye.

I spun away from him. 'Try it on again and I'll brain you.'

'No need to lose your goddamn temper.'

Panting, unsteady, my mind in a whirl, I straightened my clothes.

'I thought you were up for it. That's what you led me to believe,' he said.

'Well, you were wrong. Now go.'

Putting on his jacket, his swelling eye closing of its own accord he said sulkily, 'You can't blame me for this. You wanted it too,' and left.

I banged the door after him. What a night! As if I didn't have enough problems without this. All I'd wanted was a bit of sympathy and comfort, not an orgy.

★   ★   ★

Next morning I showered and dressed, nursing a massive hangover. I dreaded a confrontation with Louis, already anticipating the oppression in the office. I crept in and went to my desk, deciding to tell nobody about the previous night's shenanigans. The morning post was piled high, and there was a brusque e-mail from Louis letting me know that he would be absent all morning. I sat in front of my screen, hoping that if neither of us mentioned the previous night we would both forget about it in time.

There was no hope of that, though, because when Louis finally appeared at three o'clock he was sporting a black eye.

'Good Lord, what happened to you?' Sophie asked, staring at the purple bruise that was spreading half-way down his jaw. 'Have you been in a fight?'

'That's a real shiner you've got there,' said Charlie, going over to inspect it.

'Walked into a door,' said Louis, staring at me.

My face flamed.

'Can I get you a cup of coffee, Louis?' asked Sophie, dying to find out how it had really happened.

'Yes,' Louis said, going to the filing cabinet and pulling out documents.

As soon as Louis had disappeared behind his glass door Charlie wandered over to my desk.

'You did that to him, didn't you?' he said, giving me a curious glance.

I swallowed hard.

'You were snoggin' him when I saw you last. What went wrong?'

Sophie, going by with Louis's coffee, heard this remark. She looked at me incredulously. 'You were shaggin' Louis?'

'Snogging is what he said. Not shagging.'

'Almost as bad. God, what is it with you, Jenny? One minute it's hunky Hugo Hunter, and the next it's lecherous Louis. Who'll it be next? Hannibal Lecter?'

'Oh, shut up. It was only a bit of fun.'

Wrinkling her pretty nose in disdain she said, 'Fun! I don't think Louis would agree with that.'

'You must have given him a right smack,' said Charlie.

'I was aiming for his jaw.'

'I can imagine what he did to deserve it,' said Sophie, sitting down at her desk and drinking the coffee herself.

Louis reappeared to reprimand me for not leaving the previous day's letters on his desk for signature. The next encounter was worse. Shoving a draft document under my nose he ordered me to get my act together and make something presentable out of it.

'I'm fed up with him hurling abuse at me,' I said to Sophie.

She said, 'Tell him to put his dodgy document where the monkey put the crooked sixpence.'

'Next he'll be showing you how to use the telephone,' laughed Charlie.

'You're being punished for having the effrontery to belt him one,' said Sandy Smith.

Sophie said, 'Tell him where to stick his job, I dare you.'

'I'll do that,' I said, calling her bluff, marching over to his office, saying, 'Could I have a word, Louis?'

'Yes?' He looked up at me out of his good eye.

That wasn't fair. He was making me feel ashamed, the bastard, as if he hadn't done anything wrong.

I said, nervous as a bold child, 'I imagine you'll want me to find another job.'

He looked at me quizzically. 'Why?'

'I mean . . . after last night. I thought, under the circumstances, it might be the solution to the problem.'

'What problem?'

'Oh, for Christ's sake, Louis, you know what I mean. You and me occupying the same space is embarrassing.'

'Spare me your blushes, Jenny. You leaving is out of the question at the moment. Can't you see how busy we are?' His face turned crimson as he said, 'What happened last night was regrettable, I know, but your behaviour wasn't so wonderful either, up for it one minute, giving me a black eye the next. But I'm not going to let my private life interfere with the office. I'm damned if I'm going to let you go. I couldn't possibly manage without you.'

'But I thought — '

'Of course, if you can't stand another minute of being in close proximity to me, and you really *want* to go, that's different. But don't expect to find another job as good as this one. Well, that's that, then.' He glanced at his watch. 'Now, I've got a meeting in RTE at four o'clock and you've got plenty to do, so if that's all?' Standing up and smoothing down his shirt, he glanced at me. 'Oh, if you wouldn't mind, cancel the table I booked at Roberto's with the Swedish ambassador and his group for tomorrow night. I can't go looking like this.'

I returned to my desk, furious with myself for getting involved with Louis in the first place. I'd let myself down by getting drunk with him, letting him practically seduce me. For the rest of the day Sophie smirked superciliously every time Louis appeared, gloating over his humiliation. I could have kicked them both. When half past five came I was glad to escape from them all.

26

On my way home I called to see Mum.

'Jenny!' she said. 'How are you coping?'

I looked at her in surprise. 'With what?'

'Hugo Hunter's engagement.'

'Oh, that!'

'It's to be a June wedding.'

'Who told you that?'

'Lilian heard it in Kilbeg. It's the talk of the parish. I wouldn't mind but Hugo was very taken with you,' said Mum. 'Didn't he take you out to dinner and everything?'

Dad was skulking behind his newspaper as usual, pretending to be reading it, not a page turning. 'You missed your chance there, my girl,' he piped up.

'Yeah, you missed a golden opportunity,' commented Mum annoyingly.

'Well, if I'm not bothered I don't see why you should be,' I said. 'It's not as if I was looking for a husband.'

'You should be thinking of marriage,' Mum said.

'You need a man,' said Dad, in agreement with her for the first time in my memory.

'I don't. Least of all one with the problems

Hugo Hunter has.'

'Seemed a nice chap to me,' Mum remarked regretfully. 'You could put up with a lot if you lived in a place like that.'

'So much for my hopes of becoming related to the gentry. Gone down the pan with your wedding prospects,' put in Dad.

'Dad! You didn't really expect me to marry Hugo Hunter, did you?'

'I bloody did, and why not?'

'Never mind,' Mum consoled him. 'You'll do all right with a local lad.'

'Yes, but you could've done with spreading your wings a bit. You were on to a real good thing going there. I even had me acceptance speech all ready for when he asked me for your hand in marriage.'

'What were you going to say?'

'I was going to say, 'Well, Hugo, me lad, you might as well have it. You've had every other part of her.' '

'Dad!'

'No need for vulgarity,' Mum said.

'It's the bloody truth. When I think of what you missed out on.'

'Don't be greedy,' Mum chastised him. 'Much wants more,' she said, and brought the subject back to Hugo by saying, 'Lilian thinks he's being nudged down the aisle by that Natalie Singer.'

I gritted my teeth. 'Natalie Mason, Mum. She's a singer.'

'I know that,' Mum said crossly. 'Everyone's amazed she's finally cornered him.'

'There's many a slip between the cup and the lip. She hasn't nabbed him yet,' said Dad knowledgeably, taking a cigarette out of his packet, glancing surreptitiously in Mum's direction, as he rose out of his chair.

'No smoking,' Mum said, grabbing the packet out of his hand. 'Dr Brady told you to give them up.'

'He also said I was to give up the stress in me life too, but I didn't. I'm still stuck with you,' he said, snatching them back. 'You're like a broken bloody record.' He slumped out the door.

'Off to the Maiden's Arms, Dad?' I asked, just to be civil.

He nodded. 'To drown me sorrows. Would you blame me?'

'He was in great form telling all his pals at the pub about the Manor contract,' Mum said. 'He really got a buzz out of it.'

I stared at her. 'You're joking!'

'Oh, yes. He even had a word with Bert Brennan and Johnny Dillon about giving him a dig out if things went well. Ah, well, it's not to be.'

'Mum, can we get off this subject, *please*?'

'We only want your happiness, love, when all is said and done. What about that nice Louis Leech you work for? I had a chat with Sophie today and she told me he's quite keen on you. You could do worse than an advertising executive in the city.' She leaned towards me. 'I believe he's very up and coming.'

'You could say that.' I thought if only she knew just how up and coming he really was she wouldn't be trying to fob off her only daughter on him.

'Very ambitious, according to Sophie.'

'Mum, give it a rest, please. You're like a dog with a bone.'

'All right, calm down,' said Mum, getting down to our weekly chat, her subjects ranging from how Adam was progressing in school to who was knocking around with whom in the neighbourhood, marriage never far from her mind.

Back at the flat I flopped down in front of the telly. Oh, what the hell! I was alive. I'd a family who loved me and friends too. The phone rang. It was Louis.

'Jenny, how do you feel about going out for a drink tonight?'

There was a pause.

'If you're frightened I'll get carried away again, I promise I won't. I'll be on my best

290

behaviour. I just want to have a chat with you.'

'No, thanks, Louis. I'm still recovering from last night,' I said, as politely as I could, and put the phone down. I'd had enough hassle for one day. I just wanted to be alone. The phone rang again. This time it was Cathy.

'Jenny! I suppose you heard the news about Hugo.'

'Me and the rest of the world.'

'I couldn't believe it. Not after what he'd said to you.'

'Well, I found it hard to believe too.'

'You poor love. I hope you're not letting it get you down too much. If it's any consolation to you I saw him in Kilbeg today, and he looked very down. He barely said hello. Rushed off before I'd time to congratulate him. Not like him at all. He's usually full of exuberance.'

'Hardly sounds like a man who's just got engaged to the stunning Natalie.'

'He knows she'll keep him on his toes with her efficiency and her schedules, her band and her parties, not to mention her trips abroad.'

'It's obviously what he wants.'

'Which reminds me, he's got the house to himself again. She's off touring with Rick and her band somewhere.'

'I thought she was staying to organise the Manor.'

'That plan didn't last long.'

'You'll probably get an invitation to the wedding,' I said, trying not to sound too forlorn.

'No, thanks. I couldn't bear it. By then I'll be really fat and frumpy, and about to produce.'

'It'd take your mind off things.'

'I'd feel positively scruffy among that posh lot, all looking down on me. No, I'll give it a miss. It's all too boring to contemplate. Anyway, I mightn't get an invitation.'

'Well, I definitely won't. How are the aunts?'

'That's the other thing I wanted to say to you. I'm scared Mum'll tell Ned about the baby. She's threatening to phone him if I don't phone him myself.'

'Oh, no.'

'She said he had a right to know, and got all huffy when I refused to contact him. At least I have this place to retreat to whenever there's a storm brewing. That makes for slightly better relationships.'

Suddenly her voice changed and she dropped the bravado. 'Oh, Jenny, I'm scared she'll tell him. I don't want him to know yet.

Not until I've come to terms with it. Can you come over next weekend? I could do with a bit of moral support and comfort.'

'Of course I will.'

'Thanks. You're an angel.'

For a long time after we had hung up I thought about Cathy and Ned, and wondered if he'd come back. His last trip had been disastrous, which was a pity because he'd tried to patch things up between them. True, he'd been angry when she'd spewed out his faults at him, but he had listened when she had ranted on about how he had broken her heart, and shattered her dreams. Even though she had sent him away, he had made it plain that he wanted her back. He couldn't say any more than that, and he couldn't phone her because she refused to talk to him. One thing stood out in all of it and that was that he was consistent in his desire to have her back, which would probably bring him to Ireland again eventually.

27

In bed that night I thought of Hugo in years to come, giving his garden parties with Natalie beside him, stunning in a plain Yves St Laurent gown, smiling, greeting her celebrity friends. 'My husband, you know, Hugo Hunter.' Bound by good manners he would stand beside her, securely under her thumb, and look helplessly at her as she said, 'Hugo's diet is macrobiotic,' or 'Hugo only likes French wine.' The talk would be of stock-exchange prices, the men nodding, the women bored.

I kept seeing Natalie's face, her beauty complementing the Manor, and the well-dressed guests, with glasses in their hands, admiring the neatly trimmed lawns, the high fences that protected Hugo and the Manor from the outside world, and the huge paintings shipped in from God knew where. I could see Hugo, his neck stiff as he greeted guests, giving nothing away.

My mind projected to the future: Hugo, his shoulders hunched, his eyes dull, beside a doll-like Natalie. I saw him sitting in the library on the leather winged back chair, reading the racing pages of the newspaper, Natalie in the chair opposite him, the one I'd sat in the day of the press reception, with her tapestry. The stereo in the background would be playing one of Natalie's old hits. Eventually, Alice would limp in, their nightcaps on a silver tray: white wine for Natalie, brandy for Hugo. She'd tell him that Rick had phoned to say that her songs were making a comeback, and that she might have to go on tour again. She would be very busy but he could come too, if he didn't mind being on his own in strange hotels because she would have to see important, record company people.

Relieved, Hugo's eyes would brighten. He knew he'd only be a burden, and he would say casually, to hide his elation, 'Oh, well, if you're up to it, go ahead without me.' Laughing she would say how strong she felt, oh, and she'd forgotten to tell him that she'd phoned Felix, their son, who was in his first turbulent year at Oxford. She would sip her drink thoughtfully and say she hoped he'd settle down soon, that she couldn't under-stand why he was so unhappy with the other boys he was sharing with, and wanted to move in with this one particular pal, Danny. And Hugo would look at her blankly, without interest, a tired, silent man, and make no comment even though he'd read between the lines and guessed that Felix was gay. No point in bothering Natalie with it. She had fixed ideas about things like that. Secretly, Hugo was afraid it would only start a row, and send Natalie striding off through her fortress, her high-heels resounding on the marble floors, the guard dogs snapping at her heels.

But she wouldn't be interested in the Manor for long. She wouldn't want to know about Hugo's meetings, his phone calls from the chairman of this board or that board, his plotting, planning. The Manor would turn out to be a bottomless pit into which she had to toss all her money and energy, and which would keep her husband away from her.

Their whole marriage would be different from what I envisaged for Hugo and me. With me he'd have been alive and animated; chasing up to our bedroom to tell me about this deal or that deal. He'd talk nineteen to the dozen about his next venture, or where we'd spend the weekend together.

I would be running the office, racing out to the stables or the milking parlour to give him some important news, raising my voice to be heard above the machinery. Hugo, his arm resting on my shoulder, would listen, smiling. The older children would be picking blackberries in the woods, while the younger ones rode their ponies.

The reality was that I was trying to get on with Louis and trying not to think about Hugo, the awful hollow that his engagement had left in the pit of my stomach. Still, there was Cathy and the weekend to look forward to.

★   ★   ★

On Friday evening when I arrived at the gate lodge it was stormy. It had rained all that day, and the farm was washed out. Great pools of water had appeared in the fields. It ran in rivulets down the yard, where chickens balanced in the wind, their feathers swaying, and aborted all Aunt Mary's attempts at a gate-lodge garden. Apart from a few irrepressible plants hunched against the walls, there was only a green pool in its hollow centre.

Cathy came out of the house, and as soon as I switched off the car engine she threw open the door. 'Jenny!'

'I don't think you should be out in the wet. You don't want to get a chill in your condition.'

'Oh, don't you start.' She laughed. 'I hear that all the time from Mum. Come in. Sorry about the mess. You'll have to step over everything. I'm in the middle of making curtains.'

The sofa was strewn with swatches of fabric, colour charts, wallpaper samples, a notebook filled with measurements. On the table in the corner were a sewing-machine, cream-coloured material and a bottle of wine.

'What a beautiful shade.'

'That's for the curtains, and the blue is for the sofa. Here, have a glass of this new French wine I bought yesterday,' she said, taking it into the kitchen and putting it down on the cluttered table. 'I should have cleared this up.'

I would have liked to tidy up for her, but I felt that would be rude. She poured the wine, her hands fluttering as she repeated things the doctor had said on her last visit to him. She hated the shape her body was taking.

'It was so hard in that surgery, with the damned doctor so sure of himself. There I was, babbling on, and he wasn't even listening.' She was breathless with exasperation.

Together we made lunch: chicken I'd bought in a delicatessen *en route*, salad, and brown bread baked that morning by Aunt Mary. Cathy's movements were swift, her voice light as she set the table, found the cheese platter, all the time sipping her wine and talking. But when she sat down to her meal she could barely eat, and left most of her meal.

'What about Ned? Any word of him?'

'I haven't heard. Mum's very silent on the subject.'

'Surely she'd tell you if he was coming over.'

'Doubt it. She'd be afraid I might scarper.'

'How do you feel about him now?'

My heart went out to her as she sank into a chair, bone tired. 'I can't say *what* I'm feeling. I'm all mixed up. I have one picture of him that I like, the carefree Ned he was before we got married. Then there's the Ned I'm married to, who I don't like at all. To tell you the truth, Jen, I'm confused as to which Ned he really is.'

'He couldn't have changed that much in such a short time, and if, when you see him again, he's the first Ned, the one you fell for, might you not fall for him again?'

'That's possible. But, oh, Jenny, I loathed the Ned I married. I mean it. I used to wish he'd disappear, or die or something.'

'A lot of women wish their husbands dead. More than you'd imagine. I think he's probably both Neds.'

'I expect you're right.'

'How will he react to you being pregnant?'

'I can't bear to think about it.'

There was no denying the aversion to him that she still felt. It was written all over her face.

She sighed, as she said. 'The baby has made my world even more chaotic than it was before. But one thing I do know is that there's no use pretending that everything is fixable just because I'm pregnant. I have to be honest on this.' She shivered. 'I hope he *doesn't* come over because I don't want trouble.'

'There's bound to be a certain amount.'

'I know, and God knows, I've had enough of his anger to last me a lifetime.' She was thoughtful for a moment. 'Maybe if he behaved more lovingly towards me I could love him again.'

I couldn't help wondering what was going to happen, and if perhaps the Ned Cathy had fallen in love with had been a figment of her imagination. If so, it had been inevitable that she'd turn away from the real Ned when she finally discovered him. I felt so sorry for her.

'I'm keeping away from Mum. I refuse to have dinner there any more.'

She opened another bottle of wine.

Later, contented and vague, the two wine bottles empty, she went to bed for a rest, half drunk and drowsy. Climbing the stairs slowly, she called back, 'Be an angel and put up the fireguard, will you?'

While she rested I went for a walk, letting the fine rain fall on my hair. On the back road to the Manor I stopped and looked through the trees at the gardens. When I came to the lychgate I gazed up at the terraces for a long time, remembering the last dinner party there: the grey-stone balustrade above the flowers and trees, people laughing, talking, glasses clinking.

The sun was sinking behind the trees, leaving a red- and gold-streaked sky, and I was clinging to wisps of memory: the smell of Hugo, the feel of him, how he looked, how he laughed, the sound of his voice. My heart breaking I turned away. Just as I was about to go I heard voices, and suddenly Hugo was standing there, tall and gaunt, his profile in shadow. I stood still, holding my breath. I could go up to him, touch his arm and say, 'Hugo!' softly. But what if he didn't want to see me?

Two men joined him, their faces shadowy, their voices indistinct. The faint smell of burning leaves drifted towards me. I walked away, down past the tennis court, the back of the barn and on to the road. Soon the Manor would be changed inside and out under Natalie's influence. Pulled apart, it would be improved beyond recognition. In the coming years Natalie would cajole Hugo into carrying out her plans. She would spend her money on what she needed, and it would all be done in the name of her love for him.

I walked on. If only I could have talked to him, just for a few minutes, heard his rich laughter just once more. Dark clouds gathered, birds settled in the trees, the sky turned plum. There was nothing more to be done, nothing more to be said. I knew that what I had never had would never now be mine.

Slowly I walked back to Coolbawn, my heart yearning, wishing I could soar up into the air like a bird, fly far away into a golden sunlight where pain did not exist.

Aunt Lilian came into the hall to meet me. She said immediately, 'Come into the sitting room. The fire's lit. I want to have a word with you in private about Cathy.'

'What about her?' I said warily.

'Did she ever tell you that Ned hit her?'

'Yes, she did.'

'Well, I asked Ned, and he says it's a lot of nonsense.'

The blood rushed to my face. 'I believe every word of it. She was badly bruised when she first came to me at the flat.'

'She's made too much of the whole thing. I

think she led him a merry dance too.'

'From what she told me, she seems to have had strong reasons for her defection.'

'What *has* she told you?'

Aunt Lilian listened anxiously to my account of Cathy's tale. To my surprise she believed it. But when I said, 'Her marriage was a tragedy from the beginning,' she balked, denying it vehemently.

'No, no, dear. The real tragedy is how it affects her today. Tucked away here, people avoiding her. She can't expect to continue living like that.'

★ ★ ★

Later, in the kitchen, Aunt Mary said, 'Everything's changed since Lilian spoke to Ned on the phone. She feels Cathy's been lying about him.'

'Does Cathy know she phoned him?'

'No, but she's all on Ned's side. She won't face the fact that Cathy's marriage is over. D'you know, she even pretends to the neighbours that Cathy's gone back?'

'But that's awful. It means that Cathy's a prisoner in her own home.'

Aunt Mary nodded. 'Cathy doesn't know what's going on,' she said. 'We must help her to find herself, while there's still time. Or she might take off somewhere preposterous without telling us, even go off her head. You won't do that, dear, will you?'

'Do what?'

'Go off your head because of Hugo Hunter. You'll stay sane, won't you?'

Startled, I looked at her. 'Why should I do that?'

'Well, you were chasing rainbows with him, and it all came to nothing as we discovered.'

'Yes,' I agreed.

'But cheer up. I have an alternative to offer you.'

'You have?'

From the excited expression on her face she looked as if she was about to pull a man out of her sleeve.

'I'll let you in on a little secret. I've bought Bluebell Cottage, the little house up on the hill, and the parcel of land that goes with it.'

'But why? You'll never leave Coolbawn.'

She laughed. 'That's where you're wrong. It's a bolthole, somewhere I can have a bit of peace. But it's for you when I'm gone. I'm leaving it to you in my will.'

'Aunt Mary! I can't believe it.'

'Let's face it, Cathy'll inherit all this, and you'll have nothing, same as your poor mother.'

'I have my career.'

'I know you have. But there's nothing like a bit of land to give a girl status. Now, you mustn't tell a soul. If Lilian got wind of it she'd have a fit.'

'Can I tell Cathy?'

'Especially not Cathy. Not until it's all sealed, and signed over to me.'

★ ★ ★

The following evening Cathy and I went to the hotel for a drink.

'I'll have a Coke,' she said, settling herself into a comfortable chair by the log fire. 'I'm giving up alcohol for the rest of the pregnancy.'

'Very sensible,' I said, delighted with her decision.

When I went up to the bar to pay for the drinks I bumped straight into Hugo.

He stared at me, and I stared back. For one awful moment I thought he was going to walk by. I stood back to let him pass, but he stayed rooted to the spot.

'I didn't expect to see you here,' he said, and touched my hair.

I recoiled.

'Jenny, let me explain.'

'No.' I shook off his hand. 'I've had enough of your lies. Asking me to wait for you, and then going off to get engaged. Or had you intended marrying Natalie all along? I wish you'd let me know. Wouldn't have been such a shock then to read about it.'

'Listen, Jenny — '

'No, you listen,' I shouted, jabbing a finger at him. 'You're a two-timing conniving bastard, Hugo Hunter, stringing me along with a whole load of bullshit after the meal at the restaurant, finally convincing me and then doing the dirty. You're despicable, that's what you are.'

There was a collective gasp of shock in the bar. Then Cathy was beside me, taking my arm. 'Come on,' she coaxed. 'Let's go.'

'No! I'm not going until I've let him know what an idiot he made of me, fabricating all those stories about not leaving poor, helpless Natalie until she was well again, and all the time he was preparing to marry her. What a joke that turned out to be, a joke at my expense. You made a complete fool out of me, Hugo.'

Hugo blinked at me, horrified. 'Jenny, listen. You've got it all wrong. That's not what happened.'

'Wasn't it? Well, there's no way you can deny it. I read it in black and white. Unless, of course, you've got some other cock-and-bull story.'

Cathy made another attempt to steer me away. 'It's not going to make much difference now, Jenny.'

I shook her off. People had stopped drinking. Not as much as a glass clinked while all eyes were riveted on Hugo and me.

'Well, go on. I'm waiting.' I folded my arms. 'Talk yourself out of this one.'

I was really getting into my stride, and the gawkers were waiting with bated breath, eager to hear him extricate himself from the tight corner I'd put him in.

'What's going on here?' said a burly barman.

'This woman is causing a scene,' said a man, pointing his index finger at me.

'Out!' the barman said, grabbing my arm, leading me towards the door. 'Out of here before I'm forced to call the police.'

'No, you don't understand. It's all right, she's with me,' Hugo explained, following us.

'I am not with you,' I contradicted him over my shoulder. 'I wouldn't be seen dead with you.'

Hugo's face dropped.

Chin up, quick as I could, I walked through the foyer, escorted by the barman, the crowd gaping after me.

'Not if you were the last man on this planet!' I shouted at Hugo from the door.

'Out!' the barman roared, his face turning dark red. 'And don't come back.'

Once outside, I stood for a moment in the darkness, my heart thumping.

'That's telling him,' I said to Cathy, as I marched to the car with all the dignity I could muster.

'It sure was,' she said.

'Jenny, stop. Wait!' It was Hugo running up the road after us.

He grabbed my arm as I was unlocking the car door. 'Jenny, you've *got* to listen.'

'I don't have to do anything,' I spat, shaking him off. 'And I certainly don't want to hear any more of your lies. Now, if you don't mind, could you please go away and let me get into my car? Or I'll call the police and have you arrested for menace,' I shouted.

'Right, I will, then,' he thundered back, dropping my arm. 'And perhaps when you're ready to listen you'll let me know.'

'That'll be never.'

We were off, driving away.

'What a disaster,' I said. 'Oh, God! He'll think I planned it, that I hung around the hotel waiting for him.'

'Don't be silly. Of course he won't. You couldn't have planned an attack like that,' Cathy assured me.

'He looked terrible, didn't he?'

'Tortured, I'd say. You were worse than the Gestapo.'

'What do I care? He led me up the garden path. Now he's about to marry the most beautiful woman in the world. A woman I could never match up to. Oh, God! What a fool I was.' I blinked back the tears, imagining him sitting there, at the bar, longing for Natalie. It wasn't so long ago that he'd longed for me.

28

'Why, why, why? Why must he come?' said Cathy tearfully, on the phone to me in the office after Aunt Lilian had told her that Ned was arriving the next day.

'Do you want me to come over? Or will I be in the way?'

'Please come,' she begged.

I drove over that evening.

'I can't face him,' she said, as soon as she saw me.

'But, Cathy, things must be sorted out.'

'And how do you think he'll react when he sees the state of me?' Cathy looked down at her slightly swelling stomach.

'He's delighted with the good news, and he agrees with me that you can't remain hidden away for the rest of your life. You've got to face up to your responsibilities,' said Aunt Lilian.

Frustrated, Cathy cried, 'Oh, why does he have to come now, just as I was getting on fine without him?'

From her heartbroken expression it looked as if she wouldn't cope with Ned's arrival. 'What do I look like, Jenny? Do I look awful?'

'You're positively blooming,' I said. 'I've never seen you look so lovely in your life.'

'Maybe it's just as well you're going to see him. Get it over with,' added Aunt Mary, trying to console her.

'I suppose you're right,' Cathy said, but remained unconvinced.

When Ned arrived, tired and dishevelled after his long journey, Cathy was nowhere to be found.

Aunt Lilian, prepared to do anything to make his stay pleasant, had the best bedroom ready and a warm welcome for him. 'Had a good journey?' she enquired solicitously.

'Not bad,' he said, looking around for Cathy, surprised that she wasn't at the door waiting for him.

Aunt Lilian, anxious to get thing on to a good footing said, 'Cathy gets confused about things. You must be patient with her. Sometimes she behaves like a spoilt child.'

Aunt Mary heard this remark and was furious. Straightening up, she said, 'Nonsense! Cathy's not spoilt. How could she be, having you for a mother?'

Aunt Lilian looked at her in surprise, this intrusion unexpected and unwelcome.

Cathy was waiting for Ned in the garden,

311

along the path, some distance from the house, not wanting Aunt Lilian to interfere in their private exchange. Walking up and down, she was a vision in her long blue going-away dress, her hair red-gold in the sunlight.

I sneaked out to her. 'He's here,' I warned her. Then I went to hide behind the hedge in case she needed me.

A few minutes later I heard Cathy say, 'Oh! There you are.'

'G'day,' said Ned.

Here he was, indeed, the overworked stockbroker with only two goals in view: making loads of money and playing rugby for Australia, looking down at her awkwardly, waiting to resolve their differences.

Since they'd last met the bitterness they'd felt towards one another had receded slightly with their separation, and Cathy was ready to be tolerant.

'It was good of you to come,' she said.

'It's not my idea of fun to have to fly thousands of miles to see my wife but what could I do? How are you?'

'I'm fine, thank you.'

'You look well. It's great about the baby. I'm delighted.'

'Thanks.'

'The thing is, I'm expecting us to work

312

something out so we can get our lives back to normal.'

'What do you propose?' Anxiously, she looked up at him.

'I want you to come back home with me, of course.'

Taken aback, Cathy said, 'Not just yet.'

'But why not?' he said.

'I need more time.'

'You've had plenty of time. And it's not just about us any more. We've got a baby to consider. That was the whole idea of me coming over. I've got your ticket.'

I was watching them through the gap in the hedge.

'We can't just brush aside the problems,' Cathy said. 'You know as well as I do that things will have to change before I could even consider going back there.'

'Look, Cathy, I've cut down on the drink.' He sounded contrite as he said this. She looked up sharply. If he had taken such a step, he must be serious. However, obstinacy forbade her to concede this.

Seeing her trembling lower lip, he said, 'I want things to go right for us. How about we go out to dinner tonight? You could do yourself up a bit. What do you say?' He moved towards her slowly.

She stood still; her head on one side.

'All right, as long as you realise that we can't expect to solve all our problems in one go.'

'I told you I've eased up on the booze.'

'There were other things.'

'Like what?'

'You hiding things from me. That awful business with Fawn.'

'Fawn's a friend, that's all.'

'That's another thing. I don't like your friends.'

His voice rose as he said, 'What do you want me to do? Change my whole lifestyle just because you don't like my friends?'

'No. Just see less of them, and spend more time with me.'

'And what about you? What changes are you prepared to make?'

She looked up at him. 'What did you have in mind?'

'Sex, for instance. Maybe you could get interested in it again. You've been doing everything to avoid it.'

'Anything else?'

'In fact, you haven't liked much of anything to do with me recently. Quite honestly, Cathy, you were becoming quite a handful before you left.'

'Oh!' The colour drained from her face. 'So why do you still want to bother with me?'

'Because you're my wife and, what's more, you'll remain my wife. I don't believe in divorce, especially not now that you're expecting my child.'

Cathy turned away. Her pregnancy was squeezing out her freedom, pushing her further into Ned's boring lifestyle with his rugby-playing friends, and their lavatory jokes. He would make few concessions, after all.

Then Ned went on, 'And I want my son to be born and reared in Australia.'

'And if I don't want to live in Australia again?'

'You'll hand the baby over to me.'

'What? If you think I'm going to waddle around for nine months, go through the pain of giving birth only to give my baby away, you can think again.'

'I'm its father. That's hardly giving it away.'

In the silence that followed she said, 'I don't expect you to understand. How could you? You're a man.'

He let that go. Like all men, he was a past master at evasion, but she would never know how close to tears he was then, and he would never know how near she was to turning on her heel and walking off.

He took her arm. 'It's rather chilly. Let's go inside.'

Shrinking away, she said, 'Don't you dare touch me. And don't insult me either by making impossible demands on me.' With one vicious thrust she pushed him away.

'Listen, Cathy, how about you come back with me, stay for the duration of the pregnancy, and see how we get on? We should have things worked out by then.'

'And if we haven't?'

His expression clouded over. 'You can leave, but you'll get nothing and I'll fight you through every court for the baby.'

Then Aunt Mary interrupted them. 'Aren't you cold?' she asked. 'Would you like some tea?'

Ned didn't hear her. He was shaking his fist. 'I'll do anything to get my baby. I'll have you branded an unfit mother. You with your hysterics, throwing up your hands and stomping off when something doesn't suit you.'

He was gone, storming back to the house, leaving Cathy standing there, her arms hanging loosely by her sides, tears rippling down her face.

'Cathy!' I ran to her, and held her in my arms.

Something in Aunt Mary snapped and she came to life.

'How dare he speak to you like that?' she

said. Her anger knew no bounds. The cheek of the fellow with his disregard for everything and everyone but himself. 'Why should this ridiculous situation continue a moment longer?' she said to Cathy. 'Dry your eyes. Cut your losses. Let him loose. Don't take any more of his insults. There's no pleasure in being married to someone like him. If he can take an aeroplane to Ireland at the drop of a hat he can return home to Australia just as fast.'

Cathy gaped at her.

'I'm serious,' she said. 'What right has he to make demands on a child that isn't even born yet? You've stood enough nonsense. You've paid over and over again for this marriage. Throw him out. He's a monster.' Aunt Mary's face was crimson and her eyes bright with fury. For the first time in her life she looked dangerous.

Cathy stood rooted to the spot.

'Come on,' I said, taking her arm, drawing her back towards the house. 'You have to be strong, for your baby's sake as well as your own.'

Slowly we made our way back, Aunt Mary saying, 'You really will have to get a solicitor. I'll come with you to see Dick Daly. He's been the family lawyer for donkey's years.'

Aunt Lilian was coming to meet us, her

back erect, two red blotches of anger her cheeks. 'What is the meaning of this hullabaloo with Ned? I caught him just in time. He was phoning for a taxi. Had I not apologised on your behalf he would have picked up his bag and gone.'

Aunt Mary said, 'And good riddance.'

'What? Really! You astound me, Mary. And you, Cathy! How could you let him get into such a state?' She looked at Cathy, appalled. 'The poor fellow came all this way only to be met with such hostility.'

'He was pretty hostile to me,' Cathy said.

'Could you blame him? Have you stopped to consider what a lot of stupid nonsense you're making out of this whole business?'

'What do you mean?' Cathy looked at her.

'Ned's trying to get you to see reason. How can he maintain any sort of balance in this matter with you refusing to co-operate? Do you realise that if you don't come to some agreement you'll be left with nothing? No money, no future, no dignity.' Aunt Lilian was dancing with temper.

Ned appeared at the front door.

'It's true,' he cried. 'I'm not being a bastard just for the hell of it.'

'Oh, there you are, Ned. I thought you'd gone to your room.' Aunt Lilian smiled brightly at him. 'I was just saying to Cathy

318

that it's all a lot of fuss about nothing. This pregnancy is making her see things strangely.'

'You don't have to make excuses for her,' said Ned. 'As far as she's concerned, she's done nothing wrong. She thinks it's my fault. I'm the one who's fouled up.'

There was a horrible silence.

Aunt Mary said, 'Let's all have a cup of tea to calm us down.'

There was a circus-like quality to the whole scene, with Aunt Lilian, leaping around, angry, self-righteous, Cathy gaping at her. Ned, for all the tricks he'd had up his sleeve, was still losing his wife, and being offered tea as consolation.

Cathy was swaying under the dreadful pressure of it all. Why hadn't she realised sooner that Ned would expect her to be a docile, undemanding, gentle, easily satisfied wife? Someone who would do things his way.

She wasn't prepared to wear the same hair-shirt of responsibility, worry and strain for Ned that her mother had taken on for her husband and Coolbawn all those years ago, because she saw the nonsense of it all. It had made an ogre out of her mother and her own childhood miserable.

Aunt Lilian said, 'Cathy, if I were you I'd listen to Ned. You should both start afresh, and take your chances together.'

319

'I'm not going back with him, and don't ask me to change my mind because I won't,' Cathy said.

'You're making a terrible mistake. Think of the poor baby, homeless before it's born,' said Ned.

'It won't be homeless. It'll be here in Coolbawn with us.'

'Oh, no, it won't. You won't be welcome to stay here.' Aunt Lilian's face was resolute. 'Not with a fatherless child.' Aunt Mary turned away in distress.

For the first time since she'd tied the knot with Ned, Cathy felt uncertain of the future. 'I don't feel well. I'm going to have a rest,' she said, turning away to go back to the gate lodge.

There, she lay on the sofa, and I made some tea, although Cathy wouldn't drink it — it still turned her stomach.

'No doubt when Ned has gone things will settle down again, and Aunt Lilian will let you stay at least until you've found a place,' I said. Cathy's own mother would hardly put her out on the street, however harsh her threat had sounded.

'I feel such a failure,' said Cathy. At last the whole situation was becoming real to her, she said. She was going to suffer as a single parent, but meantime she'd make herself useful, prepare for her baby. And out of this horrific muddle something could be retrieved. She found herself suddenly looking forward. It would be good to have her child.

Later we returned to the house, and faced Ned in the sitting room.

'Let's sit by the fire.' He spoke distantly.

She sat down.

'Is there anything you'd like me to get you?'

'I just want a bit of peace.'

He produced a bottle of whiskey from his pocket.

'I thought you'd given it up,' Cathy said, surprised.

'I said I'd cut back. We're both fraught. A drink won't do us any harm. It might relax us.'

'Not for me. I don't like whiskey.'

Taking some notes out of his wallet he counted them carefully, and put them into her hand. 'If you're not coming back with me now you'll need cash for your journey when you do decide to come.'

As he did so, the awfulness of the situation reared up again, and a sense of injury overtook her. 'It's been quite a day, hasn't it? Not a civil word spoken to one another, and now you're giving me money for a journey I've no intention of taking,' she said.

'No more of this,' he snapped. 'Your mother agrees with me that you're coming back to Sydney at some stage, and that's that.'

His presumption was the ultimate insult. Cathy had reached the point where everything was out of proportion, the love they'd shared turning into hatred. She handed him back his money. 'I don't want it. I don't want anything from you. I'm sorry, but I've made up my mind. I'm not going back to Australia — ever.'

'And what am I supposed to do without my wife?'

'Just carry on as before. Get someone in to cook and clean for you and you won't even notice I'm not there. Go back to living the life of a bachelor. I'm sure Fawn or some other tart will be available for nookey, when you're not too pissed to enjoy it.'

Ned spun round, and grabbed her arm. 'If you think I'm going to let you get away with this you're wrong. You don't know what you're letting yourself in for. Think of all those nasty court cases — you branded as an unfit wife and mother, and the loss of your child at the end of it.'

Cathy contemplated her bleak future: a life alone, a child to rear on social security. Then she said, 'If you take my advice you'll leave now. I'll order a taxi for you.'

Astounded, Ned stood rigid, his back to the fireplace. He said, 'Why the undue haste?' and subsided into the nearest chair.

'To make sure you get the next flight.'

'What an idea! My flight's not until the day after tomorrow.'

'Others change their air tickets, why can't you?'

'Having come all this way, I certainly will not.'

'We can go on like this for the next couple of days but, really, there's nothing more to be said. I've made up my mind. I'm not going back to Australia. Now, why don't you cut your losses and go?'

Her eyes were on the clock on the mantelpiece as she said, 'I've decided. I want a divorce, and that's final.'

'Don't say that.' He leaped out of the chair, and clasped her hand.

'Let me go.' Her voice was as cold as ice. Then she went out to phone Paddy Reilly for a cab.

At this the aunts came hurriedly into the hall.

'Don't tell me Ned's leaving already,' said Aunt Lilian.

Trembling, Cathy held on to the back of the hall chair. 'I've just phoned for a taxi.'

Ned gave Aunt Lilian a hopeless glance. 'I'd better get my bag,' he said. As he left the room he looked ill and sad, which seemed appropriate somehow.

'There's the taxi now,' said Cathy. 'He came quickly.'

Paddy Reilly paused at the door. 'Is the passenger ready?'

Ned came slowly down the stairs, knowing that his presence had become an embarrassment, but still reluctant to go.

'Don't let us delay you,' said Aunt Mary. 'We know you're anxious to be off.'

'Don't worry, I'm going,' he said, and shrugged himself into his jacket, Aunt Mary helping him.

All the glamour had left him as he walked gracelessly out of the door. He was no longer the stylish, purposeful young bridegroom who had stood at Cathy's side on their wedding day.

'Thank you for coming,' said Aunt Lilian, following him sheepishly out of the door, Aunt Mary behind her, like a shadow, her expression grim.

He turned back, paused, and looked at Cathy, who gazed blindly ahead, the life gone out of her.

Finally Ned was in the taxi, his head down, and relief was in the air as Aunt Lilian said goodbye. A relief that was short-lived.

His head popped out of the window of the taxi and he said to Cathy, 'Just one last thing. I did my share to make things right. I gave you every chance to do the same. But you, you stubborn bitch, wouldn't budge.'

'Calm down,' called Aunt Mary.

Fists clenched he said, 'You'll be hearing from my solicitor about my rights to the baby.'

'Righto!' said Aunt Mary, waving frantically, wishing Paddy would drive off, seeing more trouble looming.

'Please don't repeat this to anyone, will you?' said Aunt Lilian to Paddy her voice quivering.

'Fearful business, right enough,' he said, his day livened up by the exchange. 'Sure I wouldn't breathe a word of it. Cross me heart and hope to die.'

'Thank you,' said Aunt Lilian. She stared after the car, devastated. 'You're in the soup now,' she said to Cathy, as they turned to go indoors.

'To think he wants rights already!' said Aunt Mary.

'Oh, yes, indeed, you're for it now,' reiterated Aunt Lilian, as she walked ahead. 'Absolutely. No question about it. He means business.'

'Yes, it's quite nasty,' said Aunt Mary, speaking as if they were discussing a dreadful disease.

'There'll be changes now,' said Aunt Lilian, shutting windows and doors.

'Yes,' Cathy agreed.

'Sometimes people should be left alone to sort themselves out,' Aunt Mary said. 'They don't want our advice.'

'What would you know, Mary?'

'I haven't seen much of life, I know, but I'm old and wise.'

'I'll not have Cathy make a fool of herself,' Aunt Lilian said. 'He wants his baby and he intends to get it.' She said this in an I-told-you-so voice.

Aunt Mary's head lifted above such trivialities. 'That's one worry that'll have to wait,' she said, patting Cathy protectively. 'Be brave, don't cry, my poor child. Things can only get better now that he's gone.'

29

Cathy lay on her bed. She couldn't go up to the house because Aunt Lilian had made it clear she wasn't welcome. She couldn't go into the village. She couldn't go anywhere, not just because of the pregnancy, but because of that stupid Paddy Reilly, who'd told everyone about Ned's disastrous visit. Aunt Lilian insisted she stay out of the way until the gossip had died down. She'd no friends to talk to. She felt very sorry for herself cooped up like a dead bird in a matchbox. Clumsily, I tried to comfort her.

'Oh, God! I'll really have to leave here now,' she said.

'Aunt Lilian doesn't mean it. You know that.'

'Oh, she means it all right. There's no way she'll let me stay here. Single mother! Divorced! My God! What would Canon Devine and the rest of the parish have to say about that?'

'Don't think about it. Aunt Lilian'll forget all about them when she sees the baby.'

Cathy considered this. 'Do you really think so?'

'Yes, I do.'

'I'm not convinced, and even if Mum does allow me to stay here I'll be condemned to bed for the duration.'

'Listen, Cathy, one way or the other you won't be on your own for long, not a girl like you. Some gorgeous hunk will come along and snap you up.'

'Looking like this? And with a baby? I don't think so. Oh, God, what a mess.'

'Rubbish. I know a man who married after his wife died, and he had three children.'

'It's easier for a man to remarry than for a woman. Everyone knows that. You've been reading too many fairy stories, Jen, that's your trouble.' She subsided into the cushions, calmer now but still miserable.

Aunt Mary chose that day to announce her purchase of Bluebell Cottage.

'Bluebell Cottage! Oh, Aunt Mary, how wonderful,' Cathy said.

'It's riddled with damp,' said Aunt Lilian. 'You can't move there.'

'I can and I will, Lilian.'

Aunt Lilian blew up. 'You're crazy.' She was at the end of her tether with this stubborn sister-in-law, who was suddenly against her in everything. 'You're taking a dreadful risk. It's falling down.'

'It's the sanest thing I've ever done in my life. I'll do it up.'

'With what? After the purchase and solicitor's fees you won't have enough money for food and clothes.'

Aunt Mary was implacable. 'There's a little of my father's legacy left. Also, I'll have an income from the farm, and with lambs, chickens, a couple of cows for milk, butter, cream and eggs, I won't starve. And don't forget the river's full of salmon.'

'River of salmon, indeed. All that salmon gets poached and sold to the hotel. What about the electricity and phone bills? You haven't thought of them, have you?'

'I've taken everything into consideration, Lilian.'

'It must be at least five miles from the church.'

'I might buy myself a little car.'

'You can't drive.'

'I can learn,' said Aunt Mary bravely.

'More expense,' Aunt Lilian said unpleasantly.

'I'll raise more money if I have to,' said Aunt Mary, who had always been evasive on the unpleasant issue of finance.

'And you'll have no one to give you a hand.'

'I manage more or less on my own,' said

Aunt Mary, putting Aunt Lilian in her place.

'Nonsense,' said Aunt Lilian. 'I've always been at hand to help.'

'Hmm!' Aunt Mary swivelled to meet her gaze. 'You've been here, true, but you never did much in the way of housekeeping.'

'There was never any time, what with the farm and everything. You can't walk out on us like this, Mary. Have sense. What about Cathy and the baby?'

'I'm quite capable of looking after myself,' interrupted Cathy, who up to now had been listening in silence.

'I'm sorry, but I've made up my mind, and Cathy's coming with me.'

Aunt Mary looked at Cathy, drawing her into her own world of conspiracy.

'Am I?' Cathy hugged her.

Aunt Lilian gaped. 'That's impossible. Where would she sleep in that hideous damp place, with its leaking roof, broken windows and the wallpaper falling off the walls?'

'I'll make it comfortable for her. I'd carry her on my back, if I had to.'

There was a pause.

'We'll do it up,' Aunt Mary continued. 'Buy the best beds. Cathy'll have the big bedroom.'

Cathy's glowing face irritated Aunt Lilian. 'What if she's suddenly taken ill, or you for that matter? You're not getting any younger.'

'I'll have to risk that,' said Aunt Mary.

'Distance can only be an advantage, with all the gossip that's flying around,' said Cathy.

'You don't understand the principle of the thing, Lilian,' Aunt Mary said. 'I've given you the best years of my life. I've had nothing but hard work and heartbreak. And now, when I should be coming into a quiet, peaceful time, you're worse than ever with your rudeness and your intolerance of Cathy's situation.' Aunt Mary got to her feet.

Aunt Lilian was stunned at her directness.

Cathy burst out laughing, the sound in the silence like breaking glass, shattering the serious mood. Her beautiful face had strength in it as she said, 'Oh, Aunt Mary, you're terrific.'

'Well, I'll have plenty to do looking after you, Cathy,' said Aunt Mary, 'but I'll be back and forth to check on you, Lilian, and you, Jenny, will be there at weekends.'

'Thanks, Aunt Mary, I'd love to come.'

'Well, don't worry about me,' said Aunt Lilian, brave all of a sudden. 'I can take care of myself.'

'But I've always worried about you, Lilian. Why should I stop now?'

Cathy gave Aunt Mary an adoring smile. 'So, we'll all see plenty of each other.' She couldn't hide her excitement.

Aunt Lilian laughed with derision. 'I expected better things of you, Mary.'

'Try to understand,' said Aunt Mary.

'Give her a chance, Mum.'

Aunt Lilian left, her dignified steps heavy across the floor, the condemned woman doomed to a life alone. At the door she said, 'That it should come to this! Take it from me, Mary. Your eyes will be opened for you over there on the bleak side of the hill. Poor Ambrose, I'm glad he's not here to see this day.'

Cathy and Aunt Mary were left alone with me.

'Oh, wasn't that awful?' said Cathy.

'It was like being scolded when I was a child,' said Aunt Mary.

Cathy slipped across to her, something secret in her expression. Pleased as a child herself she put her arms around her aunt, and gave her a bear-hug. 'Thank you for letting me come to live with you, Aunt Mary,' she said.

'I'm doing it for you, dear, and don't worry, we won't be long licking the place into shape,' she said. 'You'll help won't you, Jenny?'

'Of course I will.'

A new fire sprang up in Aunt Mary,

Cathy's pregnancy fanning its flame. Enchanted with her new plans, all the years of tumult and drudges lifted from her shoulders as she moved about with a lighter step.

Before dark we went to see Bluebell Cottage. Small, undemanding, manageable, it stood neglected at the end of the sea road, battered by the wind from the mountains and lashed by the rain. Wet leaves were plastered to the gravel, old rose trees and shrubs were submerged under the garden wall among tall grass.

But it was a doll's house, built on a bank where thyme, bluebells and violets grew in springtime. While Cathy and Aunt Mary examined the kitchen I looked around the tiny porch and hall. It was cold and strange, the walls discoloured, a bloom on the wooden floor, the windows fogged.

It would be good for Aunt Mary to live here, where she would have peace. Soon relations and friends would fill it. She would easily get someone to help her manage the farm, and Cathy could handle the sale of wheat and lambs.

'It's such a delightful house,' Cathy said, tripping lightly down the hall, looking like the cat who'd got the cream. 'Come on up and have a look round.'

Aunt Lilian hadn't managed to extinguish

her zest for living. Her frivolity and determination to enjoy life that she'd inherited from her father were returning. Aunt Mary would share in her fun, even throughout the pregnancy. To all intent and purposes Cathy was her child, the one she never had, to be minded and cosseted.

'This will be the nursery,' Aunt Mary said, her voice reaching a note of delight.

The strain and worry that had made her old beyond her years drained out of her as she unfolded her plans to us.

'Blue, for an unruly boy, or pink for a shockingly beautiful girl,' said Cathy wittily.

'But what do you think it will be?' said Aunt Mary, already, in her mind, pushing it out in its pram, changing its nappies, making fairy sandwiches for dolls' tea-parties.

'Do you think Mum'll come round to the idea of a baby?' Suddenly Cathy looked pale and anxious again, her voice falling away.

'Probably, when she's sees it.'

As we wandered through the rooms I visualised Bluebell Cottage being just as pretty inside as out, decorated with muted shades and soft Persian rugs,

'It's going to be a new beginning,' cried Aunt Mary, in a voice that sounded like a child's.

The next time I saw Bluebell Cottage, work

was underway: builders, building materials and ladders were everywhere. White with exhaustion, Aunt Mary had been on the go all the time, doing chores, plodding back and forth bringing the builders their lunch, holding the ladders, generally getting in their way, in a constant effort to get everything shipshape.

'The roof needed a lot of money spent on it,' she said to me, 'but don't worry, I've still got a bit salted away, and we'll get a bit of a mortgage, if necessary, won't we, Cathy? It's the thing to have nowadays, isn't it?'

We both laughed but Aunt Mary wore an expression of responsibility. After all this time she was the head of her own household. She could do as she liked. Upstairs the water plopped like thunder into the old zinc bath. 'And we'll have a new bathroom fitted,' she said, with determination.

30

I stood in front of the wardrobe, trying to decide what clothes to take. This was my first brush with the film world and I didn't know what to expect, apart from glamorous actors, expensive restaurants. Warm jumpers and jeans, evening wear — I bundled everything I possessed into my bag.

Louis woke me at five the next morning by banging on the door. When he saw my bag, he said, 'It's only a bloody commercial we're shooting, not a whole film,' and groaned under the weight as he carried it down to the car.

'At least I can't be accused of not being prepared for all occasions,' I retorted, my mind on the ordeal of having to face Hugo again.

I didn't want to go back to the Manor, but Louis had given me no choice. There was work to be done and, as far as he was concerned, sentiment didn't enter into it. I had to go and that was that.

Also, it was the first time I had been alone with Louis since that awful episode at my flat, and the atmosphere was strained. As we moved off he said, 'Look, Jenny, I'm really sorry for what happened at your place.'

'Forget it.'

'I should have apologised properly to you before now but I never seemed to find the right moment, and I blamed you for giving me the green light.'

'Yes,' I admitted. 'I suppose I did.'

'I just want you to know that it won't ever happen again, especially now that I know where I stand with you.'

'And where's that?'

'You don't fancy me, and that's that.'

The penny had dropped.

'Thanks, Louis. I appreciate that.'

For the rest of the journey he hardly spoke, and I was lost in my own thoughts. I cursed myself for being nervous. I didn't want to see Hugo, I thought, but then I changed my mind. God! I'd give my eyes to see him again, and I knew Natalie wouldn't be there. There would be no harm done if I saw him just this once, with Louis there. I thought of our previous meeting, how brave and stupid I'd been, losing my temper like that, letting my tongue run wild, and shouting into his face. Oh, God! After that what could I say to him? There was nothing *to* say.

Several green trailers, lorries and vans were parked on the gravel sweep outside the

Manor. Men with beards and women in bright-coloured fleeces were rushing in and out of the open doors, unravelling cables, swinging cameras. There was no sign of Hugo. At the door a group of people with clipboards stood waiting. Large drops of rain fell on to our bare heads. Louis, looking up at the leaden sky, ran to the door, with me following. Inside, the hall was dark and cavernous, one huge spotlight shining from the vestibule door.

Louis raised his hand. 'Wait! Don't go in, they're shooting.'

As soon as the spotlight went out we entered. Inside, people surged forward. I became wedged behind the clapperloader, a stout girl in a bright yellow T-shirt and baggy jeans. Louis introduced me to Mark, the lighting cameraman, Eamon, the assistant director, Dave, the director, and Sam, the sound recordist. A group of extras stood patiently as the makeup girl, a big bag swinging from her arm, put the final touches to their faces.

The drawing room looked completely different. People sat straight in the tall chairs, and gone was the friendliness and ease of old. Gone, too, was the cream carpet, the blue button-backed sofas and gilt mirrors. Informed by Natalie's minimalist taste, there wasn't an ornament or a photograph in sight, just a huge vase of chrysanthemums on the table in the centre of the new, highly polished wooden floor. The room felt unused.

In one corner a small group was gathering near a camera. A young girl with flowing blonde hair walked up and down with trained model elegance, anxious for the action to begin, her cigarette smoke lingering in the air.

'I read about this place in the *Field*,' said a tall elderly man, who was peering at the paintings, which Natalie had allowed to remain in place, delighted with what he saw. He said to the model-like woman, 'Come here, m'dear and judge this for yourself.'

Hugo appeared out of the shadows, his head clearly visible above the throng pressing about him. He didn't see me but stood there grandly, looking handsomer than ever, his acceptance of the presence of the film crew in his home total. I longed to take a step nearer to him, but stayed where I was, the film crew between us, willing him to turn and see me.

Finally he did. 'Jenny!'

'Hello, Hugo.' I hesitated. I should have been civil enough to say, 'Let bygones be bygones. No harm done. Congratulations,' but the words stuck in my throat. I tried again, 'I hope you'll . . . ' Each word sounded flat and insincere, yet he was listening as if what I was saying had huge importance. I longed for Louis, or Sophie, or anyone to rush in and rescue me. Just as Hugo was about to say something to me Louis and Sophie arrived. Louis, agitated, grabbed Hugo, calling his attention to the cameraman in the hall. 'He wants to shoot you with your ancestors,' he said.

'Good for him,' said Sophie, under her breath. 'They deserve shooting, the whole bloody lot of them.'

'Excusing himself, Hugo was gone, stepping over wires and cables to stand beneath his forebears who gazed down grimly from their frames. She was right. Let the past go. Why open up old wounds? I would avoid Hugo for the rest of the day.

Later, I saw him on a tour of his rogues' gallery, explaining his ancestors' battles, while big lights with flat lids were trained on their faces.

Suddenly, Natalie floated into the room, the artificial light bouncing off her sleek hair, her perfect makeup and the electric smile she trained on Dave, the director, who bustled over to her.

Divine in a tiny pink cashmere cardigan, her slashed black skirt revealing her long brown legs, she stood posed as a dancer. When she saw me she said rudely, 'What are you doing here?' Antagonism blazed in her eyes.

'I'm working,' I said, clutching my clipboard.

'Still Louis's dogsbody? Fancy that I thought you'd have left by now for a more interesting job. Something you could sink your teeth into.'

'I'm happy enough where I am,' I said, wanting to sink my teeth into *her*. 'I'm just as surprised to see you here. Louis didn't tell me you were involved in this commercial.'

Natalie raised her eyebrows. 'I'm not officially,' she said gaily. 'I wouldn't want to be professionally linked with any kind of advertising. I'm just here to make sure things are handled properly. Obviously, in my profession, I know a lot about camera technique, lighting and makeup.'

Mark, the cameraman, drooling over her, said, 'A nice close-up of you at that window would be really sexy. How about it? Then we could home in on you walking in the garden.'

'Oh, all right, I'll do it,' said Natalie, yielding reluctantly, swayed by her assurance and vanity.

'I'll go and ask Louis,' Dave said.

'I'll get him,' I offered, dying to get away from her.

Leaning forward she said, 'There's no

need. I can make my own decisions.' Delighted with herself she swanned off, leading the way, Dave and Mark following her.

I went to find Louis. 'Why didn't you warn me that she'd be here?' I cried.

'I didn't know.'

'She's got a nerve,' I spluttered. 'One more insult out of her and I'll give her a piece of my mind.'

Louis, his mobile stuck to his ear, said, 'Take no notice of her. She's only trying to make mischief. And you've got to get on. There's loads more important things for you to be doing.'

After the coffee break Louis headed in the direction of the garden with Dave to check out the best location to film from before the crew descended on it. Outside the rain had stopped, and the air was warmer than it had been for some time. The sun came out and there was the sweet smell of earth after rain.

I took a short cut into the conservatory and walked along beside the plants. Red roses trailed up alongside mauve wisteria, their heavy scent mingling with the scent of climbing pink geraniums. Sky blue *plumbago capensis*, high up under the cool glass dome, shaded the light. *Clivia miniata*'s glossy strap-like leaves were spectacular against the soft white petals of a nerium, its deep orange clusters beside peach trees, and muscatel vines. Pots of waxy cymbidium were ranged alongside huge ferns, the constant drip of water keeping their dark jungle foliage moist.

In here, amid his exotic plants, Hugo stood stoic and gracious with his group, their notebooks in hand, their biros poised. I ached to go to him, hold the hand that was hanging limply by his side, touch the beloved face that had looked at me so lovingly in the past. But that was impossible. Hot and dizzy I left.

Outside the greenhouse, the gardener explained boxes of cuttings under glass, looking as if he'd been talking for hours. Down by the pond, ducks skittered around in a frenzy of excitement as Natalie, spectacular in an emerald green cloak, stood silhouetted against the backdrop of the Manor, her hair streaming in the wind as the cameras whirred and lights flashed. This was the culmination of Hugo's struggle to hold on to his inheritance, and she was a major part of it.

During the break refreshments were served in the splendid new tea-rooms, built for the public to sit and savour the past with their delicious cakes. All the difficulties of re-creating the Manor — the advertising campaign, the decisions, the arguments, discussions, changes, doubts — had been ironed out. Louis had done his job well, looking after Hugo's interests with the dedication of a brother, protecting him from everything but the success of the venture.

For the rest of the week I went through the motions, following Louis's instructions, helping to get everything done, but I couldn't wait for it to be over. Everybody was excited about the party Hugo was throwing on the Saturday night, relieved that the commercial was in the can.

Louis invited Cathy to the party.

'I can't gatecrash!' she protested.

'Course you can,' said Louis, happy that it was all over. 'Anyway, you wouldn't be gatecrashing. You'd be with me.'

'I would?'

'Course you would. Isn't that why I'm inviting you? I'll pick you up around seven.'

31

On Saturday afternoon Cathy was drooped over a chair, clothes flung all around her, her hands up to her face.

'Help me find something to wear,' she said, in despair. 'I look grotesque in everything I possess. I need some sexy new clothes, and this short hair doesn't help. Oh, why did I get it cut?'

'It's grown quite a lot and it's lovely. Try something on and let me have a look.'

She put on clothes she'd had before her marriage then flung them off again, because they were all too tight now. 'I won't bother going,' she said. 'I really haven't got a thing to wear.'

'But you *have* to go. Louis's invited you. He'll be upset if you don't. Come on, try something of mine on.'

She finally settled on my black palazzo pants, which had a drawstring waist. The pale blue shirt she teamed them with was a size too small, accentuating her new boobs, giving her curves she'd never had before. I spent ages doing her makeup, mascara and lip-gloss, then backcombing her hair to make it fuller round her face.

'Now,' I said, pleased with the effect, turning her towards the mirror.

'Oh, my God! I look like I've been plugged into an electric socket!' she yelped, staring at herself.

'You look terrific.'

'Terrifying, you mean.' She smoothed down my handiwork with her fingertips.

'Thanks,' I said crossly.

She returned to the mirror, twisting and turning before it. She looked gorgeous, and I told her so.

'Not as gorgeous as you,' she said encouragingly, knowing my real reluctance to go to this party.

Louis arrived.

Cathy came down the stairs, stood before him and said, 'How do I look?' as if his approval really mattered, her years of independence, of roaming the world, falling from her like a cloak.

'Beautiful,' he confirmed, delight in his eyes.

Touched by his attention she was excited, her cheeks tinted with the breath of romance in the air.

Louis took her arm and led her out of the house. All her loneliness was forgotten, for tonight her troubles would be swept aside.

For tonight she would forget the past, and her uncertain future.

The Manor was throbbing with a glittering crowd. Louis led Cathy inside, introducing her proudly to everyone as they proceeded through the hall. I stood still, my eyes wandering among the glamorous groups dressed in black and silver, sipping champagne. Excitement ran high among the film crew, as they clapped one another on the back. Champagne popped and fizzed. Everyone was enjoying the party, laughing, talking, drinking, the happy atmosphere surging through the house.

Sam, the sound recordist, brought me a glass of champagne. 'Here's to having a good time,' he said, raising his glass to mine.

Louis looked triumphant: In his developing romance with Cathy he was losing his brashness.

Then Natalie made a dramatic entrance, Rick close behind her. Her gauzy silver lace dress left her shoulders bare. With her hair in plaits, her feet in light silver sandals, there was a fairy quality to her. Here she was, rejoicing in her beauty, using every opportunity to show herself off. It was as if she was saying, 'I'm the greatest person here, and I know it.'

'Time to party,' she quipped to everyone

347

who gathered round her, laughing, clamouring for her attention.

'Surely not without Hugo,' said Louis, looking annoyed. 'Where is he?'

Hugo walked in then and went to stand beside Natalie.

'There you are,' she said to him, making a tremendous effort to appear casual.

Then she was talking too fast, Rick playing along brilliantly with her. Hugo looked uneasy with her false gaiety, which brought a chill to the air. He looked as if he'd have liked to say to her, 'Do you have to make such an exhibition of yourself?'

She went further, telling jokes, angry with Hugo because he refused to be part of her game.

Gradually he pulled further away from her, remaining poised and aloof, expressing his distaste without words, while the other men shouted with laughter.

'You were born to be on stage, Natalie,' said Rick. 'Wasn't she, Hugo?'

Hugo ignored him.

Resentful, Natalie said, 'Hugo, you should try to be polite to Rick. At least answer him when he speaks to you.'

Wishing I were thousands of miles away, I kept out of the way.

Louis didn't seem to notice, but Sophie,

her eye on Sam, said to me, 'Hugo doesn't seem himself. What's wrong with him?'

'Natalie,' I said, keeping a stiff upper lip as they posed for photographs for the national newspapers.

'She's a bitch,' said Sophie, watching her posture for the cameras.

'Need a drink?' Cathy asked.

'Badly.'

We scuttled off to the makeshift bar in the library. It was no longer a peaceful place for a quiet read or a smoke. It was stuffed with people: groups of girls chatted to one another, their glasses held aloft, glancing at the men who stood talking together, ignoring them. Not for long, though, because the girls became daring, sidling up to them, laughing.

Supper seemed endless. Oysters were devoured with champagne and Guinness, and there were tiny sandwiches, bite-size savouries and cocktail sausages on sticks.

We sipped our drinks, everyone talking around us, then Sophie went off in search of Sam. I wanted to go but Louis insisted we stay a little longer. He was going to make the most of this party. There would be other parties at the Manor, given by Hugo and Natalie, but as far as Louis was concerned tonight was his night.

It was a night to remember. A night to be

relived in the years to come. Louis had schemed and plotted and planned to put the Manor on the map, and tonight he was going to enjoy the fruits of his labour. He'd worked his magic on it, and now he held sway over it, as if the place was his own, and Hugo his best friend.

Natalie was everywhere, first with this one, then with that one, giving her all, Rick at her side, as attentive as a detective.

'Well, dear,' said Aunt Flo, coming towards me in a lilac dress that brought out the colour of her eyes. 'It's been a wonderful evening, hasn't it, Jenny? Though, mind you, some of the dresses are hideous, don't you think?'

'We're off,' said Uncle Tom. 'I know Hugo won't mind, he's exhausted too.'

'I don't have any sympathy for him,' said Aunt Flo. 'He brought it on himself. All calculated for the money.' She continued, 'He looks so miserable.' For once she kept her voice down.

'He had to do it to ensure the survival of the Manor,' I said.

'It'll only skim the top off his debts. He'll have to wait until he lets the cottages for the real money,' said Uncle Tom knowledgeably.

Someone started playing the piano, and everyone was taking to the floor, dancing energetically.

Suddenly Hugo was beside me. 'I haven't had a chance to get to you all evening,' he said. 'Will you dance with me?'

'No, thanks.'

Taken aback he said, 'You don't hate me, do you, Jenny? I never meant it to happen. I must see you again.' His voice close to my ear set my blood racing, obliterating the pain he'd caused me.

I shouldn't be thinking of him like this. It's not fair to Natalie or to me.

He moved his head back slightly, his eyes meeting mine as he said, 'We're still friends?'

'Friends?'

'Aren't we?' he asked.

Was that what I was to him? A friend? That was something I never wanted to be. The hurt twisted in me like a knife, almost choking me. I said, 'We were never friends. Bob Crowe is your friend, Louis's your friend. I'm not. You have Natalie now. She'll make you a wonderful wife.'

I'd said it. The pain I'd grown used to seeing in his eyes was back. All pretence was gone, leaving us both separate and alone once more in frightening reality.

'Hugo!' Natalie was calling him.

His eyes never leaving my face, he said, 'Excuse me, please.' He was gone, his back stiff as he moved among the dancers.

My throat constricted as if I was about to burst into tears. Let him go to his beautiful bride-to-be. What did I care? If he had stayed to explain or argue I'd have died. I was so tired, oh, so tired, and my feet ached. Everything was suddenly so awful that I wanted to shriek. But I couldn't. I had to stand my ground as someone called for a song from Natalie.

An inspired performer, she couldn't resist the request. Eyes glittering, she moved to the centre of the room and stood beside the piano, the light from the chandelier framing her oval face and plunging her into an eerie silver glow. She began to sing:

> 'A mountain steep,
> I'd dart and leap,
> Through seas I'd hurry,
> Let nothing stand in my way,
> To get you.'
>
> If ruthless storms,
> Flung me down,
> I'd headlong go,
> To get you,
> To get you.'

Eyes shut, she dropped her head forward, her voice rising, her body moving to the rhythm.

'I've learned to fight,
For what is right,
You're all I want,
And I've got you.
I've got you.'

Her voice grew louder as she gave herself up to her song, sweeping us off on a tide, Hugo's presence a fierce undercurrent. I looked to my left. There he was, so close, so grave, gazing into my eyes, his own dark and glittering mysteriously. Was it my imagination, or did he wink at me? I couldn't think.

A burst of wild applause followed. And Natalie's singing snatched the party from Hugo, to make it her own. But behind it all a deep sense of resentment lurked, more powerful than Natalie and the happiness she was so desperate to convey.

I didn't see Hugo again until the party was nearly over.

Everyone was saying goodbye, profuse in their thanks and praise. The last of the cars were driving off and Natalie was going down the steps in the rain, surrounded by a group of people, calling over her shoulder, 'Leave the door open. I'll shut it when I come in.'

Hugo followed me out. Suddenly we found ourselves alone in the cold wet garden. Self-conscious, I stood stiffly not knowing what to say, knowing that things between Hugo and Natalie were at breaking-point, and things between us were at breaking-point too.

'Jenny.' Rain was plastering down his hair, his dinner jacket was getting soaked and his eyes were intense, forlorn. Seeing him like that, I loved him all the more. 'I'd like to talk to you.' There was anguish in his voice.

Pain, sadness, defeat, fear, and regret were written on his face. His Manor and his guests had been marshalled in Natalie's favour. Never would she crawl away in surrender now. No, she would go only if it suited her, in her own time, not at Hugo's insistence.

'I don't want to talk.' I walked on.

'Jenny! Wait!'

I kept going.

'Jenny!' It was an exasperated Hugo who caught up with me and swung me round to face him. His face was wretched as he said, 'Jenny, listen! I've let you down. I've failed you and I'm sorry.'

Without warning he kissed me, a dangerous, delicious kiss I would never forget.

'Oh!' I moved back from him, taking control of myself. 'I must go.'

'Don't go. We must talk about us.'

'I can't talk to you. I've tried and tried!' I

354

looked into his strained face, saw the pain in his eyes too.

'Can't you let me explain?' He was pleading. 'You see . . . ' He touched my shoulder.

'No, I don't want to see.' My hands were shaking as I faced him in the gloom, the falling rain a curtain between us. 'I don't want to see, and I don't want to know. I've had too much champagne and I'm tired.'

I was gone, stumbling across the grass before he could catch hold of me again. He was calling me, his voice crying out like a voice in the wilderness. Into the excruciating silence that followed came Louis and Cathy. They stood talking to Hugo. I watched Louis lean towards him, say something in his ear, and they moved back towards the house.

I went and stood by Louis's car, looking up at the huge, dark Manor, shadowy in the moonlight, bidding it farewell, knowing I would never see it again, sad at the parting. I couldn't think straight. I wanted him so dreadfully and he was out of reach. Did he feel the same way about me? That strange, perilous kiss had seemed to say so.

But what did he feel about me when he was away from me? Did he feel the awful longing that could never be sated because he didn't have the strength to do something about it?

It was at that precise moment that I saw them at the side of the Manor, near the trees, their arms round each other. Silhouetted in the light of the moon they kissed, drew apart, then came together again, prolonging their embrace, as if they couldn't bear to be parted.

Oh, my God! My hand flew to my mouth to stifle my gasp of shock. I stayed there rooted to the spot, staring at them across the lawn, the mist from the mountains descending. I wasn't prepared for *this* truth.

Rick of all people! He wasn't her type. But there they were, kissing before my eyes. So she's been skulking off with him all the time, I thought incredulously. It was Rick and Natalie, not Natalie and Hugo. While they stood talking I studied them as if in a dream, thinking of their blatant nerve in carrying on like that outside the Manor. All right, it was dark, but what they were doing was dangerous.

Finally Rick got into his car and drove off. Natalie, a sliver of silver in the moonlight, ran back across the grass, her dress clouding around her, her plaits swinging. I wanted to grab her and say, 'Stop! Enough! Go away and never come back.' But it was useless. She would always come back, if only to drive Hugo mad. Up the steps and in through the great doors she went. They closed behind her, and just then the whole world seemed empty, all dreams shattered.

I wouldn't mention what I'd seen. No need to breathe a word of it to anyone. Why would anyone need to know? As far as Natalie was concerned, the night had gone well. For anyone to see what I had seen had been beyond her scheming plan. Suddenly the doors opened again. Cathy and Louis emerged, Louis's arm protectively around her.

'Sorry about that,' Louis said, coming towards me, opening the car door. 'Natalie locked us in by mistake. We were having a quick look at Hugo's golf-course plans.'

That night I stayed with Cathy. 'Why are you standing there?' she asked, coming into my room to say goodnight. 'You'll catch cold. Aren't you getting into bed? What's the matter, Jenny?'

Stiff with the cold, my feet like ice, I said, 'I'm frozen.'

'Come on, into bed.' She helped me undress, got me into my nightdress, went downstairs and returned with a hot-water bottle, and a cup of tea.

Climbing into bed with me she pulled the duvet around us. We talked for a long time about the adventures of the night, her arms holding me, patient until the tears dried.

'The thought of seeing Hugo ever again is unbearable,' I told her, and I made a decision, there and then: I would not see him again.

32

Next morning we went to the supermarket. Cathy, huddled into her coat and wearing a woolly hat, was energetic and cheerful. Afterwards we stumbled into the gate lodge under the weight of the grocery bags, laughing at some joke. Louis was coming for lunch and Cathy cooked chicken with a lemon and herb sauce, a Robbie Williams CD blaring in the background. She swayed to the rhythm, interrupting herself every so often to tell me something that had just occurred to her about her workmates in Australia, or an idea she had had for an interior design. I made a salad, set the table and opened the wine. Together we moved around in harmony, Cathy lost in the beat of the music, her face glistening with sweat under the kitchen light.

'Delicious,' she said, tasting the sauce. 'This reminds me of our adolescence, just the two of us together. Remember us sneaking off to be on our own, no interfering adults?' There was a look of pure innocence on her face. 'I can't wait to get away from Coolbawn and Mum.'

Louis arrived with wine and vodka. Not the

businessman any more, he took over, pouring drinks, organising the chairs, talking to Cathy. She told him of her dream to have her own interior-design business, how she wanted to specialise in commercial assignments.

'You're young and pretty. It'll be difficult for you to get the big boys to take you seriously,' he said, shaking his head.

Cathy bit her lip. 'So, how do I get started?' she asked, frustrated.

'Get a few small, worthwhile assignments under your belt first, build up contacts, make a name for yourself in Galway. Convince the big boys you can do it. It's the only way to make them take you seriously.'

'I'm as good as any of them.'

'You have to be ten times better because you're a woman.'

'I want to study more, take an advanced degree.'

'You've already got a good degree,' I protested.

'You know enough,' Louis said. 'Now you must act as if you know you're good enough.'

'I can't wait to get going. I'm so bored at the moment.'

'One step at a time,' Louis said, and told her of premises he thought might be suitable. He said he'd make enquiries for her. 'Landlords are cowboys, most of them. You want to know who you're dealing with.'

Louis was solicitous of Cathy, touching her in silent support. She told him about her former clients, their likes and dislikes. They discussed modern designs and patterns. The talk took a serious downturn when Louis said, 'But what about the baby? How'll you manage when it's born?'

'I haven't worked that out yet,' Cathy said simply, 'but I'm sure Aunt Mary'll help.'

Louis said, 'It must be awful for you having to go it alone.'

'I don't really mind,' Cathy said, resting her head on the arm of the sofa.

'You're bound to feel different with another life growing inside you,' he said.

'I get nervous thinking about it.' She giggled.

'But isn't it awful for you, alone here?' Louis said again, looking around.

'I'm not really alone. Mum and Aunt Mary are up at the house, and we'll be moving to Bluebell Cottage as soon as it's ready.'

'What about the birth?'

'I'm dreading it. I'm a coward when it comes to pain, aren't I, Jenny?' she asked.

'No worse than anyone else,' I said.

'You won't be on your own for the birth, will you?'

'I hadn't thought that far ahead.'

'You mustn't be alone. I'll come and be with you, if you'd like me to,' he offered. 'I'd be brilliant at holding your hand, mopping your brow. I did a first-aid course at college. I thought about doing medicine, you know, but — '

'You didn't have the brains,' I interjected.

'Jenny! Don't be so rude,' said Cathy.

'Only teasing.'

Ignoring me, Louis said, 'Oh, I wouldn't like to intrude. It's only if you'd like me to be there.'

Cathy became serious. 'It's sweet of you, Louis,' she said, her eyes shining with pleasure.

'Listen to you two. Anyone would think you were about to give birth any minute.'

I left them to wash the dishes, Cathy giggling wildly at the notion of Louis being there to help deliver the baby, Louis teasing her about becoming a mother. For the time being I was left out. They had discovered something between them that didn't include anyone else. When I returned they were talking in low, intimate voices. Louis's hand was resting on Cathy's stomach.

'You won't feel it kicking yet, it's too soon,' she was saying.

'Well, you just take it easy. Just lie there and rest, and if you need anything I'll be right back to get it for you,' Louis said, and went to make a phone call.

'I've never known Louis to lighten up so much,' I said, 'or seen him so happy. You're good for him.'

'Do you think so?'

'He's falling in love with you.'

Cathy couldn't hide her delight as she said, 'Really? Do you think so?'

Louis came back into the room, glowing, saying, 'Come on, Jenny, let's get going before I change my mind and stay here for good.'

Cathy laughed.

'It's been a perfect day,' Louis said to her, taking her hands in his. 'Why don't I come over soon again and take you out to dinner, just the two of us?'

On the journey back to Dublin he said, 'I know she makes light of it but I still think it's hard for her in that gate lodge all by herself.'

'That's the way she wants it. It's difficult for her up at the house with Aunt Lilian. She thinks Cathy's wrong not to stay in her marriage.'

'I suppose you think it's wrong of her to get involved with me.'

'It's up to Cathy to decide how she's going to live her life.'

'What brought the two of you so close

363

together?' he asked, curiosity in his smile.

'We practically grew up together.'

'There's more to it than that. I grew up with my brother but we're not close like you two.'

'Call it a conspiracy of women.'

'Hmm. That sounds suspicious.'

'We talk to each other about our feelings.'

'Ah. What sort of feelings?' he asked.

'Mainly about what it's like to be women living in a male-dominated world,' I said, to annoy him.

'That's a pretty ambiguous answer.'

'You don't think I'm going to tell you our secrets?'

'I'm jealous.' Thoughtfully he said, 'Tell me about Cathy's marriage. What did the bastard do to her?'

'Why do you assume he's a bastard?'

'Aren't all men bastards?'

I laughed. 'Coming from you that's a joke — but I can't talk about Cathy's marriage. It's her business. She'll tell you herself, in her own good time. I know she will. She wants to, when you get to know each other better.'

'The fact that she's a married woman doesn't put me off, you know.'

'I gathered that from the amount of attention you were paying her.'

'But I'm not going to get involved with the

moralities of the situation.' He was adamant. 'She's making her own arrangements with her husband, and the arrangements she makes with me, whatever they might be, will be different.'

'I agree with you. Just because her marriage failed doesn't mean she can't have another chance. But she may not be ready to make a commitment yet. You have to understand, Louis, that she's going through a bad patch.'

'I know that, but I still think it's not right for a woman like her to be on her own at a time like this. Or at any time. She needs a man. Someone to love her and take care of her.'

'Someone like you.'

'Yes.'

If Cathy had done nothing else for him she had given him a wonderful day. Everything she had done and said had charmed him.

'Believe it or not she's coping admirably,' I said. 'I just hope it works out at Bluebell Cottage.'

'Time will tell,' was all he said.

33

Life in the office got back to normal. Well, on the surface it did. I worked harder than ever and tried not to think about Hugo or his anguished face as I left the party. I tried not to think of us in the Manor that first summer evening, or of the day we went to Galway and walked along the narrow streets, stopping on the bridge to look at the river. I also kept away from Connemara to give myself a chance to get over him.

Cathy phoned regularly with a progress report on her pregnancy.

'You're obviously doing well,' I said.

'You too,' she said, hearing my cheerful voice.

I didn't tell her that I couldn't sleep, that I took sleeping pills that gave me terrible dreams. Or that I had decided to change my life. Maybe I would go to America or Australia for a year. Other people had left and survived. Why couldn't I? As long as I worked for Louis I'd be ducking and diving, doing somersaults to avoid Hugo. I wouldn't hear about him for weeks, months maybe, and then, one day, Louis would come roaring into my office saying, 'Hugo Hunter was on the phone. He wants us to do this or that,' and we'd be off again, Louis expecting his enthusiasm to carry me along. But I was dying inside. I thought about Cathy and her baby, and thought that it would be all right to leave her. Aunt Mary would take care of her, and Louis, too, by the looks of things.

Sam, the sound recordist, phoned me, inviting me to a party next Saturday night. I told him I'd think about it and let him know. Why not? He was good-looking, and he had a nice body. I phoned him back. We arranged to meet in Searson's in Baggot Street. There, he introduced me to his friends in the film world, all dressed in worn jeans and bizarre-coloured sweatshirts, some with beards, all talking passionately about film as if they'd invented it. After Sam had negotiated his way to the bar and back, we sat apart from the others and he talked about the various locations abroad where he had worked.

'That's my other great passion,' he said.

'Travel?' I asked.

He nodded. 'I've been everywhere,' he said, and told me about the therapeutic value of backpacking between shoots in scenic places like the Swiss Alps, where they had made a toothpaste commercial, and Lake Garda, where they had filmed one for swimsuits. All night we talked about films, discovering while we danced that we shared a passion for classic black-and-white movies like *Casablanca* and *Brief Encounter*. The time flew by. I liked Sam's dedication to his profession. I also liked the way his eyes crinkled at the edges when he smiled, and he smiled a lot.

As we said goodbye, the taxi engine humming beside us, Sam cleared his throat, and said, 'I've got the *Casablanca* video if you'd like to see it some night.'

I hesitated. 'Maybe in a couple of weeks' time,' I said.

Touched by his gentleness, I was trying to find a way not to hurt his feelings.

'No pressure. It's up to you.' He smiled. 'Give me a ring any time you feel like coming over. We'll arrange it.'

★ ★ ★

'Were you out with Sam on Saturday night?' Sophie asked me, first thing on Monday morning.

'Yes, I was. Why?'

'You might have told me,' she said peevishly.

'Can I not go on a date without everyone knowing about it?'

'I'm not everyone,' she slammed at me. 'I

just happen to be your friend, and you know I fancy Sam.'

'Well, I'm sorry but I was the one he asked out. What was I supposed to do? Say, 'Sorry, Sam, I can't go out with you because Sophie fancies you and she's my friend'?'

'Something like that.'

'Don't be daft. If he'd wanted to ask you out he would have. Anyway, it was only a date. I'm not starting an affair with him.'

'No. You have Hugo in your life. He might be weak but he's all you want.'

Furious, she refused to speak to me. Louis, in a foul mood because Cathy had put him off visiting her, blew me out in front of everyone. 'Jenny, you're not listening. I asked you to find me the Kitten Soft file an hour ago.'

'Tell him go shove his head up his arse,' Charlie advised.

I kept calm, didn't answer him. That evening I went back to the flat cursing Louis, Sophie and the whole ruddy office. I was getting nowhere in this job except right up Louis's nose. Sophie would have a massive huff on for weeks over my date with Sam — and Sam? I didn't want to get involved with him, or anyone else for that matter, because I didn't want to have to extricate myself from the mess in a couple of months' time when it would be over.

★ ★ ★

Time was flying by, and one day Mum rang to remind me that it was my birthday in a few days' time, on 21 April, and to ask me what present I would like.

'I haven't even thought about it. I'll let you know,' I said, not wanting to be reminded.

'We could meet on Saturday morning. Adam's going to his granny's for the weekend so I'm free until twelve.'

'Great.'

'You're quiet. What's up?'

'Nothing. Just a bit tired.'

'So, what about your birthday? Louis taking you somewhere nice?'

'Louis! He's my boss, Mum, not my boyfriend.' Not Twenty bloody Questions again. 'He doesn't even know about my birthday.'

'But I thought he'd taken a shine to you.'

'He's fallen hook, line and sinker for Cathy.'

'Cathy? But she's pregnant.'

'So! Some men prefer pregnant women.'

'Jenny! Don't be so disgusting.'

'It's true. I read somewhere — '

'You scare them off! You know that? That's what you do, you scare them off.' She sounded furious.

'No, I don't. I haven't met Mr Right yet, that's all.'

'You wouldn't know Mr Right if he jumped up and bit you.'

'That's hardly likely to happen.'

'When I think of the opportunities you let go by! Time's ticking on, you know. You'll be thirty before you know it.'

I held the phone away from me.

'Anyway, how are you going to celebrate your birthday?' she squawked. 'We could have a party here, invite a few of your close friends.'

'No, thanks. I'll be in Connemara. Cathy wants me to take her shopping to Galway. She wants to get a few bits and pieces together in case she gets a sudden call,' I said. 'Thanks all the same, Mum.'

After she rang off I gazed into the mirror, checking the wrinkles, the bags under my eyes, the sagging jawline for signs of further ageing. That's what I'd like for my birthday, a face-lift. I tried to imagine what Dad would have to say to that. I drowned my sorrows in a vodka and Diet Coke then sank into a hot, lavender-scented bath, before retiring to bed with a copy of *Hello! magazine*.

★ ★ ★

The next day Louis was in a serious mood when I went into his office. 'I hear Natalie's in New York,' he said.

'Oh, really?'

'Apparently she's making a video of her new single there with Rick and the band. Strange, they're always going off together for rehearsals, concerts and tours.'

'That's what show-business people do all the time. He is her manager, after all.'

He thought for a minute. 'Odd, though, how he cropped up at the party. There he was, bowled over by her, hanging on her every word, dancing with her. Odd that Hugo didn't object.'

'He may not have cared.'

'Or he might be hiding from the truth.'

'What are you getting at?'

'You don't think there's anything going on between them?'

'Like what?'

'Like an affair.'

I stared at him, flummoxed, not wanting to say what I'd seen.

'I don't have a clue. It's been a while since that party.'

'There's something so false about the way she bitches about being away all the time, and being homesick for Hugo and all that crap.'

'We gazed at one another.

'Do you think she's cheating on Hugo? I mean, she's got the perfect alibi.' Louis looked directly at me.

'Rick's not her type. He's a bit rough round the edges for her,' I said, trying to put him off, I don't know why. Anyway, if that's the case why doesn't she go off with him? She's much stronger now, a real toughie. She doesn't need Hugo any more.'

'Hugo's got the Manor.'

'And a load of debts.'

'Ah, but his potential to make money is enormous, and she's virtually penniless.'

'What?'

'So I heard. Natalie's career has gone down the pan since her accident. In fact, I'd say her accident had more to do with her waning popularity than anything Hugo did or said,' Louis observed.

'But I thought she was rich. What about the new album she's just released, and this video she's making, and everything? What about all those tours abroad? She's famous, for God's sake. Her last single was a hit.'

'Her single is a hit, yes, but her album's a flop. So was her last tour. Cancellations all over the place.'

'She did come back early.'

'Why do you think she wanted to be in our commercial? It isn't exactly her scene, now, is it? She knew we'd be sending it to European tourist boards and the States. I mean, she didn't charge us a penny for her appearance.'

'I thought that was to help Hugo flog the Manor. It came across as if she was doing us all a favour by being in it.'

'Doing her career a favour. She wouldn't want anyone to know how far down she's dropped. She's spent a fortune trying to resuscitate it. After the accident she didn't get any work because the record companies lost faith in her, mainly because of her erratic behaviour. She's broke from having to pay for her own publicity. That's why she's off making this video. It's a desperate bid to claw back her fans,' Louis said.

'I'd no idea. She comes across as so successful.'

'That's just her image. The reality's different. Not that she can keep up the pretence for much longer.'

'I wonder if Hugo knows the truth.'

'He knows. Why do you think he didn't object to her being in the commercial? He's probably bailing her out even as we speak. But he doesn't know about Rick and her.'

'There might be nothing to it. Why risk

Hugo and that lovely house if she's such a gold-digger?'

'I don't know, but someone ought to have a word with him about what's going on,' Louis said.

'There's no proof.'

'If I find out I'll go and see Hugo myself. Put him straight.'

'What?' I gasped.

'I owe it to him, Jenny. He's been a good friend to me.'

34

Bluebell Cottage had changed beyond all recognition. It was delightful. In its new coat of blue paint it stood out against the mountains. Two bow windows had been built on to the south face of the house, overlooking the garden, the surrounding fields and the mountains.

The mood of spring was everywhere. Birds whistled. A sharp wind rose and fell ruffling the bluebells, and wild cherry embroidered the green boundary hedge with its snowy blossoms.

This was the life from which Cathy could never escape. It was the world where she belonged. Aunt Mary and she were at the door to welcome me, their arms entwined, their excitement at my arrival in their faces.

Inside, the house was lovely, with its creamy walls, its polished wooden floors, its shining white bathroom full of delicious scents, and its soft beds made up with the finest pastel-coloured sheets, and matching curtains at the windows. In her own way, Aunt Mary had provided luxury for Cathy and herself.

'I can't believe it's the same place,' I said, as I sank into a deep sofa.

Cathy was changing before my very eyes. Away from the shadow of Aunt Lilian she was no longer the difficult girl that her mother thought her. She was rounding into a mature woman.

'Has Aunt Lilian seen it yet?' I asked.

'No. We're keeping out of her way as much as we can.'

'Has she warmed to the idea of the baby?'

She shook her head. 'She can't stand to look at me with this bump.'

'You look beautiful,' I said.

Delighted, Cathy said, 'Wait until I get enormous. I'm dreading it. I'm going to get slower and slower as I get bigger and bigger. It's going to be awful. I'll have to wear huge tents of things to hide it.'

'We'll go shopping. Some sexy clothes to show off your legs,' I consoled her.

'Louis says he wants to take care of me.' She smiled. 'In fact, he says he'd like to marry me some day.'

'How would you feel about that?'

'It's far too early to say. But Louis is so kind, and I trust him.'

Since he'd taken up with Cathy, Louis's obtuseness had vanished. Sitting by the fire, her face glowing, she spoke calmly about him. 'I'm happy the way things are here with Aunt Mary looking after me.'

'That's all right for now while you need someone to take care of you, but you won't always want to live like this. And Louis's patience won't last for ever.'

'I realise that,' she said.

Louis was hardly able to endure the strain of their separations while she was calm about them. But part of her appeal to him was in the way she managed to keep him at bay, yet never letting him quite out of her sight. He accepted this reluctantly because he loved her. They were two people together, even when they were apart.

'What does Aunt Mary think of this romance?'

'She likes Louis, and she's quite happy to watch and wait, provided I take things slowly.'

Sitting by the fire I felt her happiness. She was becoming more confident and less vulnerable with Louis. With him she felt a stronger current of excitement than she'd ever experienced with Ned, but she didn't want to dwell on it yet — she had no idea where it might lead. Also, she'd no idea of the emancipation she'd undergone since her marriage with Ned. This time, without fully realising it, she wasn't prepared to be captured and imprisoned like a bird in a cage.

'What really counts now is whether its love or infatuation,' she said.

'It's love on Louis's part. I've never known him so happy, and he's much easier to work with.'

'Good,' laughed Cathy. She became serious suddenly. 'I have to stop living haphazardly like this without planning in advance.'

'What do you mean?'

'I'm going to have a child in June, which Mum will never forgive me for, and I'm living out here with poor Aunt Mary whom I have no right to trouble.'

Aunt Mary, coming in, said. 'You mustn't think like that, Cathy. I'll always have a place for you here, and the longer you can be with me the better. I know it's difficult for you now but you have plenty of time after the baby is born to make plans.'

Cathy didn't contradict her. But I suspected she was thinking about getting a place of her own, perhaps her desire for freedom and Louis uppermost in her mind.

'And Aunt Lilian,' I asked. 'What do you think she'll say when she comes to visit?'

'I don't know.'

Cathy was dreading the next outburst from her mother, but all she said to me was, 'There's bound to be trouble yet.'

On Saturday I was on my own, Cathy at

the market, Aunt Mary out on the farm, when the doorbell rang. I nearly jumped out of my skin. I peered out from behind the curtain in the sitting room and recognised Aunt Lilian's old felt gardening hat. I shrank back, panic-stricken, casting around for somewhere to hide, wishing I could run out of the back door and down to the meadow. The doorbell rang again, violently this time. I had no alternative but to answer it.

'Aunt Lilian, what a nice surprise!' I said.

'Hello, Jenny. Where's everyone?' she asked, marching in.

'Aunt Mary's out on the farm. Cathy has gone to deliver eggs and butter to the market.'

'Good God! What a nice place.' She stood looking around, her hands in the deep pockets of her coat.

'Let me take your coat,' I said, realising she was nervous. 'Can I get you a cup of coffee or a drink?'

'I'll wait for Cathy,' she said, ill at ease, wandering around, me trailing after her.

The house was warm and flowers were everywhere. Cathy's favourite blend of Jamaica coffee was percolating, but there was no sign of Cathy returning. When she did appear she bade Aunt Lilian a quick hello, and stood leafing through a magazine, a shaft of sun turning her hair to spun gold, and highlighting her mother's pale-faced disapproval.

Miffed, Aunt Lilian said, 'So I said to myself, 'Why don't you drive to Bluebell Cottage and see it for yourself?' Little did I know I'd be kept waiting while you were out.'

Cathy, knowing it did Aunt Lilian good to jibe at her, let it go, and went into the kitchen. Her mother followed her.

'You've been keeping to yourself,' said Aunt Lilian. 'You haven't been to see me since you left. Anything could have happened to me.'

'Like what?' Cathy asked.

Aunt Lilian pursed her lips. 'A great deal can go wrong when you're living alone on a farm. My arthritis has been at me, and I lost some sheep. They fell down Moran's cliff. I wake up in the mornings and I don't know what's going to happen next,' she said huffily. 'Of course you don't care.'

'You're always so down on me I thought you'd prefer me to keep away.'

Aunt Lilian looked around. 'Such a lady you're becoming, snug in this place with good land all around you, and little to do while the rest of us slave our fingers to the bone.'

Cathy gave her mother a look of animosity

before she sank into her chair. 'I do my share,' she said.

'I'm amazed at you going about in public like that, I really am,' Aunt Lilian said.

'Why?' Cathy asked, turning away from her mother in a hopeless attempt to conceal the thickening lines of her body. 'I'm determined to lead a normal life right up until the birth, if possible.'

'You're not fit. Anyway, it's awful behaviour. Haven't you brought enough disgrace to your family without bringing attention to yourself at every hand's turn?'

Cathy lifted her hand to her eyes. 'I am fit.' Uncovering her face she added, 'Nobody took any notice of me today.'

I was thinking of the long weeks and months ahead, and the scourge of Aunt Lilian whom she thought she'd escaped.

Aunt Lilian said lightly, 'Any other news?'

'Not much,' Cathy said, in an impersonal way, displeased with her mother's unexpected visit, and desperately hoping, I suspected, that Louis wouldn't arrive while she was there.

Aunt Lilian stood erect, fingering her wedding ring, her lips pursed. Flushed with annoyance she walked round the sitting room touching the polished surfaces of the new furniture, the loss of Aunt Mary at

Coolbawn a sharp pain, though she wouldn't admit it.

The truth of the matter was that Aunt Mary wouldn't let Aunt Lilian share much of her life any more, and Cathy didn't listen to her complaints. She saw them as self-indulgence.

Aunt Lilian gazed into the oval mirror over the fireplace. 'I need my roots done,' she said. 'It wouldn't do to let myself go just because I'm on my own.'

When Aunt Mary returned she greeted Aunt Lilian graciously, and poured her a glass of sherry.

'It's good to see you, Lilian,' she said.

Aunt Lilian drank quickly, the sherry relaxing her. She sat listening to Aunt Mary's account of her trips around the shops on her buying expeditions as if it were a thrilling story.

'I think I'll go for a little stroll in the garden,' Aunt Lilian said. 'Come on, Cathy. You can show me around.'

Cathy rose with unfamiliar slowness, said, 'I don't feel well.' She sank into her chair again, her face white, her hands sweating.

'Oh, Cathy!' I ran to her.

She gasped, 'I hope it's not the baby coming.'

'She's in labour,' said Aunt Lilian.

'It's too early,' said Cathy, taking deep breaths.

'You'll be all right,' I said, and phoned Dr Kelly.

When he came downstairs he said, 'Everything's normal, apart from her blood pressure. It's slightly raised. Has anything occurred out of the ordinary?'

'Nothing,' said Aunt Lilian. 'Except, of course, she's always had a tendency to race around doing lots of things at once. She's highly strung, you know.'

'The baby's probably turning,' said Dr Kelly. 'No running around until after the birth. Complete rest is vital.'

'Will she be all right?' asked Aunt Mary anxiously.

Dr Kelly said that Cathy, being only a few weeks from her confinement, should stay in bed for a few days.

'She should be in her own home,' said Aunt Lilian.

'She's staying here.' Aunt Mary stood firm, supported by Dr Kelly who shook his head at Aunt Lilian.

'Arguments of any kind aren't good for her. You must not trouble her.'

He spoke a few more words to Aunt Mary, then left.

Fuming, Aunt Lilian was heading for the

stairs and Cathy's room when Aunt Mary stopped her. 'My dear, you must go now and leave her alone. I'll manage everything.'

Aunt Lilian gazed at her. 'I will not go. You're not qualified to take care of Cathy.'

Unruffled, Aunt Mary said, 'You must go now, Lilian, and let her rest.'

'What impertinence,' said Aunt Lilian, 'denying me the right to my own daughter.'

But the pack was turning on Aunt Lilian. 'I'll walk you to your car,' I said.

Speechless, clutching her car keys like a lifeline, she stalked out. Before she drove off she called. 'I'll be back to find out how you're looking after her.'

After a long sleep Cathy felt better. Aunt Mary said, 'You're bound to feel exhausted after your mother's visit.'

'I wish she wouldn't call,' said Cathy.

'The trouble is, she doesn't realise you've grown up.'

'You're right. And I should have been more polite to her.'

'No one person could have put up with her,' said Aunt Mary. Looking out of the window she said, 'Here come the chickens for their food.'

'I'll feed them,' said Cathy, rising.

'Nonsense,' said Aunt Mary. 'You stay there and rest.'

'But I love feeding them,' Cathy protested.

Watching them, I knew that these two never could be parted for long because of their love.

Much later Louis arrived looking happy and casual in sweater and jeans. He kissed Aunt Mary's cheek.

'Where's Cathy?' he asked.

'She took a bad turn earlier and she's resting,' I said, leading him upstairs.

'Cathy!' he exclaimed. He went to her as if she was all that mattered to him in the world.

'I'm all right now,' Cathy assured him.

He sat in her bedroom for the rest of the evening, his hand in hers.

When I popped in, Cathy was sitting up in bed her hair soft and feathery around her face, her bare arms smooth against the soft peach of her pyjamas. Louis was leaning over her, his head close to hers. Seeing me standing in the doorway Cathy blushed.

'You're growing more beautiful by the day,' he said.

'Well, there's certainly more of me,' she joked.

'All the more for me to love.' He laughed.

When eventually he came downstairs to go home, he said, 'Don't let her do anything that might make it come. You stay on another day or two, Jenny, to keep an eye on her. We'll manage in the office.' The old arrogant Louis had gone.

Bluebell Cottage was isolated from neighbours and no one knew of Louis's comings and goings, that sometimes he stayed in the guest bedroom. Or that Aunt Mary went out of her way to provide him with lovely meals, no questions asked. Aunt Mary had hidden herself away in the years after her brother's death, when she could have had a man and marriage. She regretted this now, and was determined that the same wouldn't happen to Cathy.

35

On my return to Dublin I called to see Mum.

'Your dad's not here,' she said, disgruntled. 'He never seems to be at home much any more.'

'How is he?' I asked.

Mum sighed. 'Much the same. Lately he's been keeping his movements secret. I don't know what he's up to, but there's no use me asking because he won't tell me. He was out last Friday all day and when I said, 'Might I ask where you've been?' he just said, 'Now, let me see, where was I? What day is today?' '

I shrugged. 'What's new?'

'I made a mistake. I should never have let him persuade me to give up minding poor little Adam. He insisted it was too much for me but I can't cope with the loneliness of this place without him.'

'Have you said this to Dad?'

'He couldn't begin to understand.'

'Do you want me to talk to him?'

'It's too late for that now. Adam's gone to Rita Murphy up the road.' She gazed out at the lawn her eyes unseeing.

'You've put up with so much from him,

Mum, why don't you just leave him for a while to cool his heels?'

'Oh, I couldn't do that,' she said. 'I couldn't bear to leave him alone in this house, having to look after himself.'

'But Dad is well able to look after himself. As you say, he's only here at weekends.'

'And if I did leave him what would the neighbours say? What about that Smyth one at number twenty? She's been after him since he sorted out her ballcock last winter.'

'Oh, Mum, that's not true. I'm sure he's not interested in Mrs Smyth.'

'She's itching to get her claws into him. She's always down in the pub. Jenny, you wouldn't think I'd invent a thing like that?'

'I suppose not.' I sighed. 'But Dad wouldn't behave badly, Mum.'

'Well, I'm annoyed,' replied Mum. 'I respected his wishes, let Adam go. I should have planned my life better for when you'd be gone. If I did go I'd have nothing. No home, nothing.' Her voice broke. 'Anyway, where would I go? What would I do? No one would want me.'

'You could go and live with Aunt Lilian,' I said, knowing it was what Aunt Lilian was always hoping for. Mum would be so useful to her, praising her endeavours on the farm, helping with the cooking, keeping her company. For years Aunt Lilian had wanted her to go and live there.

'Think of the trouble it would cause. No, it's too late,' she said. 'Anyway, there's you to consider.'

'You don't have to worry about me. I'm a big girl now.'

'But how would it look for you if your parents were separated? Think about the harm it might do to you.'

'Rubbish. That has nothing to do with it. The only reason you won't leave Dad is because you're afraid to strike out on your own.'

'You're cruel, Jenny, to say such a thing. That's what you are. You could make life a bit easier for me by moving back home but, no, you think of no one but yourself. You certainly don't think of me.'

True I'd escaped from my mother's power, but I did feel sorry for her.

I said, 'Listen, I'm going to Connemara on Friday. Why don't you come with me for a bit of a holiday? I could pick you up early and we could do a bit of shopping in Galway.'

'That would be nice,' she said, grudgingly.

She was waiting at the door when I arrived, her suitcase beside her. We drove to Galway City, stopping for a snack in a pub. The shops were full of busy customers. In Moon's I laughed when Mum suggested I try on a pink, gossamer-fine dress that in her opinion was ideal for a party.

'You haven't celebrated your birthday properly yet,' she said.

'Oh, Mum, forget about my birthday.' Desperate to distract her I marched her off to the makeup department where I'd spied an offer of a free makeover on the Clinique counter.

'This stuff is not suitable for me.' She glared at the yellow-haired assistant, whose heavy makeup was melting in the heat of the store.

'Have a manicure, then,' I suggested. 'They're doing them at the Cutex counter if you buy two bottles of nail polish. You'll feel better.'

'I don't need to spend a fortune to feel good.'

'I'll treat you. Go on, sit down there and relax.'

The assistant glanced at Mum's ragged nails and wrinkled her nose disdainfully. Then she picked out a colour from the huge assortment that she thought might be suitable.

'I'll be back,' I said to Mum, leaving her facing the cuticle remover.

I bought the pink dress, and went off to look at shoes.

There he was, in the men's department, head and shoulders above the other shoppers, tanned and more handsome than I'd ever seen him. I stared at him, hardly believing my eyes. At any second he'd see me. He'd turn around. But he didn't. His eyes were on a row of handmade shirts. He wouldn't want to see me, not when I'd turned away from him when he'd tried to talk to me at the party. Since then I'd composed notes to him, torn them up, written others. Now I was looking at him, and I couldn't resist him.

'Hugo,' I called, but he was gone, lost amid the other shoppers.

I followed in the direction I thought he might have taken, looking left and right as I headed through the men's department and out the other side, moving as fast as I could, inhibited by the surge of shoppers coming towards me. I went down the escalator to the ground floor, scanning the crowds. He was nowhere to be seen. I pushed my way to the entrance, thinking he might have left. Outside people bustled past as I went down the busy street and round the corner. No luck. He'd disappeared.

'Jenny!'

I turned.

Our eyes locked, his startled.

'Hello,' I said. Like the first time we had met on the train no words were spoken but a huge surge of longing rose in me, threatening to overwhelm me. I felt giddy. My knees were knocking, but there was nowhere to sit down. Slowly he walked towards me, amazement still in his eyes. The realisation that he, too, was struggling with all sorts of emotions dawned on me as the shock subsided from his face. He smiled. 'So, what brings you to Galway?' he asked.

'It's just a flying visit to drop Mum off at Aunt Lilian's.'

'How are you?'

'I'm fine.' I was hoping he wouldn't see the truth in my face. 'And you?'

'Fine. How's Cathy?'

'Oh, not too bad. Coping.'

'That's good. Like a drink?' he suggested.

'Yes, why not?'

We went into the lounge of the Great Southern Hotel.

'How have you been?' I asked, when he returned with the glasses.

'Miserable. And you?'

'The same.'

'How's work?'

'Fine.'

'Louis in good form?'

'Yes. He's smitten with Cathy.'

'Seems so.' He nodded.

'I heard you'd been away.'

'Travelling around Europe, flogging Western Tourism.'

'Went well, did it?'

'Fine. Plenty of interest from Germany and Holland.'

'Good. And the Manor?' I felt my breath catch as I mentioned it. 'Are they interested in that too?'

'Yes. There's a man called Gerhard Sauther, with pots of money, who loves Ireland. He comes to visit the Manor when he's over on business. He wants to buy it.'

'You wouldn't sell it to him, would you?'

He shook his head. 'No. Happily we seemed to have turned the corner. Things are looking up.'

'That's great. I'll tell Louis. It's like a baby to him too, you know.'

He smiled.

Silence.

'You didn't return my call,' he said.

'No. I didn't see the point.'

'Look, Jenny, I don't want to embarrass you, but I'd like to try to explain the whole thing. Not here, of course,' he added, looking around. 'Could we go somewhere?'

'I don't really want to get into it all again.'

394

'Just the same, let me tell you the truth.'

'There's no need.' I was afraid to look at him.

'There's every need.'

'What's the point, Hugo? You've got Natalie, and the Manor and everything.'

Hugo was shaking his head. 'None of it's any good to me without you. And, anyway, it's over with Natalie.' He looked at me, his face wretched.

'Does she know how you feel about me?'

Hugo looked faintly worried. 'I don't think I mentioned it — not in so many words. But she will know, and soon.'

'How will she?'

'Because I'm about to tell her.' His voice was resolute.

I'd waited months for this but my sudden joy at hearing him say it turned to anguish as I thought of how people would call him a bastard for ditching Natalie and turn against him. Yet I knew that he'd been Natalie's victim. She'd been too strong for him.

'I tried to explain it all to you the night of the party, Jenny, but you wouldn't listen. You were so remote the last time we met.'

'You could hardly blame me for that. It was so difficult with Natalie there, and with the engagement just announced.'

'I know.'

'Do you?'

He paused before he answered. 'I know I promised you more than I could give, and I don't feel proud of the way I treated you, Jenny, but I don't know what else I could have done.'

I looked away, not knowing what to say.

'What about us, Jenny? Where do we go from here?' he asked, with a touch of awkwardness. 'Couldn't we try again, make a fresh start?' He took my hand. 'We could see each other again, have dinner or something?'

What was he offering? To be a lover, or a husband? I only knew with certainty that I didn't want any more promises that couldn't be fulfilled. The memory of Hugo's rejection crept over me. What a fool I am, I told myself. He's only being friendly and kind because he's got time on his hands. And Natalie could wrap him round her little finger — she could get him back whenever she wanted him. He was beyond my reach.

He took my hand. 'Perhaps we could go somewhere for a quiet dinner together, just the two of us?'

'I don't think I could manage dinner.' I looked at him. 'It's no use, Hugo. I'm too scared to get involved again.'

'Jenny, I told you. It's over with Natalie.'

'It's no use, Hugo. I don't trust you.'

He let go of my hand suddenly and stood up. 'Is that your final answer?'

'I nodded.

'Fine, that's it, then.' He downed his drink. 'If ever you're ready to trust me again, get in touch.'

He was gone, striding out of the lounge. I grabbed my bag and ran out after him. The door swung behind me and I flew down the steps, out into the square, past a fat woman in a floral frock and an old man.

Hugo was at the corner. He turned and walked on briskly, not once looking back, his coat flapping around him as he crossed the road and went quickly to his car. Then he was heading off in the opposite direction.

Mum! Oh, God! I'd forgotten all about her!

My heart was pounding as I ran to Moon's. Mum would be in a panic. She'd have alerted the store manager by now, perhaps even called the police. Willing myself to calm down I shot up the escalator.

There she was, her face beautifully made-up, mascara thick on her eyelashes, her lips glossed. She looked fabulous.

'Jenny!' she called, waving her freshly painted nails at me theatrically. 'What'd you think? Aren't they gorgeous? And there's a hair promotion on all week. All sorts of special offers in cuts and colours. I might book an appointment,' she said, gazing at herself. 'According to Toyah here, the best colour for my complexion would be beige blonde.'

'Yes,' I said, distractedly. If only I'd caught up with Hugo. I should've listened to him this time, not run off like a frightened rabbit like I did on the night of the party at the Manor.

'And you know what they say about blondes? They have more fun. Isn't that right, Toyah?' She addressed her as if she were her bosom pal.

'Well, we get dirtier quicker.' Toyah sniggered.

'Really! How interesting,' Mum said, considering the meaning of this puzzling remark. Then she was off on a different tack. 'I'm going to find a job,' she said. 'No use hanging around the house wasting all this.'

'You could get one in Kilbeg.'

'I wouldn't like to live in Connemara.'

Not for her the quiet countryside, the country neighbours, their secret country faces prying over their fences, behind which they led their indifferent lives.

36

Aunt Lilian was alone in the sitting room at Coolbawn, the faint crackle of the fire the only sound to disturb the quiet.

'You're late,' she snapped. 'Your dinner's destroyed.'

'I'm so sorry, Lilian,' Mum apologised. 'Jenny insisted that I have a makeover in Galway.'

'What's she trying to do to you?' Aunt Lilian looked at her critically. 'You know what they say,

> 'A little bit of powder,
> A little bit of paint,
> Makes the coarsest woman
> Into something that she ain't.' '

'Lilian, that's not very nice.'

'I think Mum looks beautiful,' I said, not really concerned about Aunt Lilian's opinion. I had other things to think about — Cathy, for instance. I would have to see her as quickly as possible, and tell her everything that had just happened. My heart sank when I thought of Hugo. I could never face him again. Not now, after what had just happened.

I was grateful for the chit-chat over dinner, Aunt Lilian telling Mum that Aunt Mary had caught a bad chill. 'I told her not to buy that damp, God-forsaken place, but would she listen? Now she's laid low with a chest infection. I wouldn't be surprised if she gets pleurisy out of it.'

I was worried about Aunt Mary, her illness obliging me to concentrate on something else other than Hugo for a short time.

'I'm sure she'll be better soon,' I said.

'Would you drive over to Bluebell Cottage later, Jenny? Take them some homemade soup and bread?'

'Certainly,' I said, delighted with the excuse.

'Tell Mary that we'll call over tomorrow if she's feeling up to having visitors,' said Aunt Lilian.

The cold evening wind blew in the hall as Cathy opened the door. 'I thought you were staying at Mum's,' she said.

'She sent me over with soup. How's Aunt Mary?'

'Much better this evening. Come on up and see her.'

'Come in,' Aunt Mary called, when I knocked on her bedroom door.

Pressed back against her pillows she looked small and pale. 'How lovely to see you, Jenny.' Her voice was weak.

Her cheek smelt of flowers as I kissed her.

'She was asleep,' said Cathy, brushing back Aunt Mary's hair gently and straightening her duvet.

I sat on the edge of her bed. 'I hope I haven't disturbed you,' I said.

'Not at all, I was just dozing. How's your mother? How's Lilian?'

'They're fine. They're calling over to see you tomorrow.'

We talked for a little while, then I kissed her goodnight and went downstairs with Cathy.

'I saw Hugo today,' I said to her.

'You did?' Her eyes widened.

I told her every detail of our meeting.

'So,' she said, infuriatingly casual as she fiddled with her hair, 'what are you going to do now?'

'Nothing. I've blown it this time, telling him I didn't trust him.'

'I'm sure you could work something out.'

'I don't think I want to.'

Back at Coolbawn I told Aunt Lilian that Aunt Mary was improving.

'I hope so,' sighed Aunt Lilian.

Soon it was bedtime, and my head was

filled with impossible thoughts. I should have seen how difficult it was for Hugo to reach me through the confusion of the past. I should have made an effort to understand. That meeting had gone all wrong. I concentrated hard, bringing his image before me: the tilt of his head, the strong, clear lines of his face, the way he walked. If I could see him once more, persuade him of how difficult it all was for me . . .

★ ★ ★

Aunt Mary took a turn for the worse: she caught another chill and developed pneumonia. Mum and I went over to the hospital on a glorious spring day.

'She's dying,' said Aunt Lilian dramatically, as we all gathered around her bed.

She was slipping into unconsciousness, the nurses fussing about her. Aunt Mary, always strong, always there taking care of everyone, was slipping away in bouts of uncontrollable coughing, so weak that it was doubtful she could see or hear any of us. I watched her, feeling that she was going and I was being left behind. I wanted to put out my hand and hold on to her as I had when I was a child.

She didn't die. Her willpower stopped her on the downward slope, and she rallied, her mind as sharp as ever, and concerned about Cathy, if she was eating properly and taking enough exercise.

Soon she was out of danger, and returned home. Aunt Lilian, mellow for the duration of her illness, lost her peevishness, and being practical, arrived at Bluebell Cottage regularly with interesting nourishing food.

One day, Aunt Flo called to Coolbawn, where she found me.

'Have you heard about Hugo?' she asked me, when we were alone.

'No!'

'Oh, the nerve of her. She had poor Hugo fooled with her coy, winsome ways, dragging him into her clutches after her accident. I watched him fall in love with you. I warned you off, not realising that she's a loathsome girl, trampling poor Hugo into the ground with her possessiveness, never letting him out of her sight, at the same time playing away with that uncouth manager of hers. I watched him becoming more and more unhappy, you know. Hugo, who's always protected her, I must say I felt so sorry for him.'

That afternoon when I went to visit Aunt Mary and Cathy, Cathy said, in a rush, 'Jenny, Hugo phoned me.'

'He phoned you!' I repeated, stunned.

'Ostensibly to ask after Aunt Mary but

really to talk about you.'

'Oh! Was he in good form?'

'Not really.' She leaned nearer to me. 'He wants you to call over to the Manor.'

I stepped backwards, shaken. 'Go over to the Manor?'

'Yes. Will you? He wants you to. He said any afternoon this week, about three o'clock. He'll be there waiting.'

'Oh, Cathy.' I sighed with indecision. 'What did you say to him?'

'I said that I'd try to talk you into going, but that I couldn't promise anything.'

I began pacing up and down. 'I can't go.'

'Of course you can.'

'Don't you see? It's only because he feels sorry for me. Oh, God!' I covered my face with my hands. 'I can't go! I'd feel such a fool.'

'Oh, you're hopeless, Jenny. Course he's not sorry for you. You have to go to him, loving him as much as you do. You have to go, Jenny. There's no other way. If you put it off it'll only make matters worse. You're bound to bump into one another — and think of the complications.'

Though I loved Cathy for trying to convince me that I should go, I couldn't help my fear of Natalie's probable return.

'And Natalie?' I asked her.

404

'Forget Natalie. She's off the scene.'

'Are you sure about that?'

'Certain. Aunt Flo said so, and she knows because Hugo and Uncle Tom are quite close.'

'God! I can't believe it.'

'He needs you, Jenny. Come on downstairs.'

I followed her slowly downstairs, feeling like a child who is being led by the hand.

37

It took severe mental effort to go to the Manor. I drove slowly, wondering why Hugo had asked me to call. But I knew I had to see him. I was no longer fearful of wagging tongues, or the wrath of Natalie.

Returning to the Manor after such a long time away was strange. In the sunshine it looked welcoming, the gardens promising in their springtime clothes. Foxgloves, lambs' tongues and alpine plants were sprinkled over the steep slopes of the terraces, red tulips shining out of the recess among the trees, the leaves of the beech trees pale and transparent in the sunshine.

My car crunched to a halt. Slowly I got out. Hugo came out to meet me. He said, quickly and unemotionally, 'It's so good of you to come,' but there was no mistaking the leap of delight in his eyes.

Slipping an arm through mine carelessly he led me towards the house. 'Would you like a drink here, or would you rather a walk to the pub?' he asked, as we mounted the steps.

'I'd love a walk to the pub.'

The sound of a car, which we glimpsed

then through the trees, brought us to a sudden halt. Who could it be? Hugo glanced at his watch. 'I'm not expecting anyone.'

It was Aunt Flo in a pale pink suit, her gold earrings shining in the sun.

'Hello there,' she called to the puzzled Hugo. 'Raffle-ticket money.' She waved her pink handbag in the air. 'You said to call over any afternoon. You haven't forgotten, have you?'

'Of course,' said Hugo, hitting his forehead, well and truly caught out.

Smiling dutifully, he went down the steps to meet her, murmuring apologies, leading her up them.

'Jenny!' she cried. 'Well, isn't that the devil? Never expected to see you here.'

'Hello, Aunt Flo.' I kissed her cheek.

We walked into the drawing room, and sat her down by the fire. She crossed her legs and settled back, no doubt for the duration of the afternoon. Hugo's eyes met mine in acknowledgement of the fix we were in.

'Tea?' he asked. 'Or would you like something stronger?'

'I'll have a crème-de-menthe,' she said smacking her lips. 'What are you up to, Jenny? Chasing Hugo again?' she asked as soon as he'd left the room, and tittered. There was excitement in her eyes as she said, 'Mind you, men are made to be chased — and caught.' She giggled in a way that reminded me of stories I'd heard about her wild youth in the days when young girls' behaviour was expected to be nothing short of exemplary. She'd been 'a one', as Mum often remarked.

'Now, tell me, Jenny, have you . . . you know?'

'Have I what, Aunt Flo?'

'You *know*.' She smirked, leaning forward. 'Done the deed?' she mouthed, her eyes swivelling to the ceiling.

'Aunt Flo!'

I usually took little notice of her, but today there was something sordid in her questions. She was making me feel like a slut and she knew it.

I wished she would go.

'See, you're blushing. I caught you out.' She giggled obscenely. 'I know what your game is. I was like you once, you know. Rash!' She chuckled at my embarrassment.

'I'm here at Hugo's invitation to clear up a misunderstanding,' I retaliated. I wished, there and then, that I hadn't come, that I'd never let Hugo back into my life, and that our long-ago love had died into the past, leaving only a wonderful memory.

Hugo returned with the drinks. Glancing at

me, he lifted his glass to say, 'Your good health!'

Aunt Flo added, 'Happy days,' raising her glass, 'and nights!'

She drank greedily, a flush spreading over her cheeks as she chattered on.

Hugo, tall and gracious, standing by the fireplace, listened to her tolerantly. As she pressed on recklessly with her suggestive chatter my answers grew terse. Silly old fool. She didn't mean any harm but couldn't she see that I was embarrassed? I ran my hand across my forehead. I needed to escape from her and her innuendos, get down to the beach until she was gone. Leave Hugo at her mercy.

I gulped down my drink, placed my glass on the coffee table, and excused myself, saying, 'I'll leave you and Hugo to get on with things, Aunt Flo,' and gave her a peck on the cheek.

'You've smudged your lipstick, dear,' said she. 'I can't allow you to go out like that.' She wiped off the smear with her hand.

For once she looked serious as she whispered, 'Listen, Jenny, remember there's usually only one 'once' in every lifetime. You're lucky enough to have been given a second chance. Don't spoil it.' Then she said aloud, 'I won't stay long. See you soon.'

'Where are you going?' Hugo followed me

out of the drawing room in alarm.

'Down to the beach till she's gone,' I said.

'I'll follow you. Wait for me,' he said.

That was better, I thought, as I strode off. She'd probably go home after another drink and lie down in her darkened bedroom until dinnertime.

Ten minutes later he joined me. We walked along the beach to the point, where we stood with our eyes on each other. His were clouded and unhappy. It seemed a long time ago since we'd been here last, not knowing then that the happiness we'd shared would be so brief.

'So, is Natalie really gone for good this time?' I asked, getting straight to the point.

'Yes. We hadn't been getting along, you knew that. We could only be civil to one another when we were apart.'

'But you got engaged.'

He sighed sadly. 'I'm afraid that was a publicity stunt Natalie pulled. *I* didn't know a thing about it until I read it. She wanted to give the impression to the people in her profession who count that she was settling down. She asked me to go along with it until she got a deal signed. She was desperate for it, and threw herself into trying to get everything exactly right.

'I did as she asked, but as time went on it

became more and more difficult. I suggested we split, she said we could make a go of it. But we were spending most of our time apart. The last couple of times she stayed here we practically tore each other's hair out.'

'I see.'

'Things got out of control. I knew I didn't want to spend the rest of my life with her.'

'Why did you let it go on for so long?'

'As you know, it was the accident that did it,' he said. 'Now it seems like an eternity ago, but at the time I felt I couldn't throw her out. Some days I'd wake up astonished that I could keep on going. When I tried to talk to her she backed off. Oh, she did all kinds of things to avoid discussing it. It was so painful. I got angry, switched off, acted as if she wasn't there, which wasn't difficult because most of the time she wasn't.'

There was no mistaking the quiet desperation in his eyes, and his need to be honest.

'I knew that Natalie wasn't happy, and that she wasn't interested in either me or the Manor. Her career came first and she was only holding on until it took off again.'

'You must have loved her once.'

'I did.'

I held my breath.

'But obviously not enough to make it work. And seeing you at the Manor on the night of

411

the party made me realise that I couldn't bear it if I was never to see you again.'

I looked at him. 'I thought you'd got over me. That you'd decided to spend your life with Natalie, and that was it.'

'Natalie's gone, Jenny. She won't be coming back. I don't think she's too upset about it.'

'Why do you say that?'

He looked at me. 'She didn't tell me about Rick, but I knew. I guessed a long time ago.'

I was barely breathing, remembering the two of them kissing.

'Did you?'

'Yes.'

'If you hadn't discovered it for yourself, would you still be with her?'

He shook his head. 'No. I'd had enough. I had to look after her until she was on her feet again. It was such a near thing that first attempt. God! I hated leaving her alone. I never knew what she might do.' He spoke so impersonally that it bore home to me, as nothing else would, how much he'd suffered.

'What are we to do now, Jenny?' he asked.

'Do? Now?'

'We could make a fresh start, couldn't we?' Hugo spoke as if it was the most natural thing in the world, while I saw only difficulties. 'I want to make it up to you. I want it to be like

412

it was,' he said. There was a hungry look in his eyes.

'Jenny, all the time you were away from me I used to think up plans to get you back. I know I'm going to want you for always.'

The apprehension in his face melted the ice around my heart and the pain subsided.

We stood watching the tiny frills of white lace on the shore, the sea breeze in our faces. The tide was rising, slapping against the sea wall. Further along boats bobbed around. We sat in the shelter of the rocks, under the wall. I told him how confused I'd been, so much so that I couldn't work, couldn't think, and couldn't make sense out of any of it.

'I'm so sorry,' he said, and he repeated, 'I never meant to hurt you. But I can't let you go. When I saw you on the film-set, all on your own, I wanted to . . . I won't tell you what I wanted to do. I just hope it's not too late for us.'

At that moment Hugo's golden retriever came sidling up to him, her eyes saying, 'I trust you. I'd go with you to the end of the world.' Hugo patted her head.

I listened to him carefully, heard the regret in his voice. The sincerity in his eyes touched me. The space between us filled as he moved closer. 'I never meant to hurt you. Do you believe me?'

'Yes.' He stood up, reached out his hand and pulled me up beside him.

'We've been given a second chance. We should take it,' he breathed into my ear.

'But, Hugo . . . '

'No more buts, darling.'

The world around me rocked and the constraint between us melted as he smiled and pulled me to him. Then his arms were round me and he placed a whisper of a kiss on my cheek. He was looking at me. I lowered my eyes seductively. I felt the warmth of his body, felt his smooth skin against mine, absorbed his familiar smell as he bent to kiss me. Our lips touched briefly. Then I drew back.

'What is it?' he asked.

'I'm scared.'

'Don't be. I'll take care of you, I promise.'

We gazed into each other's eyes, a flicker of flame in his, and I rested my cheek against his. I could feel his soft breath.

'Come on, let's get back, it's chilly down here.' Holding hands we turned back to the Manor, the fields all around it swathed in the pink glow of the setting sun.

I stood in the dim room in the west wing, nervous, looking around at the cool white walls, the half-closed curtains pulled across the two windows, casting a strip of light across the sheer white bedspread, and lace-trimmed pillows.

'I had this room redecorated just for us. You like it?'

'I think it's very romantic.'

We were moving to the bed, lying down together, intertwined, Hugo wooing me with loving words, stroking me lightly, sending shivers down my spine. It was so good to be close and warm, hearing each other breathing, feeling the sensation of desire. We were postponing the moment of possessing one another, yet powerless to resist. Feverishly we clasped one another. The dam burst, the floodgates opened, releasing all the tension and pain, such love as we had to give to each other filling the void that had been empty for so long.

He bent over me. 'I love you.'

I looked into his face. The sadness was gone. In its place there was contentment. We lay in the stillness, peace and happiness invading us.

I was conscious only of a deep feeling of gratitude to Cathy for making me come back to the Manor, and a lack of anxiety for the future.

Later, the phone rang. Hugo answered it. My heart leaped into my mouth as a voice shrill with surprise and tension came on the line. What was it this time?

Hugo hung up and turned to me. 'That was Louis. Cathy's had the baby. It's a girl. She's going to call her Lilian.'

I heard the news with a mixture of excitement and gladness. It was bound to warm Aunt Lilian's heart and break the ice between her and her daughter.

'Louis wants to marry her,' Hugo continued. 'And why not? He adores Cathy.'

'Why not indeed?' In his turn, Louis captivated Cathy. It was there for all to see. She was alone, and had been for most of her pregnancy, and she was lonely. She was frightened, too, of her age, of love, and of losing her looks.

But Louis wanted Cathy, and he was going to have her. He'd gladly wait for her until she was free of Ned. Since he'd met her he'd become less selfish, less demanding. I felt happy for Cathy in all her joy, and looked on Louis as her saviour.

We went down the short flight of steps to the lawn, stopping together and leaning over a rosebush to admire its perfect golden blooms, which drenched the air with their perfume.

'It's called Warm Welcome,' said Hugo, and took me in his arms.